Sofia lost her mother eight months ago, and her friends were one hundred percent there for her. Now it's a new year, and they're ready for Sofia to move on.

Problem is, Sofia can't bounce back, can't recharge like a cell phone. She decides to write Dear Kate, an advice columnist for *Fifteen Magazine*, and is surprised to receive a fast reply. Soon the two are exchanging emails, and Sofia opens up and spills all, including a few worries that are totally embarrassing. Turns out even advice columnists don't have all the answers, and one day Sofia learns a secret that flips her world upside down.

Speed of Life is the heartbreaking, heartwarming story of a girl who thinks her life is over when really it's just beginning. It's a novel about love, family, grief, and growing up.

Praise for *Speed of Life*

"Perceptive, funny, and moving... I found myself nodding with recognition and scribbling 'exactly' in the margins... I laughed out loud and I teared up while reading this novel."

—*New York Times*

"*Speed of Life* is the kind of book that you want to read speedily, all at once, because the characters are so engaging, the voice of the narrator pitch perfect, the situations convincingly real and raw, the humor and liveliness of the prose such fun to follow, and the feelings of that time in a teenager's life when everything can go from awful to awesome in a heartbeat are so vividly captured. You won't want to put it down. But my advice is slow down and savor this delightful book, full of cariño, funny and heartfelt, and (spoiler alert) not just for teens."

—Julia Alvarez, award-winning, bestselling author of *In the Time of the Butterflies* and *Return to Sender*

"[A] wonderful book that takes us from loss to laughter."

—Richard Peck, author of *The Best Man* and Newbery Gold Medalist for *A Year Down Yonder*

"Sofia and her dad try to move forward in the wake of her mother's death last year. After the 'Dear Kate' columnist visits her school, Sofia turns to her for advice. But then her dad drops a bombshell... Sofia's world just got way more complicated."

—Young Adult Library Services Association, YALSA 2018 Best Fiction for Young Adults

"As a middle school librarian at an all-girls school, I can't stop recommending this book to my students. It is realistic fiction at its best."

—Beth Abramovitz, former librarian at
Columbus School for Girls

★ "The multicultural cast is led by the completely likable Sofia, whose mother was Spanish and whose abuelo's comforting presence remains across the ocean. Her story has no fast, easy answers, but there is a clear message that while time does not necessarily heal, it helps. The advice of not to fall too hard, too fast, or too far is real, not preachy. Complex characters and a strong voice make this one stand out."

—*Kirkus Reviews*, Starred Review

★ "This slice-of-life story echoes the author's own experience as a teen magazine advice columnist and addresses all sorts of issues: death, grieving, moving, parental dating, parental sexuality, stepsibling conflict, new schools, self-esteem, and relationships…but eventually Sofia does get to a better place… Weston isn't afraid to tackle the squirm-inducing questions common to high school freshmen too embarrassed to seek sound information from reliable sources."

—*School Library Journal*, Starred Review

★ "This novel is jam-packed with important, dramatic, and inevitable aspects of adolescence, from pimples to periods to popularity… The narrative effectively contrasts the diversity of a city environment with that of suburban life…a solid, affecting tale of maturing and coming to grips with one's reality."

—*Booklist*, Starred Review

★ "Sofia's growth—amid unexpected interest from boys, her first relationship, new additions to her family, and grief—is both relatable and moving."

—*Publishers Weekly*, Starred Review

"Weston imparts insights about life and loss throughout, tracing Sofia's increasing maturity. Supported by sympathetic friends and family, Sofia faces each new challenge in her life with honesty, bravery, and humor."

—*Horn Book* magazine

"A letter-writing habit turns hairy in Carol Weston's *Speed of Life*."

—*Vanity Fair*, Hot Type

"A sweet, moving tale about grief and growing up."

—Mackenzie Dawson, *New York Post*, Required Reading

"This is, perhaps, the most perfect eighth grade girl book I have ever read. In fact, it was excruciating to read (in the best possible way) as I felt I was right back in middle school myself. It reminded me of nothing more than the Judy Blume books I read at that age, but current for today's readers."

—Teen Librarian Toolbox, *School Library Journal*

"This poignant story for tweens and early teens follows Sofia's struggles…with help from her friends, her dad, and an advice columnist who will eventually take part in a major plot twist."

—*Yale Magazine*

ALSO BY CAROL WESTON

Ava and Pip
Ava and Taco Cat
Ava XOX

Speed of Life

CAROL WESTON

sourcebooks
jabberwocky

Published by Sourcebooks Jabberwocky, an imprint of Sourcebooks, Inc.
P.O. Box 4410, Naperville, Illinois 60567-4410
(630) 961-3900
Fax: (630) 961-2168
sourcebooks.com

The Library of Congress has cataloged the hardcover edition as follows:

Names: Weston, Carol, author.
Title: Speed of life / Carol Weston.
Description: Naperville, Illinois : Sourcebooks Jabberwocky, [2017] |
    Summary: "Fourteen-year-old Sofia Wolfe has her fair share of problems,
    and she doesn't have anyone to talk to...until she finds 'Dear Kate.'"
    Provided by publisher.
Identifiers: LCCN 2016051104 | (alk. paper)
Classification: LCC PZ7.W526285 Sp 2017
LC record available at https://lccn.loc.gov/2016051104

Source of Production: Marquis Book Printing, Montreal, Canada
Date of Production: June 2018
Run Number: 5012537

Printed and bound in Canada.
MBP 10 9 8 7 6 5 4 3 2 1

TO MY MOM AND DAD—
WISHING I COULD SIGN A COPY FOR THEM

WARNING: THIS IS KIND OF a sad story. At least at first. So if you don't like sad stories, maybe you shouldn't read this. I mean, I'd understand if you put it down and watched cat videos instead.

I like cat videos too.

Then again, this book is already in your hands.

It starts and ends on January 1, and I was thinking of calling it *The Year My Whole Life Changed.* Or *Life, Death, and Kisses.* Or maybe even *The Year I Grew Up.*

For me, being fourteen was hard. Really hard. Childhood was a piece of cake. Being a kid in New York City and spending summers in Spain, that was all pretty perfect, looking back. But being fourteen was like climbing a mountain in the rain. In flip-flops. I hoped I'd wind up in a different place, but I kept tripping and slipping and falling and wishing it weren't way too late to turn around.

This book does have funny parts. And I learned two giant facts.

Number one: everything can change in an instant—for worse, sure, but also for better. Number two: sometimes, if you just keep climbing, you get an amazing view. You see what's behind you and what's ahead of you and—the big surprise—what's inside you.

PART ONE

JANUARY

"GUESS WHO'S COMING TO ASSEMBLY," Kiki said. We'd agreed to meet in my lobby and walk across Central Park together. I'd told her I didn't want to go to my building's New Year's Day party, and she didn't push me, which I appreciated.

Kiki was bundled up in her new blue coat and looked gorgeous. *Drop-dead gorgeous*, I thought, though I'd come to hate that expression.

We'd been best friends since West Side Montessori. She lived eight blocks north, and we always used to play "school" and "restaurant" and, since we were city kids, "elevator." We'd step inside my hallway closet, press pretend numbers, and make-believe we were going up and down, up and down.

Now Kiki was fourteen—like me—but seemed older. Half Vietnamese, half Brazilian, with dark eyes and cocoa skin, she became a boy magnet right around the time I became a girl that some kids avoided. Guys from Buckley, St. Bernard's, and Hunter began to text her just as the few boys I considered friends vanished.

"Sofia, guess who's coming!" she said, impatient.

"I give up. Who?" I checked the lobby mirror to adjust my wool scarf and make sure nothing was caught in my braces.

"Dear Kate! Can you believe it? Dr. G just told me. God, it's so weird to see a *teacher* outside of school. And on vacation!"

"I'm used to it," I said. Halsey Tower, my home since birth, was right across from our school. Nicknamed Teacher Tower, it was like a vertical village of teachers. "But who's Dear Kate again?" The name rang a distant bell.

Kiki stared at me. "You don't remember?" She waited.

"Oh, right." I *did* remember. Dear Kate was the advice columnist for *Fifteen Magazine.* At a sleepover at Kiki's the previous summer, Kiki was taking a shower, and I'd stumbled on an email exchange she had printed out. I hadn't meant to snoop. I just hadn't known we had secrets.

Dear Kate,
My BFF's mom died a few months ago and she's still sad all the time and I don't know how to help.
Wanting to Help

Dear Wanting to Help,
You're already helping—your best friend is lucky to have you. Tell her that if she wants to talk about her mom, you're there for her. And if you're tempted to share a happy memory, don't hesitate. You won't be reminding her of her mother; she's already thinking of her. Her sadness is understandable, and your kindness means more than you realize.
Kate

At the time, I was hurt and offended. Did Kiki think of me as a charity case? "Oh, *please*," Kiki had said. "I thought she could help."

"No one can help!" I'd said and considered storming off. But I didn't. I couldn't afford to lose Kiki.

Now we were in the park, heading toward Bloomingdale's. The trees were sticks. The duck pond was frozen. The sky was impossibly blue.

"So what's Dear Kate going to talk about?" I asked.

"Probably the ABC's of adolescence."

"The ABC's?"

"Anorexia, Bulimia, and Cutting!" Kiki laughed. "And maybe the *P*'s?"

"The *P*'s? You've lost me."

"Pimples, Periods, and Popularity!" Kiki was cracking herself up. "And definitely the *S*'s!"

I rolled my eyes, but it was clear Kiki was going to wait until I started guessing. "Stress?" I finally offered.

"That's one."

"Substance abuse?" I said.

"That's two. And c'mon, Sof. What's the most important?"

I looked to make sure no one we knew was around—no boys, no parents, no teachers. "Sex?"

"Sex!" Kiki repeated loudly. "And sexually transmitted diseases!"

"Ugh, I hope she spares us. I hear enough about 'infection protection' at home." Kiki knows my dad is a gynecologist who sometimes offers random talks about STDs or unintended pregnancies.

Kiki and I passed Wollman Rink and watched a wobbly girl on ice skates clutch her mother's hand. "Dear Kate has a daughter," Kiki said. "Can you imagine being the daughter of a teen advice columnist?"

"No."

"She'll be talking to the parents too."

"The daughter?"

"The mother!" Kiki looked at me, exasperated. "We should get my mom and your dad to go." Three years earlier, Kiki's dad had moved out, and lately, Kiki had been hinting about setting up our parents. "Or at least tell me if he's going so I can tell my mom to get dressed up and save him a seat!" She laughed.

"Shut up! Your mom would kill you."

"Or thank me. He *is* an eligible bachelor, Sof. Free gyno appointments for life!"

"Kiki, stop," I said, and she backed down. I didn't like to think of my dad as "eligible." I was still getting used to "widower." And while I'd noticed a few women flirt with Dad (including Kiki's mother, Lan, whenever we went to her restaurant, Saigon Sun), I'd never seen him flirt back.

Mom used to call Dad "*Guapo*"—Handsome. But now he was fifty, and I figured he'd shut down that part of himself. Which was fine by me. I couldn't handle it if he started dating.

"What do you want to buy?" I asked, changing the subject. We were crossing Fifth Avenue heading east.

"I'm *desperate* for new jeans," Kiki answered. "What do you need?"

"Maybe a skirt for the dance with Regis. Or a sweater?" I didn't say what I really needed—more than a new skirt or sweater—was to feel like my old self again. To feel like I could breathe.

. . . .

On Sunday, Dad wanted me to help him take down our tree. It was a miracle we'd managed to put one up, and I didn't see what the big hurry was to take it down.

But Dad likes things neat, and Christmas is messy.

I'd always loved Christmas—the decorations, school concerts, presents, parties. I loved how, right after Thanksgiving, Canadian lumberjacks drove into New York City with trucks full of ever-greens and set up miniature forests on the sidewalks.

Mom, Dad, and I had our own ritual. In early December, we'd pick out a tree on Broadway and lug it home to Ninety-Third Street. Dad would stand it up in its base, Mom would water it with ginger ale, and I'd hang the first ornament. We'd trim the tree together as we listened to carols—everything from "Deck the Halls" to "Feliz Navidad." Pepper, our black cat, would race around, batting at the low-hanging mouse-size ornaments.

That was our family tradition. I thought it would last forever.

But Mom died on April 7, and I died a little that day too.

The first months without Mom were a blur. I still caught glimpses of her everywhere: chopping onions, folding laundry, disappearing into the subway. I couldn't believe Mom was dead—and spring came anyway. At school, most people were extra nice to me, but others kept their distance, as if a death in the family made conversation too awkward—or might be contagious.

I spent most of that summer before eighth grade with Abuelo, Mom's father, in Spain. He and I took dozens of walks in the hills outside Segovia. Some mornings, we'd get pastries by the Roman aqueduct and he'd point out pairs of storks nesting on towers. Or we'd pass the *Alcázar*, which looked like a castle in a fairy tale. On hot afternoons, my grandfather took a nap and I sometimes ducked into the cool Gothic cathedral and tried to picture Mom there as a schoolgirl in the choir. Tried to hear her singing.

I returned to New York before Labor Day and went back to hanging out with Kiki and Natalie and Madison. But it was a long fall, and I mean that both ways: "fall" as in autumn and "fall" as in falling. Worse, everyone—even Kiki!—seemed to expect me to have bounced back.

No one got it.

I wasn't going to bounce back. And no, I wasn't *depressed*. I was *sad*. Who wouldn't be?

On December 21, I turned fourteen and had my first unhappy birthday. The unmerry Christmas came days later, and now it was a new year, and—ready or not—Dad wanted to take down our stupid tree. It felt like a low blow. Christmas had sucked, but I still didn't want it to be over.

Strange. On TV, you never see anyone *undecorating*. Decorating, yes, every year on every show. But *undecorating*? Never. You don't see dads and daughters placing twinkly lights and plastic mistletoe back into boxes, as if in a home movie playing in the wrong direction.

I didn't have it in me to argue. So I did as I was told and became the Grinch Who Stole Christmas. I "stole" everything: the ornaments, the wooden crèche Abuelo had carved, Dad's and my crimson stockings. I tried not to think of Mom's matching stocking, neatly folded in a storage unit in the basement of our building.

We laid our bare tree on an old ripped sheet, wrapped it, and dragged it to the elevator, where we propped it up and took it outside. Then we left it, toppled on the street, with a clump of other discarded evergreens, the top ones dusted with snow.

Back inside, Dad got out the vacuum cleaner, and Pepper ran for cover. I didn't mind the noise because at least it stirred up the smell of pine needles—and happier holidays.

I checked to make sure we'd gotten rid of every last shred of Christmas. And that's when I saw the red-and-green construction-paper chain draped over a window. Mom and I had made that chain when I was in first grade. I could still feel the plastic scissors in my hand, still smell the sweet Elmer's glue.

Dad followed my eyes. "I'll take it down," he offered.

"Okay," I said, surprised at the lump in my throat. That didn't happen much anymore, thank God. I'd grown used to the reminders, the photos of the three of us at the Hippo Playground, at Jones Beach, in Madrid's *Plaza Mayor*. At first, I lost myself in every photo. Now I could usually walk by without looking, look without feeling.

"As soon as we put everything away," Dad said, "I'll take you out for dinner. Maybe Bodrum?"

"Whatever," I mumbled.

"We can talk," he said.

No, we can't, I thought.

· · · · · · · · · ·

When I was little, if I couldn't fall asleep, I'd tiptoe into my parents' room and nudge my mom. She'd stumble out of bed, groggy, then come lie down with me on my bed. She'd whisper, "*Que sueñas con los angelitos,*" which is what you say in Spain: Dream of little angels. And we'd both fall asleep under my pink canopy.

Seems like forever ago.

And also yesterday.

Mom taught Spanish at Halsey School for Girls, and those first months without her, when I couldn't sleep, instead of waking Dad, I'd stay in bed and listen to Mrs. Morris, the computer teacher in 6C, pacing above. Sometimes, the clicking of her heels bothered me. Other times, the sound kept me company.

I'd try to fall back asleep, but you can't fall asleep by making an effort, only by letting go.

Lately, though, if I couldn't sleep, I'd get out of bed and find Pepper. I'd hold him by the cold window and hissing radiator and look out at the dark buildings, some with lights still on and trees still twinkling. Or I'd look at photos of Mom and wonder if somehow she could be looking back. Sometimes, I'd be tempted to call Abuelo, since it was already early morning in Spain. But I didn't want to scare him. That summer, he'd told me it made him nervous when the phone rang at odd hours.

I'd been the one to tell him about the aneurysm. Until April 7, I'd never even heard the word. Breast cancer, heart attack, car accident: those were words to worry about. But aneurysm? Cerebral hemorrhage? Those were spelling words, not ways to die.

Dad had asked me to make the call because my Spanish was better and because, as he'd put it, "Silvio will need to hear your voice." So I'd called, broken the news, and broken his heart.

"*Abuelito, tengo noticias terribles…*"

Thinking about it later, as I often did, I was glad that at least Abuelo hadn't seen what I saw.

I'd been alone when I'd found Mom. I'd rung the doorbell, dug for my key, let myself in. I'd tossed down my backpack and shouted, "I'm home!" The apartment was pin-drop quiet, and there was no smell of simmering onions. Mom always told me when she had faculty meetings, so I was surprised by the silence. But I didn't feel the first prickle of alarm until I walked into the living room and saw the back of her head slumped unnaturally on the sofa.

"*¿Mamá?*" I said.

"*¿Mamá?*" The prickle became panic.

"MOM!" I stepped closer and saw that my mother had slipped onto her side. At first, I just stood there, as immobile as she was. Then I pushed back her dark hair. She stayed still and her face was blank and pale, though her eyes were open.

"*No!*" I screamed. "*No!*" I put my arms around her, but her arm was limp and heavy. "*No!*" I couldn't stop screaming.

I called Dad and blubbered into the phone. At first, he said, "That's not possible!" He asked me to check that there was no breath, no pulse. I did, and then I heard him crying too. He said he'd call 911 and would race home. Pepper looked at me, wide-eyed, and I tried to hold him as I phoned Mrs. Russell, our down-stairs neighbor. But he wriggled away, scratching my arm. I wanted Mrs. Russell to come over, but I also didn't. If no one else saw my mother, maybe it could all be some dreadful misunderstanding.

Mrs. Russell arrived, then Dad, then more and more and more people. There was no misunderstanding.

That evening, I looked up *aneurysm* in Spanish—*aneurisma*—and phoned my grandfather. I told him that Mom's expression was peaceful, which it was. After a long while, he said, "*una muerte dulce*," a sweet death.

Of course, we both knew there was nothing sweet about dying at age forty-two.

I did not tell Abuelo that by the time they took her away, Mom's body had gone stiff and cold. I wished I hadn't noticed.

. . . .

Two days before Dear Kate's visit to Halsey, Kiki handed me a stack of old *Fifteen*s, all open to her columns. "Read these," she'd commanded.

"What? You're giving me homework?"

"Yep." Kiki opened my closet, reached in, and took out the skirt I'd bought at Bloomie's. "Can I borrow this?" she asked, and I shrugged: sure. Then she looked at the closet floor and said, "Omigod! Your dollhouse!" She lifted up the wooden mother and father. "They're so much smaller than I remembered!"

Kiki and I used to spend hours playing with my dollhouse. Abuelo had carved it and given it to me when I turned five. The first time Kiki and I played with it, we smooshed all the wooden tables, chairs, beds, cabinets, and people onto the top floor. Mom said we could "spread out," but Kiki and I were used to apartments, not houses, and spreading out had felt unnatural. We couldn't imagine a family taking up *two* floors.

"How is your grandfather anyway?" Kiki asked as she pulled on my skirt and studied herself in my mirror.

"Okay. He's coming in March."

"Cool." She told me she was about to go meet Derek but had told her mom she was with me. "Not that she's going to call you or anything." Derek was Kiki's latest boyfriend, and I said I'd cover for her if she did call. Then Kiki left, leaving her jeans and magazines behind.

I made some hot chocolate, found Pepper, looked at the *Fifteens*, and read the "Dear Kate" columns slowly, one after another. I liked the advice. And I liked that Dear Kate never said, "Talk to your mom." She seemed to know that "parents" in plural was not a given.

FEBRUARY

I'M OBSESSED WITH HER EARRINGS," Kiki said. "And seriously, how cool are those boots?"

Kiki had saved fourth-row seats for Natalie, Madison, and me and was clutching her battered copy of *Girls' Guide*. Principal Milliman was introducing Dear Kate.

The advice columnist's eyes were blue-jean blue and her hair was strawberry blond and shoulder length. I wondered if she was going to tell us to "believe in ourselves" and "find our passions" and "follow our dreams."

She didn't. She began, "I visit a lot of schools, but I'll be honest: I like all-girls' schools best. Why? Because I can dive right in and talk about bras, periods, cliques, and crushes."

Kiki elbowed me as if to say, *See?*

"I know your plates are full of academics, but this is also the time when you're getting comfortable with your bodies. Me, I wasn't just a late bloomer—I was a member of the Itty Bitty Titty Committee! I still am." Dear Kate laughed and the audience did too. "It used to bother me, but now it doesn't. I mean, we all bloom! And big boobs are fine but so are little boobs and medium boobs."

Mr. Conklin, my Latin teacher, smiled, and I could feel myself starting to blush. Even though Mom had been a teacher, I'd never thought of the other female teachers at Halsey School for Girls as women with bodies. As for the male teachers, I wished Principal Milliman had told them to skip assembly.

"The average American girl gets her first period at about twelve and a half," Dear Kate continued. "Many start sooner or later. I didn't get mine until I was fifteen."

Kiki and Natalie had both started the previous winter; I'd started that fall and still wasn't regular. I knew I could ask my doctor dad about this, but it had been much easier when I could ask my mom.

Was thirteen the worst possible age to lose your mother? Maybe. Then again, there was no good age.

"Let's talk about putting in a tampon," Dear Kate was saying, her expression bright. "For some of you, it's a no-brainer. For others, it's like: never gonna happen." I looked around. Girls were giggling, but everyone was riveted. "If you're having trouble, you can buy the small, slender, plastic kind for first-timers. Apply a dab of Vaseline to the tip of the applicator. Then relax, take a deep breath, and give it a go but only during your time of the month—no practicing between periods!" Madison had been searching her long, blond hair for split ends but was now leaning forward. "Once you're a pro, you can go green and buy tampons that aren't plastic." Natalie nodded.

"Some girls tell me they can't figure out where the tampon goes." Dear Kate continued, arching an eyebrow. "Ladies, there are three holes down there. *Un, deux, trois.* One's for pee, one's for poo, and in the middle is the vagina. If in doubt, check a mirror!"

Everyone started laughing, and the teachers started shushing us. I looked at Principal Milliman, half expecting her to jump up and haul Dear Kate off the stage. But she remained seated as if our speakers routinely said "pee" and "poo" and "vagina" into the microphone.

"I realize this is all superpersonal," Dear Kate added. "But I get lots of female email, so I know what girls worry about. I'll share some letters with you—no names of course. Oh, and if you ever want to write me, I'm at <u>DearKate@fifteen.com</u>. Keep it short, and I'll answer."

I wondered what kind of girl would actually write to her and then remembered: Kiki, for one.

Dear Kate read us letters about everything from school lockdowns to transgender teens. When she asked for questions, a sixth grader with glittery, green fingernails asked, "Is it okay to be boy crazy?"

Dear Kate said, "Crazy is never ideal."

Madison asked how much email she gets each week. Dear Kate said, "A ton, and it doubles around Valentine's Day. I can hardly keep up."

A seventh grader asked where most of the mail comes from. "No clue," Dear Kate answered. "Letters come with return addresses, but email is often anonymous. And while I'm good at guessing a girl's age, I can't usually guess where she's from. Sexibabi, iluvcandy, lilditzy—emails can be from anywhere." She smiled. "Speaking of, when you're applying for jobs or college, change your screen names! RedHotChica won't cut it with employers or deans of admissions."

Natalie was twirling her hair and suddenly raised her hand. She asked Dear Kate if she had any general Valentine's tips.

"I'll give you four," Dear Kate replied and started counting on her fingers. "One: don't rush your crush. Two: a boyfriend should also be a friend. Three: your love life should not be your whole life. Four: Cupid can be stupid, so listen to your *head* not just your heart. How's that?"

"Helpful," Natalie said.

Dear Kate ended her talk by saying, "If you don't have a valentine, relax. Most girls don't! And if you do, try to *step* into love instead of falling in. And don't go racing around the bases. You're in middle school. Keep your pants on!"

The auditorium exploded with laughter, and Principal Milliman bounded onto the stage. "I'm afraid we're out of time! Thank you. You have certainly given us a lot to think about."

Kiki jumped up, holding her dog-eared *Girls' Guide*, and said, "Guys, come with me."

"I have to finish my science homework," Natalie said.

"I have to go get my history book," Madison said.

Kiki looked straight at me. "Sofia, no excuses."

"Go by yourself, Keeks. Since when are you shy?"

"Pleeeease! Before the line gets any longer!"

I followed Kiki onstage, mad at myself for being a tagalong shadow. Did I really used to belt out solos during recitals and musicals in this very auditorium?

The line moved slowly. When it was Kiki's turn, she asked Dear Kate to sign her book, gushing, "It's my bible. I have parts of it memorized!"

Dear Kate gave her a warm smile and asked how to spell her name.

"*K-I-K-I*," she replied. "I love your column too!"

"Thank you."

"And your earrings!" Kiki added, starstruck.

Dear Kate touched her earlobe. "These are my daughter's. She basically dresses me." She looked up at us. "I don't know how mothers without daughters stay chic!"

"She's so lucky!" Kiki said. "She must think you're a cool mom."

Dear Kate shook her head. "Oh, I don't know about that. She says, 'You don't get it' about as often as other girls." She handed back Kiki's book. "Are your parents coming tonight? I'm speaking at six. A different talk, of course."

"My mom's coming. Her dad might be," Kiki said, answering for both of us.

I felt my cheeks growing flush and willed myself to say something—anything. *Speak, Sofia, speak!*

But no. Nothing. I just stood there, mute. Then again, what was I supposed to say? There were no quick 'n' easy tips for what I was going through.

"Mind if I take a photo?" Kiki said.

"Not at all," Dear Kate replied, and Kiki took selfies of the two of them.

Finally, Kiki said, "Thanks for coming to our school!" I wiggled my fingers as though I were a baby who could wave bye-bye but not yet articulate words. It was humiliating! Did Dear Kate have that effect on other girls? Did some babble while others stood speechless?

. . . .

Pepper greeted me at the door and rubbed against my legs. Mom had called him *Pepito*. We'd rescued him from a shelter three years earlier, and when he wasn't acting like a scaredy-cat, he acted like a dog, following me everywhere.

But at night, instead of sleeping in my room, Pepper preferred to curl up on the rug in front of the radiator in my parents'—my *dad's*—bedroom. Which was a shame because at night, I could have used his warm, purring presence. My old stuffed animals, Panther, Tigger-Tiger, and Yertle, weren't as comforting as they'd used to be.

I opened the refrigerator—milk, bread, juice, a take-out carton of sesame noodles, two plastic containers of hummus and baba ghanoush.

Was I still hoping to find leftover paella or *tortilla española*, the Spanish potato omelet Mom could make at a moment's notice? When was the last time Dad and I had even tasted Manchego cheese with membrillo, that quince paste Mom and I both loved?

Pepper jumped onto the counter and padded to the faucet. I didn't scold him, and he settled by the sink and looked at me, his green eyes round and hopeful. I twisted the handle and a thin stream of water trickled down. He tilted his head, lapping with his quick, pink tongue.

When Dad was home, Pepper behaved differently. He did not loiter by the sink or jump onto the counter or tables. But after school, when it was just girl and cat, all bets were off.

I called Dad.

"Hi, cupcake. How was school?"

"I got a ninety-eight on a Spanish quiz."

"Why not one hundred?"

"You're supposed to say, 'Way to go!'"

"Way to go! But where'd the two points go? You speak better than the new teacher." The new teacher: the one hired to replace Mom.

I told him I'd left out a written accent, then asked when he was coming home. He said, "Around six."

"You're not going to go hear the talk 'Raising Healthy, Happy Daughters'?"

"Don't I know enough about female adolescents?"

"The lady spoke at assembly today. She was good." I wondered what she'd talk to the parents about. Not the ins and outs of tampons.

"If I go," Dad said, "what will you do for dinner?"

I considered saying, *Throw a wild party*, but said, "Order in."

"Fine. I'll see you after it's over."

"Okay. Love you."

"Love you too."

Ever since April, we'd been saying that at the end of every phone call. I wasn't sure who started it—probably Dad. At first, I felt self-conscious mumbling "love you" into my cell in front of friends. But when I didn't say it, I felt worse.

Mom and I used to say, "*Te quiero*," to each other, but not after phone calls. We'd said it mostly at bedtime, when she tucked me in every night.

. . . .

I ordered dumplings and a dragon roll from Miyako, and Pepper kept me company as I ate. Back when our family dinners for three turned into dinners for two, Pepper would sometimes jump into Mom's chair, his furry, black ears and owl eyes peering out above the table. At first, even Dad didn't have the heart to shoo him down. He knew Pepper was as needy and confused as we were.

Kiki called. "Your dad's definitely going, right?"

"Right."

"Good, because my mom's putting on perfume." She laughed, excited. "And I'm going too! I want to hear her again."

"Keeks, we just heard her! And it's Antarctica out there!"

"I want to hear what she tells parents. I want to *be* her, remember? I'm picking you up in five."

"No way! We're not allowed."

"Yes way. We'll hide in the balcony."

"I have homework," I protested. *And I don't want to get in trouble—or watch your mom hit on my dad.*

"So bring your precious homework!"

I could feel myself caving. "You're a terrible influence, you know that?"

"Yep," she said proudly.

I scribbled a note in case Dad got home before I did: "At school. Back soon." I put on my coat and scarf and took the elevator down. Kiki met me in my lobby, and we hurried across the street and into Halsey.

Inez, the security guard, said, "It's a little late, girls." She pointed at the wall clock, and her gold bangles slid toward her elbow. I tried not to stare at her new nose ring.

"I need to grab my English book from my locker," Kiki lied. "We have a huuuge test tomorrow."

Was I imagining it, or did Inez's expression when she saw me switch to the one I saw so often at Halsey? Was she thinking, *Oh, that's Señora Wolfe's daughter, poor thing*? Before Mom died, everyone used to say, "You look just like your mother!" After, it felt as if everyone was still thinking it.

"Inez, we're desperate!" Kiki said.

"All right, make it quick."

We hurried around a corner, passed some posters ("Be a winner, not a whiner!" "Even Einstein Asked Questions!"), and dashed up the back stairs to the empty balcony.

Kiki and I sat on the floor and peeked over the railing. There was Dad, sixth row on the left. And there was Lan right next to him, slipping off her soft fur coat and making herself right at home.

. . . .

Principal Milliman tapped the microphone. "Good evening, parents. Our guest this evening is an advice columnist and the author of the bestselling *Girls' Guide*, which has been published in many languages—from Chinese to Czech. She was a hit this afternoon with your daughters, and I know you'll love her too. Please give a warm welcome to Katherine Baird."

I crouched behind Kiki as Dear Kate strode to center stage. Kiki whispered, "Funny to hear her real name, isn't it?"

Dear Kate thanked everyone for coming and said, "It's always the good parents who attend these evenings. Raise your hand if you have a daughter who is eleven. Twelve? Thirteen? Fourteen? Fifteen? Sixteen?" She raised her own hand at sixteen.

Kiki's eyes were on her mom and my dad. "If they got married," she whispered, "we'd be sisters."

"Kiki, shhh!" I said and tried not to feel mad at my best friend. Yes, I understood her point of view, but didn't she understand mine?

"I've been writing for teens since I was a teen," Dear Kate said. "I started when hotties were hunks, middle school was junior high, flip-flops were thongs, and thongs were G-strings. Remember those days?" There was a rustle of laughter. "A lot has changed but a lot hasn't, and the best way to know what's going on in your home is to talk and to listen. So don't just have the Talk; have an ongoing conversation."

A mother raised her hand. "But what exactly do we say about sex?"

"Whose mother asked that?" Kiki whispered, eyes wide.

"I'll take questions at the end," Dear Kate said, "but my message to girls is: 'Slow down! Sex too soon is a train wreck.' When addressing *older* teens, I always add: 'No glove, no love. No balloon, no party.'" Kiki smirked, though it took me a moment to figure out what Dear Kate was talking about. "Teens need info," she said. "It's not 'Just Say No.' It's Just Say *K-N-O-W*." A few parents nodded.

"And girls need to be clear about boundaries because while society is changing, sex is still a very big deal. It comes with *consequences*, and girls and guys of all ages need to take that seriously."

I looked down at my dad and Kiki's mom and wished I hadn't let Kiki drag me up here. Sex? I had trouble getting boys to text me back. Kiki was a virgin too, but she and several guys, including her current boyfriend Derek, had, as she put it, "done more than just kiss."

Thirty minutes later, Dear Kate was wrapping up. "Blink and your daughters will be grown. My own nest is almost empty," she said wistfully. "I encourage you to relish the privilege of parenthood and to remember that while your job is to give your kids a nest, their job is to spread their wings. I'll leave you with this quote from Christopher Morley: 'We've had bad luck with our kids. They've all grown up.'"

A man laughed. Dad? I wasn't sure. I hadn't heard him laugh in a while.

The parents applauded and Principal Milliman announced, "If you'd like a copy of *Girls' Guide*, please form a line here onstage. Exact change is appreciated."

"Let's go!" Kiki said. "I have to get back before my mom does."

"Right behind you," I said, wishing we had Harry Potter invisibility cloaks. We snuck down the balcony stairs, raced past Inez, who gave Kiki a long look, and stood outside my lobby. Kiki giggled and my fingertips started tingling from the cold. "You still want to be Dear Kate?" I asked.

"Totally! In high school, I'm starting my own column: 'Ask Kiki.'"

"Great idea!"

"So should I give my mom any advice about your dad?"

Tell her to stay away, I thought, but said, "Kiki, it hasn't even been a year!"

Kiki nodded and hurried off to Amsterdam and 101st.

. . . .

Back home, I tore up the note I'd left for Dad. Twenty minutes later, I started wondering what was taking him so long. Mom was the one who had liked to linger at Halsey events, not Dad.

She especially loved singing in the parent-teacher choir, then going out with everyone afterward. Mom had a beautiful voice. Everyone said so.

People said I did too—though no one had heard it lately. Not only had I not performed at last year's Spring Sing, but I'd also dropped out of chorus. In the fall, instead of auditioning for a lead in *The Pajama Game*, I'd volunteered to paint backdrops. I also hadn't sung at the Holiday Cabaret or Christmas Chapel, which I'd been doing since lower school.

Dad's keys finally jingled outside the door, and Pepper raced to greet him. "How was it?" I asked from the kitchen, trying to sound casual.

"Excellent."

Excellent? "Did you see Kiki's mom?"

"She sat next to me."

I was tempted to say, *Practically in your lap!*

"She wears a lot of perfume," he said. "And she told me Lan means 'orchid' in Vietnamese."

"She *is* pretty," I said to see what he'd say.

"That she is," he agreed. "Hey, I bought you *Girls' Guide*. Even got it signed. That's what took a while. And there was a car with a dead battery, so I stopped to help—"

I was afraid he might say something else about Lovely Lan, so I interrupted. "I ordered dinner," I said.

"Good. What'd you order? I'm starving."

"Sushi."

"Sushi? On this freezing night, you ordered sushi?"

"Sorry. I—"

"No, no, it's okay," he said, backing down. I could tell he didn't want to make me feel bad. We were still being extra gentle with each other, as if we were afraid the other was breakable. "Sushi is fine. And you got gyoza, right? And negimaki?"

I nodded. "Check, check."

"Then we're good to go."

"Except I already ate. Mind if I keep doing my homework?" I wasn't up for a quiet dad-daughter meal, let alone an "ongoing conversation." And it would be awkward if he wanted to discuss Dear Kate's talk, since I'd just heard every word.

"The speaker was big on family dinner—"

"Dad, I have a ton of reading."

He shrugged, defeated.

Mom would never have given up so easily. She also would have noticed my guilty expression and grilled me: "*Hija, ¿qué te pasa?*"

. . . .

"Deep down, are we shallow?" I asked Kiki as we studied ourselves in her bedroom mirror the following week. I was wearing my new pink sweater and skirt, and Kiki was wearing a purple crochet dress. We were getting ready for the Valentine's Day dance. The point was to look effortlessly incredible—a challenge that required incredible effort. We'd done our nails, blow-dried our hair, and were applying lip gloss, blush, and eye makeup.

Kiki laughed. "No. Deep down, we are deep."

"I used to love Valentine's Day," I said. "Remember my red headband?"

"How could I forget? You wore it every day in second grade."

I considered taking offense but decided not to. "And remember those giant valentines Mrs. Jenkins stapled to the wall, the red hearts on white doilies? She wrote our names with magic marker in her perfect handwriting—"

"We sat on the floor, 'crisscross applesauce,'" Kiki said, "and came up with words for each letter of everyone's names."

"My words were *sweet, open, fun, interesting,* and *awesome.* The *awesome* was because *hablo español.*"

"Mine were *kind, imaginative, knowledgeable,* and *intelligent.* The words barely fit. I was so proud."

"Now teachers act like February 14 is just another day. At least there's the dance tonight."

"Exactly! So hurry up. It's going to be fun!"

"For you. Every guy you like automatically likes you back."

Kiki couldn't even deny this. But I was hoping that for once, things might work out for me too. In December, I had hung out with a boy named Julian at a party that our girls' school had with his boys' school. We'd talked about graphic novels and had even exchanged numbers (his idea), and when I'd texted him afterward, he'd actually texted back. The first three times anyway.

"Who do you like *besides* Julian?" Kiki asked offhandedly.

"Why do I have to like anyone else?" I eyed her, my mouth open as I applied mascara. She didn't answer, so I capped the mascara. "What? Did you talk to Julian about me?"

"Derek did."

I took a breath. "What'd he say?"

"Derek said that Julian said that he likes you, but he's afraid to go out with you."

"Because I'm scary?"

"Because he doesn't want to ruin your friendship—"

"Oh, *please*! I wouldn't call us *friends*. And isn't that usually the girl's line?"

"He also said that if you went out, he'd never be able to break up with you because..."

"Seriously?" My stomach turned. "God, I am so sick of everyone feeling sorry for me! Isn't it enough that *I* feel sorry for me?"

"I thought you should know. So you don't take it personally."

"Great. Thanks. Now I won't feel bad when he avoids me tonight because, hey, I'll *understand*."

"C'mon, Sof."

"No, Keeks. Why is he thinking about how hard it would be

to dump me instead of how great it would be to go out with me?"
I threw the mascara on the floor. "You know what? *J* is for *Jerk*."

"*U* is for *Ugly*!" Kiki joined in.

"*L* is for *Loser*!" I felt bad turning on Julian—but he'd turned
on me first.

"*I* is for *Idiot*!"

"*A* is for *A-hole*!" I said, surprising myself.

"And *N* is for *Neanderthal*!" Kiki concluded with a smile.

"It's not like I wanted to get married," I said. "Just hang out."

"Hang out or hook up?"

"Maybe both." I threw a pillow at her.

. . . .

The dance sucked. Not for beautiful Kiki, Madison, and Natalie
but for mediocre me. I danced only with girls, and when it was
over, my Jerky Ugly Loser Idiot A-hole Neanderthal of an ex-crush
took a taxi back to the Upper West Side with Britt, even though
they'd *just* met.

On Monday, I saw a valentine peeking out of my locker. Inside
the envelope, it said:

> Happy Valentine's Day to Sofia the Sweet
> from Kiki the Kind

That was *Sweet*. And Kiki was *Kind*. Yet maybe what *S* really
stood for was *Starved for love*.

I never used to feel that way. According to Dad, I was the apple of my mother's eye. But lately, I felt like moldy applesauce. It still seemed absurd that Dad and I were supposed to just get by without Mom, amble along without her as though her absence hadn't drained the color out of everything.

After school, I went online and googled "Dear Kate." A pale pink website popped up, and I clicked around, watched a Love 101 video, skimmed an interview, and took a quiz. Then I saw: Contact me.

My heart began pounding. I double clicked and there was a blank email with the address filled in.

Should I start typing?

What would I say?

Maybe that I wished I could be happy again? And that I didn't like feeling jealous of my friends?

Everyone else had gotten her first kiss during summer camp or winter break or at last year's bar and bat mitzvahs or even earlier playing spin the bottle. Kiki had already had three boyfriends. And while I didn't want to kiss someone random just to get it over with, I also didn't like feeling behind.

I clicked on a few more links. There were book reviews, a Facebook fan page, a photo of a white, fluffy cat, and a black-and-white photo of a girl with braces and pigtails. Was that Dear Kate at my age? If so, she was cute.

Cute? Now that was a word I could do without. My friends said I was cute—and cute was better than not cute. But cute was not hot or beautiful.

Pepper leaped onto my desk, stepping around two green ceramic turtles I'd made in third grade. He settled in beside me and revved up his purring motor. "Pepito," I said, kissing him. "You are such a handsome boy." Then I turned back to the computer, and my hands started typing.

Dear Kate,

My mother died ten months and one week ago, and I'm still not over it. I keep wishing things would go back to normal. I think some people, especially boys, are afraid to get close to me. (When it first happened, I sometimes cried when I shouldn't have.) I'm still sad, but I don't cry as much. (Maybe I don't laugh as much either?) Anyway, I just really miss her. I'm also the only girl in my class who has never kissed a guy. I'm nervous about doing it right. I'm 14, so I'm way too old to be kissing my cat.

Signed,

Pathetic

PS It feels dumb to write you about death and kisses in the same email. Sorry.

I pressed Send and my insides tightened.

What had I done? I opened my Sent Mail and read what I'd written. I wanted to gag. "Signed, Pathetic"? I was beyond pathetic! I was an immature idiot. And for Subject, had I really written: "Life, Death, and Kisses"? Ugh! Why hadn't I pressed Delete?

Too late.

At least I hadn't used my real name or address—just my screen name: Catlover99.

I got up to make popcorn, and Pepper went with me, leaping onto the kitchen counter and peering at me from the sink. "Here," I said, adjusting the faucet to a perfect trickle. He drank while the microwave made popping noises.

I turned off the water, poured the popcorn into a bowl, and was back at my desk and halfway through my math homework when an icon on my screen started jumping, indicating a new message. It was probably spam. An email from a Nigerian widow who wanted to give me a million dollars in exchange for my bank account numbers. Or a drug company asking if I was satisfied with my "manhood." Or some "friend" demanding I write ten people in five minutes to avoid horrendous luck.

I read "Re: Life, Death and Kisses" and double clicked. An autoresponse, no doubt.

I opened it.

Oh. My. God.

Dear Not Pathetic,

I'm very sorry that your mom died and not at all surprised that you haven't gotten "over" it. Losing your mother when you are young is so sad and so hard. At first, it feels like there's a big hole in your life. But little by little, you learn how to step around the hole. Things will never go back to how they were, but you are finding a way to live with your loss. Be patient with yourself! As for being too old to kiss your cat, I still kiss my cat, and I just turned 46! In fact, my old, white cat is with me now, napping on a pile of letters on my desk.

Trust me, you are not the only one in your class who has not kissed a guy. Please don't worry about "doing it right." You'll figure it out, and there is no wrong way. Besides, boys don't like girls who have perfected their technique; boys like girls who like *them*. What's important isn't doing it right anyway. It's kissing the right boy at the right time.

Kate

PS I don't always answer so fast, but my father died when I was young, so I know how difficult it is. While there is no shortcut through grief, here's a strange parting thought: a mother dies only once, so you've already been through the very worst.

Wow. It didn't sound like an autoresponse! I was tempted to call Kiki or Dad, but then they'd ask me what I had written her, so forget it. I stared at the screen and reread the email. My mom had been big on thank-yous, so I pressed Reply and changed the Subject to "Thank You."

Dear Kate,

Thank you for the advice! I will defiantly take it into consideration.

Happy Valentine's Day.

Catlover

PS Is that your cat on your website? Was that you with braces?

I pressed Send, then reread my words. "Defiantly"?! I'd meant "definitely"! English teachers were always telling us to proofread, but I had a horrible habit of proofreading when it was too late.

The icon started bouncing.

> You're welcome. Happy V. Day to you too. Yes to both your
> questions.

I sat back. *Cool.* I considered sending another thank-you but didn't want to bug her. Who knew? I might need Dear Kate again someday.

Dad came home with red tulips from the greengrocer on our corner, and I helped him make dinner. Neither of us was a Top Chef, but I could bake box cakes, and he could make steak and blueberry-banana smoothies. That evening, I boiled water, and Dad dropped in some heart-shaped ravioli he'd bought at Zabar's.

It was kind of depressing actually. But we both knew we'd been overdoing it on ordering in. Deliverymen bicycled to our home with everything from moussaka to moo shu pork. And when we called Saigon Sun, Kiki's mom always tucked in something extra: spring rolls in the summer, curry soup in the winter. Last time, she put in free chicken satay with a note that said, "Enjoy!! Lan." Under the exclamation marks, instead of dots, she'd drawn little hearts. I was tempted to throw the note away before Dad even saw it.

After our home-cooked dinner, I read about Mesopotamia and wrote 150 words comparing two Shakespearean love sonnets. At ten, I went into the living room and announced, "I'm going to bed."

Dad looked startled and closed his laptop halfway. Weird. That's what I did when I didn't want *him* to know what I was doing.

"Good night," I said and looked at Pepper curled on the sofa, his paw over his head as though he'd had a hard day. I picked him up and slung him over my shoulder. "I'm taking my valentine with me."

"You do that." Dad smiled.

I thought about Kiki and Madison, who both had real valentines. According to Kiki, there were also two girls in our class, Steff and Terra, who were going out with each other and having lots of "sleepovers" while their parents had no clue. Steff told Kiki she was bi but that Terra was "just" gay. How could they even be so sure? And what did they do in the dark? It was more than I could think about.

I was glad I had Pepper—and that Dad wasn't out on a hot date with Lan.

. . . .

"What do you think of this shirt?" Dad asked in the kitchen the next Friday.

"I like it," I said.

"Mom used to shop with me."

"I know. You did okay."

"Good, because I also bought it in blue." Dad and I never talked about clothes. He wasn't exactly a trendsetter, and at work, he wore a doctor's smock.

"How's school?" he asked.

"Fine."

"Who got the lead in *Guys and Dolls?*"

"Madison and Natalie both got big parts. You know Madison— she's the ridiculously pretty blond." In my mind, Kiki and Madison could both be models. Maybe even Natalie, with her freckles and cinnamon curls.

"Is that…hard for you?"

"I didn't even audition. And I'm okay with being a stagehand." *Was I?*

"Where's Kiki these days?"

"She has a boyfriend." It wasn't the first time Kiki had been spending a lot of time with a guy—and a lot less with me.

"Does Natalie have a boyfriend?"

"Daaad!" I made a face. Why was he asking so many questions all of a sudden? "She has bigger news," I said. "Remember when her dad lost his job? Well, she applied to public schools—and LaGuardia took her."

"Impressive," Dad said. "So she's leaving HSG?"

"No one can believe it."

"What about you? Do you have a boyfriend?"

"Dad, this interview is over!" I went to my room and shut the door. I didn't want to tell him I'd probably never have a boyfriend.

Alone in my room, I opened my laptop.

Dear Kate,

It's me again, the one who's never kissed a boy. My BFF has a new BF, and I guess I have a question that is totally confidential. I've been noticing how beautiful a lot of my friends are, and

since no guys ever like me, I was wondering if there's a chance
I might be bi or lesbian. I know that's okay and everything, but I
don't think I really want to be.
Wondering

I pressed Send—then felt instantly worse. Why in God's name
did I write that? I wasn't conflicted about this! I just got a tiny bit
confused sometimes because my friends always talked about this
stuff. But why had I put it into words?

Maybe because writing Dear Kate was so easy. I could type
anything. Dumb stuff. Deep stuff. Whatever was on my mind. It
didn't feel real. I shuddered to think what would happen if my
email ever got forwarded or something.

It was too late to take back what I wrote, but to be safe, I
opened the Sent file and pressed Delete, then went into Recently
Deleted Mail and pressed Permanently Delete.

As I was finishing my homework, the icon started jumping.

Dear Wondering,
It's normal to be curious and to notice how pretty your friends
are, but don't be in a hurry to define or label yourself. This is
not something you need to struggle to figure out anyway. It's
something to discover naturally over time. It's not a choice or
a decision. It just is. And everyone should love who she is!
For now, the fact that you find some of your friends beautiful
doesn't mean you're gay or bi; it means you have eyes.
Kate

PS As for your busy BFF, invite her to do something—just
the two of you. And someday when *you're* the one with a BF,
remember to make time for old friends.

When *I'm* the one with the BF? *Yeah, right!*

. . . .

"Don't forget to call Grandma Pat for her birthday," Dad said. "I'm
going out to dinner." I wondered why he didn't say more. If it was
with Lan, would he say so? I wanted to ask Kiki, but she hadn't
returned my last few texts.

"I won't," I said. Hey, I was grateful for all the family I had left:
one father at home, one grandfather in Spain, one grandmother in
Florida. Sometimes, I envied Madison—she was always going to
family reunions. And because of divorce, instead of four grandparents, she had six.

I speed-dialed Tandoori Take-Out, then Grandma Pat.
"Grandma!" I said. "Happy birthday!"

"Who is this?"

"It's *Sofia*. It must be nice in Florida now."

"Yes, it's nice of you to call."

"Grandma, I'll wait while you switch to *your new phone*."
Whenever she wasn't on her special amplified-hearing phone, she
had to do a lot of guessing and I had to do a lot of shouting.

"All right. Just a moment." I waited a *minute*, not a moment,
and then we talked about weather and classes and babysitting, and

I told her that things were "going great." I did not tell her how much I missed Mom or that Dad was out on a date or that my friends were all growing up while I was staying still.

We said good-bye when the deliveryman buzzed from the lobby, and I took the elevator down, paid him, then went back up and ate alone. Afterward, I walked two flights down the stairwell to the Russells' to babysit their two-year-old, Mason. Mrs. Russell had been my math teacher in fifth grade as well as my emergency contact.

"We'll be back at eleven," she said. "There are ribs in the fridge."

"Thanks, I just ate," I said, though of course I intended to sample everything edible. Our building's New Year's party, the one I had skipped this year, was a potluck, and everyone always looked forward to Mrs. Russell's ribs. Everyone had loved Mom's Baked Alaska too.

Mason came running in and grabbed my leg. "*Sofiiiiia!*" He was barefoot and his yellow pajamas were sprinkled with airplanes.

"Mason!"

He high-fived me, and I hoisted him up. He wrapped his arms and legs around me, and his twisty hair smelled of baby shampoo.

Mrs. Russell looked at him and asked, "Who's the best little boy in the whole wide world?"

"Mason!"

"And who loves Mason soooo soooo much?"

"Mommy!"

"Give Mommy a kiss," she said, and I held him tight as he squirmed and leaned into her cheek. "Good night, darling boy!"

"G' night, dowwing Mommy!" I watched their big hug, my throat tight.

When Mrs. Russell left, Mason looked anxious. "Mommy gone?"

"Your mommy is meeting your daddy for dinner," I said. "You'll be fast asleep when they come back."

"Mommy come back?"

"Yes. Mommies go away and come back."

I felt light-headed. *Had my mommy really not come back? How was that possible? Was I really supposed to live the rest of my life without her?*

"Mommy come back!" he confirmed, his dark eyes big and trusting. "We play cars and fire engines?"

"You got it!" I said. "Cars and fire engines."

"You got it!" he repeated, beaming.

. . . .

Hours later, after I tucked Mason in and made sure he was asleep, I got out my laptop and started typing.

> Dear Kate,
> It's me. I'm babysitting. Sorry to bother you again, but is there a way I can get people to understand what I'm going through? Sometimes, the grief feels brand-new, but I can't say that— even to people I love.
> Alone a Lot

It helped that I *could* say it to Dear Kate. It felt like I could tell her anything.

No sooner had I sent the email, than I started looking for a reply. None came. It was Saturday night, and I realized that even advice columnists can't be on call round the clock.

The next morning, however, an answer was waiting.

> Dear Alone a Lot,
> You'll never be able to get everyone to understand what you're going through. But that's not your goal anyway. Your goal is to feel good and whole again. It helps if you have at least one or two people with whom you can think aloud. You'll find them. Hang in there. Things will get easier, I promise.
> Kate

I hoped she was right. I needed things to get easier.

I printed out all the Dear Kate emails and stuck them in the bottom drawer of my desk in a folder marked "Notes for History." I wanted to be able to reread her promise: "Things will get easier."

I also wanted to believe it.

MARCH

I WAS SO OVER JULIAN, I was surprised I'd ever liked him. I felt that way about a lot of ex-crushes. In fifth and sixth grade, I'd been obsessed with Daniel, but as soon as I gave up on him, I wondered why I'd fallen so hard in the first place. Maybe because Kiki and Natalie and Madison had preapproved him? As for Julian, everyone liked Julian. I'd just joined the crowd.

Right then, it felt as if I alone liked Miles. I didn't know if anyone else even knew him, but Natalie and I had noticed him the week before at French Roast, a bistro on Broadway and Eighty-Fifth that seventh and eighth grade girls were starting to go to. He was a ninth grader from Collegiate, and he was with a Trinity girl, but we decided she was probably his sister because they were both tall and had the exact same wavy, dark hair.

"He's cute, don't you think?" I'd asked.

"Yes, but not my type," Natalie said.

"Then he's mine, all mine," I'd said, and we'd laughed.

Now it was Saturday night, and Miles was sitting with us at *Twelfth Night* in the Morse Theater at Trinity. Natalie had invited me because her cousin was in the play, but she'd gotten me to go by saying, "Maybe your crush will be there. I found out his sister is playing Olivia."

The play was good. I liked the set design (especially the papier-mâché palm trees), and I liked how all the characters were confused about love. But what I liked most was that Miles had sat down right next to me.

We talked a little before the show, and at intermission, he asked, "What's your name anyway?" When I told him, he asked, "With an *f* or *p-h*?" He did *not* seem to be thinking, *Aren't you the girl whose mother died?*

"With an *f*," I said.

He smiled, so I smiled back. I introduced Natalie and said her cousin was playing Malvolio.

"Cool," he said. "My sister's playing Olivia." Neither Natalie nor I revealed that we already knew that. "Hey," Miles added, "my parents are in the country this weekend, and my older brother and I are having a party. Wanna come after the play?"

"Uh…yeah," I answered as though Natalie and I routinely accepted such invitations. Kiki sometimes snuck out to meet a guy when her mother had to work late, but I didn't have a curfew because I didn't have a nightlife.

"Um, I just have to call to make sure we can go," Natalie said, grabbing my arm. She yanked me toward the stairwell and said, "Sofia, are you crazy? My brother will never let us go!"

"Won't he be at a cast party?" I said, surprised that for once, I was the one bending the rules. "Our parents know we're together, so they'll assume we're at each other's apartments. I'll call my dad first." I pressed DAD on my cell phone while Natalie stared at me, wide-eyed.

"Hi, cupcake," Dad answered.

"Can I stay out a little later tonight? Natalie and I want to watch a movie after the play."

"Okay." Mom would have pressed for details: Whose home? Who else was there? What movie? What's it rated? "Since I know you're safe," he added, "I may stay out later too." Whoa, now *Dad* wanted to stay out?! "Will you be sleeping at Natalie's?"

I turned to Natalie. "Can I sleep over?"

She nodded, nervous. "Yes."

"Yes," I echoed.

"Great. So I'll see you in the morning."

"Okay. Love you."

"Love you too."

I frowned at the phone. Not only had I gotten away with a lie, but Dad had seemed almost glad I wasn't coming home until morning. Was he relieved I wasn't moping?

Wait. Until recently, hadn't we *both* been moping? Last Thanksgiving in Florida, he'd told Grandma Pat how hard it had been to disconnect Mom's cell phone and how he used to call it just to hear her voice. He also told her about the grief groups he was always inviting me to. I'd never gone, but when was the last time *he* had gone? Come to think of it, Dad was acting almost cheerful lately, wrestling with Pepper and going out at night.

Mom's birthday was June 22, and now she also had a death

day: April 7. Did Dad realize this anniversary was around the corner? Or had *he* turned a corner?

During the second act of *Twelfth Night*, Miles pressed his leg against mine. Or was I imagining this? I moved my knees together, but Miles's knee followed. Okay then. Should I press back a teeny tiny bit? Or not? Questions like this made it extra hard to keep track of the Shakespearean mix-ups.

After the play, Natalie and I got in a taxi with Miles and headed to his apartment. I sat in the middle. Miles's knee was against mine the whole time, and it was clear it was no accident.

Miles lived on the East Side, on Fifth Avenue, not far from Mount Sinai, the medical center where Dad worked, and not far from Natalie's old apartment. When the cab stopped, Miles paid, and the doorman greeted him as "Mr. Holmes." We walked through the marble lobby to the elevator, where a second man in uniform pressed eighteen.

Growing up in Manhattan, I'd been to lots of fancy apartments. Kiki's, I have to admit, was pretty cramped. Our place had two small bedrooms, a small living room, and a small kitchen. But Natalie's, before her dad lost his job, was a humongous penthouse with a wraparound terrace. My mom used to tell the story of how, in first grade, I'd gone to Natalie's for a playdate, and when I came home, I had asked, "Are people allowed to pick where they live?" Mom said, "Of course," and I got all bent out of shape and said, "Then why didn't you pick a penthouse?!"

Actually, Mom and Dad had started renting at Halsey Tower before I was even born. It was designed to provide "convenient and affordable faculty housing," and Dad had liked the cheap rent, and Mom had liked the "non-commute" and that everyone knew everyone. This August 1, however, Dad and I were getting, as he put it, "gently evicted." Halsey had granted us "a courtesy year" since the beloved Señora Wolfe had taught there for nearly two decades. But rules were rules, and time was up. Teacher Tower was for teachers, and Mom wasn't teaching anymore.

I didn't like thinking about leaving the only home I'd ever known.

"Nice apartment!" I said to Miles when we stepped out of the elevator into his parents' marble foyer and giant living room. It was already packed with kids. Who were they? Were they from different schools? Natalie said she was hungry and headed toward the kitchen. But I wanted to check out the view—and also get my courage up. I walked across the oriental rug, passing a piano topped with silver-framed photos of people on horseback. I looked out at the glowing street lamps of Central Park and the skyline of the Upper West Side.

"Amazing view!" I said when I realized Miles was right behind me.

"That's just what I was thinking." He looked me up and down and placed his hand on the side of my waist. I felt a tickle of excitement. He followed my gaze out the window. "My parents always have people over during the marathon. It's cool to watch the runners from here."

"Sounds cool," I said. Little Miss Conversationalist. What was amazing was to be standing with Miles in his home looking down on Central Park.

"Hey, so what can I get you?" he asked. I wasn't sure what he meant. "Vodka? Beer? Wine?"

"I don't know," I said, then realized this was a dumb answer. But I'd never really drunk alcohol, not counting sips of sangria with my family in Spain. He moved closer, spreading his fingers and subtly tugging at the hem of my shirt. He touched first the cloth, then my skin. I felt a shiver of excitement. Or was it nervousness? Should I tell him I was completely inexperienced? Or was that completely obvious?

I turned toward him, and he walked slowly forward, moving me backward, until he'd backed me into the wall. The lights were dim, and no one was nearby. I felt drawn to Miles but a little repelled too, caught in the pull and push of a magnet.

He tilted his head and leaned into me. It was as if we were slow dancing without music. Then he kissed me. His lips were dry and tasted of cigarettes. I kissed back, aware of my braces and my awkwardness. He started pressing himself against me, and I could tell he was... What did Dr. G call it in Life Skills? "Tumescent"? I wanted to keep liking Miles, wanted to want to kiss him. But I didn't like feeling cornered. Was Miles a great guy? Or a horny rich kid? And had I asked for this—led him on?

Dad often lectured me about guys, especially on Saturdays after he did pro bono work at a clinic for teenage girls. But his words had always seemed abstract. Even though I knew that a lot of Halsey girls, like Kiki, had done stuff with guys, I knew that a lot of others, like me, hadn't.

"Wait," I said to Miles, pushing him away.

"Wait? Why?"

"I just want to know you better."

He put out his right hand. "I'm Miles Holmes, and I'm crazy about you."

I shook his hand. "But you don't know me."

"I like what I see."

I wanted to feel flattered, not flustered, but he was in such a hurry. He was already kissing me again, and it didn't feel the way I wanted my first kiss to feel. His lips were on mine, but it wasn't romantic. It was rushed—it was wrong. And now his tongue was in my mouth.

I pushed weakly against his chest. "Maybe I *will* have something to drink," I mumbled. Where was Natalie? Was she okay?

"Sure." He led me by the hand to the crowded kitchen.

"Do you have flavored water?" I asked.

"Flavored water?" His eyebrows went up, and he peered down at me. "Help yourself," he said, letting go of my hand.

Just a sec—was he dumping me because I hadn't let him grind against me and didn't want to do vodka shots? I searched for Natalie and thought, *I lied to my dad for this?*

A girl with red sunglasses on top of her head shrieked, "Miles! I couldn't find you!" She rushed over and gave him a big, sloppy kiss.

Natalie appeared. "I heard he has a girlfriend. I'm assuming we're looking at her."

"She can have him. I wouldn't even mind leaving—unless you want to stay."

"No. Let's get out of here."

We jostled through the crowd toward the elevator, and some guy tripped and sloshed beer on my blouse. "Sorry!" he said, then started pawing at me as if to get the beer off. Ugh! Natalie and I darted out, and I made a mental note to drop my smelly top straight into the laundry machine rather than in the hamper. Or maybe I'd just do a load the second I got home.

Miles's doorman helped us get a cab, and I paid for it since I was the one who'd wanted to go to the East Side. Twelve dollars! I sighed, furious with myself. I'd spent a lot of time daydreaming about a boy I never even wanted to see again.

At Natalie's, we made sundaes, squirting fudge sauce onto ice cream and adding mini marshmallows.

"Your bat mitzvah was so fun," I said, remembering last winter when everything was much easier for me—and for her. "I liked when the rabbi said to 'shower you with sweetness,' and we pelted you with marshmallows."

I was glad Natalie and I were at her place. "And I even got to dance with Daniel," I said, since back then, he'd been the boy I liked.

In fourth and fifth grade, Natalie and I had both been "madly in love" with Daniel. We'd vowed not to let it come between us if he asked one of us out. Which he never did. In the beginning of sixth, he *did* drop a blueberry down Natalie's shirt—making me insanely jealous. But by the time Natalie was "called to the Torah," she and a boy in her Hebrew school had gone out, broken up, gone out again, and broken up again.

I was still the only one of our friends—our "Core Four"—who'd never gone out with a boy. As for having my first kiss, did that kiss with Miles count? I hoped not. "Natalie," I said quietly, "I don't even get what just happened. Did Miles reject me, or did I reject him?"

"Maybe it doesn't matter?" she said. "Or maybe both?"

I nodded and was going to say more about Miles, but she said, "It's weird to think that my family used to have an apartment as big as his."

"I like this apartment," I said, although I'd liked her family's bigger one too.

She shrugged. "Yeah. But my dad gets mad a lot now. He wants my mom to go back to work. I guess they lost a lot of money."

I listened. Just the other day, she and I were little kids with little problems. Were we really becoming "young adults"? Were we ready?

. . . .

On Sunday morning, when I got home, Dad was in such a good mood, I almost told him about the party. But no. Bad idea. Forget it.

Still, I wanted to talk to someone about making out with Miles. Kiki? Maybe. But if I called her, would she think I should just get over myself and grow up?

I turned on my computer.

Dear Kate,
Remember I told you I'd never kissed a guy? Well, last night I

did, but it didn't turn out like I hoped. He was kind of arrogant, and he already has a girlfriend. At least I stopped him when I did, if you know what I mean. I feel like such a little kid sometimes. I also feel bad because I didn't tell my dad about the party. But if I tell him, he'll never let me go out again. And I don't want him to worry. He's actually been acting happy lately. Is that bad? (Me lying, not him acting happy.)

Catlover

For Subject, I typed "Lies and Kisses."

I pressed Send, then stared at my screen for a few minutes. The icon didn't budge.

Oh well. Just writing it all down made me feel a little lighter. Still, I decided to call Kiki after all.

She picked up after the first ring, and I spilled my saga. She said she'd heard Miles was full of himself and had gone through a number of Nightingale and Chapin girls. She also said things were good with her boyfriend.

"You and Derek?"

"Me and Tim! He's a junior at Horace Mann."

"A *junior*?! Omigod. Your mother would kill you!"

"That's why she doesn't know."

"How *is* your mom anyway?" I wondered if her mom had said anything about my dad.

"No idea," Kiki said. "She's been working late a lot—which works for me." Kiki laughed.

I didn't.

....

Two hours later, I saw "Re: Lies and Kisses" in my inbox.

Dear Catlover,
If I were the pope or your principal, I might say you should always tell the whole truth. But life is complicated, and sometimes, people have reasons for not telling each other everything. I'm not suggesting you lie to your dad! The guilt you feel shows you're a caring daughter and self-respecting person. I'm just saying I understand. Fortunately, you got home safe, and you don't sound heartbroken. (Believe me, I know what heartbroken sounds like.) I'm sorry the evening was a disappointment, but you were smart not to let things get out of hand. It's wise to take your time and trust your gut. And yours sounds trustworthy.
Kate
PS No worries. That was your first kiss, not your last kiss.

....

Right before dinner, I was looking for my cell phone and remembered that I'd left it backstage. "I'm such an idiot," I muttered.

"Don't say that!" Dad said.

"I'm talking to *myself*, not you!"

"I get that. But no one gets to call my daughter an idiot. Not even my daughter."

"It's just that I left my phone at school," I explained.

"So let's go get it. I'll go with you." He grabbed his jacket. "I have something I want to tell you anyway."

"Dad, you can't go to school with me!" I said, alarmed. "I'm fourteen!" I shot out the door. Besides, I did *not* want to hear about his evenings with Lan, the Siren of Saigon Sun!

It was enough that I'd noticed a new *Playbill* in the blue-and-white bowl on our sideboard. That bowl used to overflow with programs of plays and musicals that Mom and Dad went to on and off Broadway. For almost a year, the bowl had been empty. Was it going to start filling up again?

. . . .

Abuelo arrived from Segovia for spring break just in time for our production of *Guys and Dolls*. He's five foot six, and in Spain, he looks short, but in America, he looks extra short. Like an elf with bushy eyebrows and twinkly eyes.

Abuelo, Dad, and I sat down to watch the show, and Abuelo complimented my backdrop for the scene when Sky Masterson takes Sarah Brown to Havana. I told him I'd spent hours painting the diner, with its turquoise booths, pink swivel stools, and tin foil stars.

"*¿Pero, Sofía, por qué no estás cantando?*"

I whispered that I wasn't singing because set design was okay. I didn't add that lately I hadn't even been singing in the shower.

We watched, and I couldn't help but think that Natalie was a good Adelaide, but I might have sung "A Person Can Develop a

Cold" with more oomph. And Madison was an okay Sarah, but I would have sung "I've Never Been in Love Before" with more heart.

Afterward, Abuelo and Dad waited while I went to tell my friends how great they were. They all looked so happy and proud, and I tried not to feel jealous, but the truth was, I didn't miss just the singing—I missed the afterglow too. The hugs and congratulations. As if reading my mind, Natalie said my set was "awesome."

Should I have pushed myself to audition? Possibly. But it's not like I could charge myself up like a cell phone—stay still and then, hours later, be good as new, one hundred percent.

The next day, Abuelo set up a worktable in our building's basement and taught me how to hold a hammer and use a screw gun and coping saw. He even showed me how he made his Christmas crèche pieces, cutting curves, carving with a chisel, smoothing edges with a file. It felt good to sit by him and learn a new skill.

We also did touristy things. One day, we walked across the Brooklyn Bridge. One evening, we saw a musical and Dad met us afterward at a revolving restaurant above Times Square.

Abuelo said that being surrounded by skyscrapers was like being in a forest of buildings. "*A María, le encantaba New York.*"

I translated: "Maria loved New York."

"She did," Dad agreed. "She was happy as a clam."

"A clom?" Abuelo looked at me.

I explained that it was like saying *feliz como una perdiz, feliz como un lombriz*, happy as a partridge, happy as a worm. And I wondered if it was easier to be happy if you were a clam or bird or worm.

I missed Mom at odd times now. During conversations about Spanish expressions. Or when the buzz of my alarm woke me up instead of her "*Buenos días.*" Even at the grocery store when Dad didn't buy Marcona almonds—or stop me from buying gummy bears.

It had been nearly a year since I'd phoned Abuelo to tell him the news. This week, he told me that that day was the saddest of his life.

Now once again, I knew something before my grandfather did: Dad was dating. I didn't know much else, and Dad had not asked me to translate anything about it. Was his relationship with the woman—Lan?—too new? Was his relationship with Abuelo too old? Whatever the reason, I kept Dad's news to myself. So when Abuelo flew back to Spain, he had no idea how fast things were changing in New York.

. . . .

"Can I come in?" Dad said a few days later.

"I'm doing my Latin."

He came in anyway. I was in my pajamas, and Pepper was on my desk under the lamplight, licking himself. Dad took off his glasses and rubbed them with his soft shirt and said, "Listen, Sof, as you know, I've been seeing someone."

Someone? Why didn't he just say Lan?

"Dad, I don't want to know!" I said, and Pepper looked at me, alarmed. He leaped off the desk and darted under the bed.

"No, I actually think you might because—"

Because what? Because then Kiki and I could share a bunk bed?
"Dad, you're wrong!"

"But, honey, I think—"

"Dad, I—"

"Sof, please give me a chance—"

"Dad, how can I make it clearer? I don't want to hear about it, okay?"

"Okay, okay." He backed out of my room.

"Close the door until it clicks!" I said.

He did, and I tried not to cry.

I got on the floor, peeked under the bed, and reached for Pepper. He was hiding next to a dusty stack of picture books and childhood board games. "Come," I pleaded, my arms outstretched. But Pepper wouldn't budge.

. . . .

I wished I could talk to Dr. Goldbrook, our middle school counselor. Some girls didn't want to confide in Dr. G because they said she was a "stranger." I didn't want to because she was a neighbor and family friend.

As a toddler in Halsey Tower, I'd been "famous" for my singing. Buckled up in my stroller, I sang nursery songs in the lobby and mail room and elevator. Apparently, I could carry a tune while doing hand motions to "Itsy Bitsy Spider" and "The Wheels on the Bus."

Mom said I made the grown-ups laugh, and Dr. G called me "Little Songbird."

So what was I supposed to do now? Knock on Dr. G's door and say I'd become a "Silent Songbird"?

I didn't know where else to turn.

. . . .

Dear Kate,

My father met someone. I still can't believe my mom is dead. Crocuses are popping up, buds are on the trees, squirrels are running around, and I'm still sad. It's hard to think about my dad with another woman, like kissing her and stuff. Please don't tell me to talk to my school counselor because I can't. I just can't.

The first anniversary of the day my mom died is coming, and I don't want to meet his girlfriend or special friend or Mystery Woman before then. I'm not in a rush to meet her afterward either!

I guess I don't want to share my dad. He's the only parent I have left. Just because he likes her, do I have to?

I hope you don't think less of me. I want my dad to be happy, but can't he wait a little? My BFF disappears when she starts going out with someone, but I never thought my dad would.

Yours truly,

Sofia

For once, I reread my email before hitting Send. I could have revised it, but it wasn't a take-home essay, and it was honest. The only thing I decided to take out was my name. I changed "Sofia" to "Still Not Over My Mom." I was surprised I'd originally typed my real name, but maybe I was beginning to feel like Dear Kate was a real friend.

Which was insane.

I didn't want to become one of those girls who makes "friends" online or who fall for guys who claim they're rock stars when they're actually serial killers.

At least Dear Kate wasn't a total stranger. I'd met her, sort of.

I picked up *To Kill A Mockingbird* so I'd stop staring at my non-bouncing icon. I couldn't believe my English teacher was giving us a quiz the first day back after vacation. I also couldn't believe it was 11:00 p.m. and Dad still wasn't home. When he and Mom used to go out, they always came back before I went to bed. But his so-called girlfriend couldn't care less about me. Maybe Dad cared less than he used to too? Before he'd left, he'd told me he'd be late, saying, "Try to understand: I saw her only once this week!"

Try to understand, I wanted to say, *I wish you weren't seeing her at all!*

I put on my pajamas, grabbed Pepper, and kept reading until I got to the last page. I was sorry when the book ended. I liked the last scene, when Atticus tucks Scout in and says most people are very nice, once you get to know them.

Would I have to get to know Dad's Mystery Woman? Would I think she was "very nice"? And if it wasn't Lan, who was it? Some widow from grief group?

I hated going to sleep in an empty apartment, but what choice did I have? I reached for Panther, Tigger-Tiger, and Yertle and wondered if other girls my age still slept with their stuffies. Impulsively, I wrote Dear Kate one more email. The subject was "Quick Dumb Question." I asked: "Is there an appropriate age for outgrowing stuffed animals?"

I pressed Send, then wanted to kick myself.

On a one to ten Scale of Pathetic-ness, I was a twenty-five.

. . . .

When I poured out my heart, it usually felt good to write everything down, but then, unless I heard back right away, I'd start to feel worse. Embarrassed and exposed.

The next morning, my inbox remained empty. Laptops and cell phones weren't allowed in school, so after a fast lunch of Moroccan tagine with couscous (Halsey "chefs" were big on inventive menus—it was part of our "culinary education"), I went to the library to use a school computer. I made sure I was alone, then signed on, hoping for a response.

And there it was:

Dear Still Not Over My Mom,
Of course I don't think less of you. You miss your mom, which shows how close you two were and how big your heart is. In fact, it would be surprising if you didn't feel conflicted about your dad's new relationship. I don't think you will ever truly get "over" your mother's death, but you've already done the difficult

job of managing without her for almost a year. That was not easy! Give yourself some credit!

How are you going to mark the anniversary? You could play her favorite music, invite friends to share memories, or plant a rose bush in your yard.

And after that? You will never ever forget your mom, but I think you will find the strength to meet your dad's new friend if it's important to him. You can also tell your dad that you just aren't quite ready.

Do you have to like her? No. But it's easier when everyone gets along. So try to be open-minded, okay?

K

PS As for outgrowing stuffed animals, no set age, no worries! And btw, I get more mail than you can imagine, and there's no such thing as a dumb question.

That evening, while setting the table, I looked at Dad and, just to be polite, asked, "Did you have fun last night?" I'd seen a new program in the culture bowl: Orpheus Chamber Orchestra at Carnegie Hall.

He poked at some marinating chicken thighs. "I did."

I hoped he wouldn't say anything else. Not one single word.

"Sofia, I'm eager for you to meet her. Maybe this weekend?"

Meet her? Then it wasn't Lan?

"I'm not quite ready," I replied, surprised to hear myself sounding so definite. I remembered when Dad had told me that I was born a week after Mom's due date and Mom had had to be induced. "Why?" I'd asked.

"You weren't quite ready," he had said.

I looked up and added, "Maybe after April 7."

"Fair enough," he said. "Hey, did you ever read that book I gave you, *Girls' Guide?*"

"Parts of it," I said and didn't add that I'd read and reread one section called "When Loved Ones Die." It had made me feel less alone and had reminded me that I wasn't the only girl in the world who seemed to be grieving in slow motion.

. . . .

I heard a crash, and Pepper came tearing out of the living room. I got up and saw that he'd knocked down a photo of Mom, Dad, and me. The three of us were face up behind cracked glass.

I tried not to feel spooked, but I couldn't help it: my family was broken. I was too.

I wanted to call Kiki or Natalie, but even if they said all the right things, they were things they'd said before: "It must be hard." "Your mom was so nice." "I wish I knew what to say."

I opened my laptop. Dear Kate *would* know what to say. She might be busy writing other girls—or hanging out with her husband and her own girl—but I needed to talk, so I typed.

Dear Kate,
My cat just broke a family photo, and it felt like a sign or omen.
Like, maybe I should accept that the past is past and agree to
meet my dad's girlfriend, even though I want to hate her guts.

Do you believe in signs?

Lost Not Found

The response was almost immediate.

Dear LNF,

I don't believe in signs, but I do believe in accepting what you cannot change. Your first family will always be safe and unbroken inside you. No cat or person can touch that. But it's good if you are willing to meet the girlfriend. Don't think of it as being disloyal to your mom but as being supportive of your dad. Are there any plusses to his having a girlfriend?

And do you think your mom would want him—and you—to be happy?

K

Was there a plus side to Dad having a girlfriend? I no longer felt sorry for him. And he wasn't bugging me as much about hanging up towels—but maybe I'd gotten better at that? He was also humming a lot—was this a plus or a minus?

Dad and I still didn't talk much, but maybe that was partly my fault. Mom and I had had an easy closeness. We spoke our own language—literally.

I decided to think about something else, something fun, like a crush. But I didn't have a crush. Not Daniel. Not Julian. Not Miles. Nobody.

Since Dear Kate was online, I decided to send her one last

horrendously mortifying question. I was pretty sure of the answer, but I'd noticed something odd, and getting her opinion might calm me down.

> Dear Kate,
> This is extremely embarrassing, but I have a tiny pink pimple with a white tip. It's like a face pimple but *down there*. I haven't had sex (!!), so it can't be an STI, right?

The reply came instantly:

> Right.

Well, good.

It was so handy having Dear Kate just a click away! She was friendly, free, and full of answers. And so many subjects were easier to type about than talk about! It felt good to be able to confide in her online anytime about anything. It was better than in person could ever be. After all, I could never in a million years ask a question like that to someone I'd have to face in real life!

APRIL

I WASN'T LOOKING FORWARD TO SATURDAY. But I'd promised Dad that after the one-year anniversary, I'd meet his Mystery Woman.

April 7 itself was drizzly. Dad had arranged for the Riverside Park Fund to plant a dogwood in Mom's honor, and now Dad and I took a walk so he could show me the tree in case I "ever wanted to visit it."

Visit it? I didn't want to go near it! I didn't want there to be a tree! But he and I were standing on the path by the muddy hill on Eighty-Ninth and looking at the dark, shiny sapling.

It was hard to think of it as "Mom's tree."

A woman in the park called out to us. She was holding hands with a child who was twirling a red umbrella dotted with yellow ducks. Under the umbrella, the child had a baby doll tucked in a sort of Snugli, its plastic head peeking out.

"Dr. Wolfe!" the woman said. "You might not remember me, but you delivered my little girl!"

Dad gave his canned answer: "Of course I remember you! And this is *my* little girl."

The woman turned to me and said she was so sorry to hear about my mother. "My niece had her for Spanish years ago. She loved her."

I didn't know what to say. That I loved her too? That I still loved her? I said, "Thank you" and waited for the mother-daughter-babydoll team to go away. I wanted the whole gray day to go away.

. . . .

At school, I told Kiki I was being forced to meet the Mystery Woman.

"So there really is an MW?" Kiki asked, a little disappointed.

"There's an MW *and* a daughter," I said, worry in my voice.

"That might help."

"Doubt it." I told Kiki we had planned to go to a Korean place downtown for bibimbap, but the daughter had a "commitment," so instead, Dad and I were going to have to drive all the way to their house in Westchester, almost an hour away.

"What a pain," Kiki said. "Still, it might go better than you think." She pointed to a cheesy poster that read, "The most important thing you can give someone is a chance." She made a face. "See? The universe is speaking to you."

"What if I don't feel like listening?"

"Maybe you and the MW and the daughter will all hit it off."

"Or maybe we'll all hate each other, and the lady will decide that free gyno appointments aren't worth it."

Kiki laughed, and I wondered if I should have been rooting

for Lan all along. Mom had liked the saying "*Mejor lo malo cono-cido que lo bueno por conocer*," which she translated as "Better the devil you know than the devil you don't."

Thing is, I didn't want any devils in my life.

Kiki and I hurried to Spanish class and sat down with a dozen other girls in pastel polo shirts and khaki pants. Because of our school dress code, we all basically matched except on Fridays, which was dress-down day.

The teacher asked me to read a passage aloud, then explained that the reason "*cuando nos veamos mañana*" ("when we see each other tomorrow") is subjunctive is that "no one can ever be certain about what will happen the next day."

Yeah, yeah, I knew all about that.

. . . .

Dad and I walked to our parking garage on Ninetieth off Amsterdam. The attendant drove up in our car, and I opened the back door the way I used to do when Mom rode up front. To cover my mistake, I dumped my bag on the backseat, then opened the front door. Dad didn't say anything.

In the car, he drummed his fingers on the steering wheel and kept peering over at me. I guess he was nervous too. When we got to 684, Dad said, "Cupcake, now I really have to tell you: My girl-friend? You've already met her."

"What do you mean?"

"Remember Katherine Baird?"

"No." I picked at a hangnail. "I mean, the name sounds sort of familiar."

"Dear Kate?"

"Dear Kate?" I repeated.

"The woman who spoke at Halsey."

Goose bumps formed on my arms. "What about her?"

"She's the one."

My neck tensed up, and I couldn't swallow.

"I wanted to tell you before, but you never let me."

I stared straight ahead.

"You'll like her. You liked her at school, remember? You're the one who told me to go hear her. Lan said Kiki's her biggest fan."

"Kiki is, but…"

"But what?"

I shut my eyes and turned away. "It's just…weird." Weird because I thought Dear Kate was on *my* side. Weird because it felt like she was being a traitor. And weird because I didn't want my father's girlfriend to know my deepest, darkest secrets! Oh God, what had I written to her about? Kissing and lying! Grief and bisexuality! Stuffed animals! I'd even vented about hating *her* guts! And oh no—that stupid, stupid pimple!

Just shoot me now! I thought.

Dad stole a sideways glance. "Weird isn't so bad, is it? Katie knows what we've been through. She's an expert at this sort of thing."

I wondered when Dear Kate had become Katie, and when our devastating personal tragedy had become "this sort of thing." I slumped in my seat. "I didn't know she was single."

"Divorced."

"How old is her daughter?"

"Sixteen."

Sixteen? If she were ten, the daughter might think I was cool. But sixteen? She might not want to have anything to do with me!

"Have you met her?"

"Once, briefly, the first time I went to their house. That's when Katie and I realized we'd known each other years ago." He told me that when he was a boy in Chappaqua, his high school girlfriend was best friends with Dear Kate's big sister. "I knew her back when she tagged along on our Trivial Pursuit games. Katie had pigtails and her last name was Dibble. Isn't that funny?"

Ha-ha-ha.

"We didn't recognize each other at HSG," Dad continued, "because I remembered her with braces, and she remembered me with long hair and a mustache!"

"A mustache?"

"A mustache! Actually, she *did* seem familiar, but of course, I can never ask a woman, 'Do I know you?' because what if she's a patient?" He shrugged. "After her talk, I walked out behind her and saw her get in her car but then get out again, looking distressed. I asked if something was wrong, and she said her car was dead. Well, I flagged a cab so we could use the cables, and I got in with her and helped her jump-start her car. And she was grateful. We had only a minute or two inside her car, but we realized we are both single parents and…"

Stop! I did *not* want to hear Dad's new how-we-met story!

I preferred the story of how he and Mom met—in the hospital where Dad was a resident and Mom was an interpreter. He always used to tell people that a Peruvian woman went into labor, and next thing you know, he was delivering twins *and* falling in love.

I also did not like that Dad had known Kate *before* he'd even met Mom. It didn't seem fair. "What's the daughter like?" I asked. "Is she nice?"

"With Dear Kate as a mom, how could she not be?"

"Dad, teenage girls are not known for their niceness." Her kid's niceness was not a given any more than kids of teachers were all geniuses, kids of ministers were all kindhearted, or kids of shrinks all had their heads screwed on straight.

"I'm sure you two will get along," Dad said and patted me on my knee as if I were eight.

At least Kiki would be impressed. She'd pee in her pants if she knew I was on my way to Dear Kate's—or that Dear Kate and Dr. Eligible were an item.

But I didn't want to have lunch with Dear Kate. I had assumed our paths would never cross again, which is why I'd always typed away, uncensored. Now what? Would she recognize me from the Halsey stage, where I'd stood, moronically mute, next to Kiki? Should I hint that she and I had a history of our own?

· · · · · · · · · ·

We drove and drove, and the city highways soon became country roads, and buildings gave way to trees wrapped in a soft, green haze.

By the time we got to Dear Kate's house, I was a nervous wreck. She was going to think she was meeting me for the first time when actually she knew my inner thoughts better than anyone.

She walked out to greet us wearing tan slacks and an apricot sweater, and she didn't seem to recognize me as Kiki's silent sidekick.

An old, white cat trundled across the lawn like a moving pillow. Kate introduced the cat as Coconut, and I heard myself saying, "I lovvve cats! I just lovvve cats!" And then I couldn't stop! I kept talking about cats—their cat, my cat, cats in general, and how much I lovvved them. Part of me must have wanted to get everything out in the open so Dear Kate would realize that I was Catlover99 and that she didn't just know my dad—she also knew *me*.

But the saner part of me wanted the idiot part to shut up. It would have been different if we could have started from scratch and if Dear Kate could have gotten to know me on less humiliating terms. I wanted her to think her new boyfriend's teen daughter was a nice, normal girl, not a whack job with crushes on the wrong boys and pimples in the wrong places.

Inside the house, Dear Kate picked up an old scrapbook with yellow-and-black flower power stickers all over it.

"Groovy!" Dad said. "Far out!"

I looked at him. "Dad! Stop!"

He morphed back into my father and asked, "Are those Peter Max stickers?"

"Yes. This was my big sister's. But wait till you see what I found inside. You ready?" Dear Kate showed us a photo of three teenage girls with poofy hair and a long-haired boy making rabbit ears behind one of them. "Look closely," she said.

"Whoa! Dad, is that you? Ms. Baird, is that you?!"

"Call me Kate, though back then, I was Katie."

"Okay," I replied, though there was no way I could say, *Okay, Kate.*

She said the photo was taken at a high school football game. "Maybe even on the day we met!" She smiled at Dad, and I felt like I had to sit down.

Next, she gave us a quick tour of her downstairs, including her office. On the shelves were teen diaries and different editions of *Girls' Guide*, half in English, half in other languages. On the wall was a framed photo of Kate with the ladies on *The View*. There was also a note that said, "I was a screwed-up teenager and your book saw me through." Next to it were a list of numbers, starting with 1–800-SUICIDE. On Kate's desk, one letter began, "Dear Kate or Whoever Cares…" On her screen were opened emails. I pictured her reading my emails at that very desk.

It was so strange. Under normal circumstances, I'd have been excited to be standing next to Dear Kate. But these were abnormal circumstances!

"Shall we have lunch?" Kate asked. She walked to the front hall and called up, "Alexa! Our guests are here." After a few minutes, she said again, "Alexa! Lunchtime!" Two minutes later, she called, "*Alexa!*"

Clearly, Kate's daughter was in no rush to meet me either.

When Alexa finally came down, she was wearing a Byram Hills volleyball sweatshirt. Like her mom, she had blue-jean eyes and strawberry-blond hair. But Alexa's was straighter and longer. She was pretty but not Kiki pretty or Madison pretty. More like athletic. Strong. Tough. "Hey," she said without smiling.

We followed Kate into the dining room and sat down, and Alexa started ladling out chicken soup. "Mom and I made it this morning," she said.

"Looks delicious," Dad said, but when he tasted it, he made a face and said, "Oh, this is spicy! Did you try it, cupcake?"

Cupcake? Did Dad really just call me "cupcake" in front of Dear Kate's sixteen-year-old daughter? I could feel my face flushing— whether from soup or embarrassment, I wasn't sure.

"I think I added a tad too much chipotle," Alexa conceded. She stifled a smile and added, "But maybe food *should* bite back."

Dad and I exchanged glances.

"I'll get some ice water," Kate said. She scowled at Alexa as she pushed through the swinging door to the kitchen.

Alexa seized her opportunity. "So, Gregg, Mom says you're a gynecologist. Sofia, is he your gynecologist?"

"I go to a pediatrician," I said, then wondered why in God's name I hadn't just said no.

She turned toward Dad. "Aren't most gynecologists women? I go to a woman."

"Nowadays, yes. When I started my residency, it was about fifty-fifty."

"What made you pick gynecology?" Alexa said. "I watched this old movie, *Animal House*, and one of the frat boys becomes a Beverly Hills gynecologist, a gyno to the stars!" She laughed.

Kate came back with a pitcher of water. "What Alexa means—"

"Fair question," Dad said, unruffled.

"You're interested in the female body?" Alexa inquired, all innocence.

"Alexa, if you can't behave—"

"*Behave?*" Alexa repeated. "Mom, I can *leave*. My friends are celebrating Nevada's birthday, remember?"

Kate frowned as she served cheese quesadillas, but Dad said, "In med school, we did a round of obstetrics, and after my first childbirth, I was hooked. Doctors speak of deliveries as being 'uneventful,' but they really are the main event, an everyday miracle. What's more beautiful than childbirth?"

"Sunsets? Rainbows? Hockey players? Help me out here, Sofia."

Huh? Alexa was looking at *me* for backup? My mouth was still on fire from her poisoned soup.

"Gregg, how many babies do you deliver each week?" Alexa asked.

"Well, there are more births around the full moon and in the summer," Dad began, "but actually last spring, after nearly twenty years, I gave up obstetrics."

"Why?"

"After Maria died, I didn't want to be on call all the time. If a baby arrived at 3:00 a.m., I didn't want to have to race out with my catcher's mitt. And if Sofia needed me or was in a musical, I didn't want to miss it."

"Paternity leave from the maternity ward?" Alexa quipped.

Dad smiled. "Exactly."

"I didn't know that's why you stopped," I mumbled.

"My colleagues have been happy to fill in."

"But, Dad, you love delivering babies." Every year, he showed me all the holiday cards with baby photos that his patients sent him.

"I've taken my practice in new directions," he said. "And now I do that pro bono work with teens."

I felt guilty. I hadn't realized Dad had made this change partly because of me.

"Isn't it funny?" Alexa said, looking at me. "Your dad and my mom have young women all figured out, inside and out, body and mind?"

I didn't say anything.

"It's nice that we share interests," Kate said and went into the kitchen. She returned with mango sorbet and a plate of Easter Peeps.

"Look how smooshed this Peep is," Alexa said, lifting up a misshapen yellow marshmallow chick. "More like a poop than a Peep!" She turned back to Dad. "I read that OB/GYNs get blamed for doing too many C-sections but that it's not their fault. It's because of rich moms who want to schedule their kids' birthdays and obese moms whose ginormous babies would get stuck coming out the regular way. Do you think that's true?"

Was Alexa always like this, or was this a performance for our benefit?

"I think that's an oversimplification—" Dad began.

Kate hopped up. "Shall we take a walk?"

"Great idea." He stood and put his arm around Kate's waist.

Alexa and I both did a double take. I'd never seen Dad put his arm around another woman, and maybe Alexa wasn't used to seeing her mom coupled up either. Kate must have sensed this because she slipped out of Dad's grasp and walked toward the sliding glass door that opened onto their deck.

"Look at the deer!" she said. Outside, two speckled fawns lifted their heads, vaguely curious. "We see deer every day," Kate added. "They're incredibly tame."

We walked toward the ball field behind their home.

"They eat everything but daffodils," Alexa said. "That's why my dad built that fence around the garden." She pointed, and I wondered where her dad was now.

We were heading toward Windmill Club, which was just beyond the ball field. The parking lot was empty, and Kate said the club was closed until Memorial Day. We started walking on the narrow road around the lake, Kate and Dad taking the lead. Alexa fell behind with me and announced, "In half an hour, I'm meeting my friends." I wondered if she'd promised her mom that she'd spend precisely thirty minutes with me—and not a nanosecond more.

After a silence, Alexa said, "What's it like going to an all-girls school?"

"I'm used to it. I've been at Halsey since kindergarten. And we hang out a lot with guys from coed and all-boys schools." *A lot? Did I just say a lot? Why not say 24/7? Why not say we have boy-girl slumber parties every weekend? No. Orgies!*

"Do you have a boyfriend?" she asked.

"No. You?"

"On again, off again." She picked up a pebble and threw it into the woods.

"Do you ever ask your mom for advice?"

That cracked her up. "God no! Do you ever ask your dad about periods?"

She may as well have pointed a remote control at me and pressed Mute.

After a while, she bent to retie her sneaker and said, "You're fourteen, right? And half Spanish?"

"Right."

"Are you going to have one of those *quinceañera* things? We learned about those last week, the 'transition from childhood to womanhood.'"

"No, no, those are big in Latin America, not Spain."

"See that red-winged blackbird?" Alexa said, changing the subject. "In the tree? Around two o'clock." She pointed to a blackbird with a splash of red on the top of its wings.

"Yes," I said, adding, "When I was little, I thought all birds were pigeons. I'd see a duck and say, 'Pigeon!' I got bees and flies confused too."

"Not too bright, huh?" Alexa said, which shut me up again.

A few minutes later, a rabbit froze in front of us, and I forced myself to break the silence. "It's cool that you have bunnies and deer around here."

"What do you have in the city? Rats and roaches?" I must have looked stricken because she said, "Kidding, kidding."

We walked along and she pointed out some robins, and then, for Kiki, I asked, "What's it like having Dear Kate as a mom?"

Alexa shrugged. "You know, reporters always ask my mom what it's like to have a real, live teenager," she began, "but no one ever asks me about living with the Answer Woman."

"So tell me about it," I said. During my quiet months, I'd learned that if I could just say, "Tell me about it," I could keep a conversation going.

"It's pretty screwed up, actually. A lot of kids get all starry-eyed around her. Like, last Halloween, a ghost, a mermaid, and Little Bo Peep came trick-or-treating, and when my mom opened the door, the mermaid whispered, 'I *told* you she lived here!'"

"Aww, that sounds cute."

"I guess," Alexa admitted. "But for me, the whole Dear Kate thing has gotten seriously old. My mother must have a million little pen pals who are convinced that she's their new best friend and that they have this *meaningful* relationship with her. It takes up way too much of her time. This morning, she and I were supposed to go for a run, but some sniveling kid emailed her from a ledge, so my mom was like, 'Alexa, I need five more minutes.' I wanted to say, 'Oh, Mom, tell the brat to jump!'"

I could feel the color rising to my cheeks.

"Her inbox is out of control," Alexa continued. "And you would not believe the letters! What a joke! 'I have boobs, but my mom won't take me bra shopping.' 'I went on a church retreat and accidentally shoplifted.' Or this one's classic: 'Sorry I haven't written in a while…' Like my mom keeps track. These kids are delusional!" Alexa snorted. "Ha! Dear Kate, patron saint of losers!" She looked at me, waiting for me to laugh along.

"A few weeks ago," she continued, "I was in her office when some girl with a zit on her vajayjay wrote my mom all spazzed out 'cause she was convinced she had an STI. The kid had never even had sex! And probably never will, little bozo. A virgin for life." Alexa was amusing herself to no end. "Basically, my mom spends half her waking hours giving out Band-Aids. She doesn't get that 'making a difference' doesn't make a difference and that she should just tell everyone to get a life once and for all."

"Do you read all her mail?" I wondered if I'd gone bubble-gum pink. Alexa probably thought I had a rare skin condition or an allergy to fresh air.

"Only when I'm beyond bored. You couldn't pay me to read it all—though she'd love for me to help her. I keep telling her I'd ruin her career. I'd tell the little freaks to dry their eyes and quit their whining. Especially the repeat customers." Alexa shook her head. "I do proofread her columns though. She makes me so she doesn't use dated slang and lose her street cred."

We'd walked about halfway around the small lake when Alexa checked the time on her cell. "Hey, want to see where we hang out around here?"

"Sure."

"Mom!" she shouted. "We'll be home in fifteen!"

"Okay," Kate shouted back. She and Dad were ahead of us, holding hands. I tried not to stare, but my stomach was in a knot.

Alexa pointed out the clubhouse and said that decades earlier, some rich guy had built an estate with a polo field, stable, and windmills. Later, Windmill Farm got divided up and houses were added, and the polo field became a ball field. "In the summer," she said, "there's a snack bar and red beach umbrellas, and people swim and go down that giant slide and play sand volleyball and stuff." I tried to picture this quiet lake bustling with people. "I used to play Ping-Pong and foosball in the Teen Room. Now we have other places to go. I mean, once you're a teen, you're not going to go to the *Teen* Room!"

Alexa led me toward an old, red windmill. The paint on the door was chipped. She tugged at the padlock, pulled back a latch, and we stepped inside. It was dark, but she walked to a ladder that led to the top. Hey, wait. Had we just broken in?

"Have you ever gone up?" I asked.

"Of course."

"Is it safe?" I could feel Alexa rolling her eyes. She checked her cell again, no doubt counting the minutes until she could leave.

"It's cool." Up we climbed. When we got to the top, we sat on a worn wooden bench and I looked out past the windmill's rusty blades to the lake below. "I mean, it's not the Empire State Building," she conceded.

"No, but I like it."

"You know what I used to call the Empire State Building?" I shook my head. "The *Umpire* State Building."

"I called it the *Entire* State Building!" I gave her a half smile, but she just stared at me.

"When are you getting your braces off?"

I felt self-conscious again, but at least I had a good answer: "Tuesday."

Her cell phone rang, and she picked up. "*Literally* on my way!" she said. "Don't you dare start without me!" She turned to me. "My friend Nevada is turning sixteen, so my friends Amanda and Mackenzie made her an epic Earth Day birthday cake with vanilla frosting polar bears on top. Amanda and I play volleyball together. We've known each other since, well, seventh grade for me, eighth for her."

Now that Alexa was about to ditch me, she was being chattier. But the second we got back to the house, she raced off like a bat out of hell.

. . . .

"All in all, that went pretty well, don't you think?" Dad asked as we drove home.

"You mean, besides your calling me 'cupcake,' the soup burning a hole in my tongue, and Alexa making me feel like I was five?"

"She's a tough cookie."

"You can say that again."

"She's a tough cookie." He smiled. "So did you soften her up, turn her into a fresh-out-of-the-oven cookie?"

I shook my head.

"Sofia, I appreciate your coming today. It means a lot to me." He paused. "She means a lot to me."

I didn't know whether to say, *That was quick* or *Me too*. I settled on, "Can we listen to music?"

"First, just answer me this: Katie's pretty nice, isn't she?"

"Yes." I sighed. "She's pretty and she's nice."

"This might be good for you too. I mean, if you ever want to confide in her, you could."

I stared out the window. He *so* didn't get it. He and I couldn't possibly share Kate. "Dad, it's not as easy for me as it is for you, okay?" I pushed a button and David Bowie started singing, "Ch-ch-ch-ch-changes…"

Dad pressed Pause. "Sweetie, talk to me."

"There's nothing to say." I blinked hard and swallowed, and warm tears started to roll down my cheeks. "Here's how it works: *you* can get a new wife, but I can't get a new mom. It's not your fault, and I'm glad Kate isn't evil or, like, twenty-eight years old, like some of Kiki's dad's girlfriends. But don't expect me to be instantly thrilled, okay?"

"Okay."

"I still don't even like sitting up front. I think of it as Mom's seat."

"I miss Mom too."

"Well, maybe I miss her more."

Dad's shoulders sagged. "It's not a contest. And you can't measure missing." His hands tightened on the wheel. "People say that the widows and widowers who were happily married are the first to remarry—not that I'm thinking about that."

"I should hope not!" I crossed my arms and surveyed the other cars, many with couples in the front seats. I pictured my parents doing the crossword, watching TV, buying groceries at Fairway. I didn't want those memories to fade.

When Dad and I had both been raw with grief, at least we

were in the gulley together: misery loves company. Neither of us had enjoyed last Christmas—the decorating or undecorating. But now it was late April, and he was moving forward—and taking Dear Kate with him. And he was not even aware that I was making a sacrifice!

In my mind, I sent one last email to Dear Kate.

> Dear Kate,
> I can't write you anymore because I found out who's taking my father away. *You!* Please don't tell him I went to that party or that I asked about kissing. And don't mention the pimple. And please forgive me for having taken up so much of your time.
> Yours truly,
> Another Delusional Loser

I was remembering how I'd hinted about my online identity by going on and on about cats, but Kate hadn't picked up on my clues. Maybe it was just as well. Still, it didn't feel right to keep our correspondence all to myself. Were secrets overrated? Mine felt like a burden. "Dad, if I tell you something, you promise not to get mad?"

"Well, honey, that depends—"

"Oh, Dad, just say yes."

"Fine. Yes. What?"

How would it feel to reveal the truth? I decided to start small. "When Kate spoke to the parents at Halsey," I began, "Kiki and I were in the balcony, hiding. I left you a note, but then I got back before you did, so I threw it away."

Dad looked unsure of how to react. "Okay…"

"Okay," I echoed and tried to determine if I felt any lighter.

No. I felt the same: hollow.

I figured it would be crazy to say anything else, so I pressed the button and let Bowie get back to singing about ch-ch-ch-ch-changes.

Dad started singing along.

"Stop," I said. "You're kind of ruining it." *You're kind of ruining everything.*

"Sorry." He stopped singing but added, "I always liked Bowie."

I knew he wanted me to press Play, but I didn't feel like doing what he wanted.

Instead, I pressed Skip and wished I had a device that worked like that in real life: whenever you got to a bad patch, you just pressed Skip.

But I didn't. So I turned off the music, and we drove home in silence.

MAY

TELL ME IF IT HURTS," Dr. Kossowan said.

"Ishokay," I mumbled. My mouth was wide-open, and the orthodontist and her assistant were probing with tools and air suckers as they removed my braces, bracket by bracket, while putting in and taking out cotton rolls damp with saliva and specks of blood. I squirmed in the big chair under the bright light.

But for once, I was happy to be there. My braces were coming off!

No more x-rays and moldings and rubber bands. No more ugly hardware in metallic colors. No more having to make up missed classes because of appointments and adjustments. No more goofy goody bags with friendly Mr. Tooth cartoons on the outside and free wax strips on the inside. I had enough dental wax to sculpt a score of tiny turtles. Now, after years of being a patient—a very patient patient—the bands and wires were going into the garbage. Good riddance!

Dr. Kossowan repositioned my chair and handed me a mirror.

"Wow!" I said. My teeth weren't crossed, there were no gaps

or spaces, and they weren't covered with unsightly metal or tiny, pointy wires that jabbed the insides of my cheeks.

I examined my smile…and smiled.

"Of course you still have to wear your retainer at home," Dr. Kossowan said.

"Of course," I said, though for a second, I'd thought I was home free.

. . . .

The next Sunday, while Dad met with a real estate agent, I walked through Riverside Park and went up to Mom's tree. I'd done this once before, and this time I hoped to stop and say something.

But it was still too hard. I couldn't do it. Not yet.

I just stood there in silence and then walked on.

A few hours later, Dad and I drove to Armonk. He turned on NPR.

When we arrived, Kate said, "I'm afraid Alexa is at an all-day SAT prep session."

"That's okay," I chimed and hoped it wasn't obvious that I was more relieved than disappointed. Dad and Kate started holding hands, and I added, "I think I'll head over to the lake." Not that I particularly felt like it.

I was amazed at how green the ball field and woods were—and more amazed when I passed a striped skunk followed by four wobbly black-and-white baby skunks. Who knew skunks were so cute?

At the lake, I took off my shoes and dipped my toes in.

Freezing! I couldn't imagine ever climbing that slide and speeding down into the water. I started looking for pebbles, then tried skipping them across the water. Each one sank.

"It's all in the wrist," said a male voice.

I whirled around, my heart beating fast.

It was a boy a little older than me. Tall and lanky, with sandy hair, he was wearing a faded black T-shirt and worn jeans. He didn't look threatening—Kiki would say he looked hot.

"I'm sorry you saw that," I said.

"Me too. Not a pretty sight." He had a slow smile.

"I've never done it before," I said shyly.

"I could tell," he teased.

"I live in the city," I said, as if that explained it.

"The *city*? New York? New London? New Delhi?" His eyes were sea green.

My face grew warm. "New York."

"Well, it's your lucky day. I happen to be an Olympic stone skipper, and I can give you one lesson for free."

"Okay…"

"First, we need the right rocks." *We?* I followed as he hunted for stones that were round, smooth, and flat. We returned to the water's edge, and he put his hand underneath mine and showed me how to send the stones spinning, not plunging. "It's like throwing a mini-Frisbee," he said. With a quick sidearm flick, he launched three stones in a row, low and parallel to the water. All three skipped repeatedly before disappearing. "See? All you have to do is defy gravity."

"You make it sound easy," I said.

"It's not easy. But you can do it."

I gave it a try. The first stone sank. So did the second. The third spun and took a tiny skip. I lifted my arms in triumph. "I did it!" For a second, I thought he might give me a congratulatory hug, but he just looked out at the lake.

We skipped a few more stones, and he asked where in the city I lived.

"Upper West Side."

"Where the dinosaurs roam?"

It took me a second, then I laughed. "Well, not *inside* the Natural History Museum."

"I used to meet my cousins there. I was all about T. rex bones and IMAX movies."

"We live about fifteen minutes away, depending on how fast you walk."

"I walk fast. I'm on the track team." He checked his cell phone. "In fact, I gotta go. I'm meeting some guys. I've been keeping them waiting."

"Okay." He started walking away, and I blurted, "I'm Sofia."

He turned and shouted back, "I'm Sam."

That night, in my room, I couldn't stop thinking about him. I couldn't remember everything he'd said about stone skipping, but I could feel his warm hand guiding mine.

. . . .

Dad got a call and hurried off to the hospital. On his desktop, I saw an email from <u>DearKate@fifteen.com</u>. It hurt to know she was writing him, not me, and I almost opened the email. But I didn't.

I was half tempted to write Dear Kate myself. I wanted to send an update signed "Stress Mess" and tell her I was happy about meeting a boy and unhappy about having to move. But I couldn't because I might be tempted to add that one thing that was weighing on me was where things were heading with Dad and his no-longer-mysterious woman. Besides, what did she even care anyway? She was deluged with letters from losers.

I called Kiki. "Meet me in Riverside Park? By the flowers?"

"The *You've Got Mail* flowers?"

"Yes." We used to watch that old movie with my mom. It was one of her favorites, and it was filmed in our neighborhood. Mom said the crew had spent days pinning yellow leaves to bare trees to make it look like autumn. "I only have half an hour," Kiki said. "I'm meeting Trevor."

"Trevor? I thought it was Tim."

"That's over. He kept saying he liked how 'exotic' I was. Creeped me out! I don't want people to like me because I'm mixed. I want them to like me because I'm awesome." I'd heard this before. "Trevor's cuter anyway."

"Just meet me. I have something to tell you."

Ten minutes later, Kiki and I stood by the community garden. It was bright with tulips and daffodils, and the nearby cherry trees were in bloom and even smelled good. Two dog walkers with a dozen dogs of all sizes sauntered by.

"I have sort of a secret," I said, cutting to the chase. I hoped Kiki wouldn't be mad that I hadn't told her about Dear Kate, but I'd needed to figure out how *I* felt before Kiki started telling me how lucky I was—or angling for an invite.

"A secret?"

"You know about my dad and the Mystery Woman?"

"Yeah, the MW in the 'burbs."

"There's something you don't know." We began walking south. "And you can't tell anyone." Boats bobbed on the Hudson.

Kiki met my eyes. "All right."

"Pinkie swear?" I knew I was being stupid, but I didn't want the whole school buzzing.

"Pinkie swear," she repeated.

"Okay, remember when Dear Kate came to Halsey?" I began. "Well, her car died that night, so she was like a damsel in distress. And my dad was like a knight in shining armor or, I don't know, maybe a do-gooder in a down parka."

"Sofia, what are you talking about?"

"The MW is Dear Kate!"

"What?!" Kiki's eyes grew wide. "Omigod! I can't believe it! Or maybe I can—my mom said that when Dear Kate signed her book for your dad, it was like they had some 'karmic connection.' I thought Mom was just jealous."

"They *did* know each other! But, Keeks, it wasn't a past life—it was this life! Dear Kate's big sister was best friends with my dad's high school girlfriend."

"Shut up! Seriously? Omigod, have you been to her *house?*"

I nodded.

"More than once?"

"Yes."

"Get out! You are so lucky! Why didn't you tell me? Or invite me!"

"Number one, you've been pretty busy lately. And number two, maybe someday."

"Is she nice? Please don't tell me Dear Kate is a nightmare in real life."

"She's nice." I paused. "Her daughter's kind of scary."

"Tell you what. Invite them over, and I'll drop by! Or take them to Saigon Sun! We'll give them freebies! Bo luc lac and curry tom—on the house!"

"Kiki, there's something else. You know how you once wrote her, and she wrote back?" Seagulls screeched above us, and I remembered once in sixth grade when Kiki and I were walking on Broadway together and a bird pooped on my jean jacket. I was freaking out because I was late for chorus, but Kiki said, "Just switch with me. I'll wash it, and we'll switch back tomorrow." We traded jackets, and off I ran, grateful to have such a friend.

"In February," I confessed, "I started writing Dear Kate—like, a *lot*. And she answered a lot. But that was before I knew—"

"She was doing your dad!"

"Eww! Please! *Dating* my dad. I'm freaked out enough."

"Sorry," Kiki mumbled.

"So now I don't know if I should tell her it was me or keep writing anonymously or change my email address before she figures it out. I don't even know if our 'special relationship' was all in my head! Her daughter said she writes a zillion girls. Do I tell her I'm one? Or *was* one? Do I thank her? Or pretend it never happened?"

"I don't know," Kiki said. "That is a tough one."

"I think I crossed some line. It would be like you asking my dad about herpes or something."

"Actually," Kiki said, "I have been worrying a little."

"About what?"

"About some of the stuff Dr. G used to try to scare us about…"

I was annoyed that the topic was slipping from my worries to Kiki's. Strange how you could feel close to someone one minute, irritated the next.

"It's just that Trevor wants to do a lot more than kiss. I guess that's my secret." She sighed. "I don't want to, but I also don't want him to break up with me."

"Didn't you just start going out?"

"More like staying in." Kiki frowned. "He also wants me to send him a photo of…"

"Oh God, Keeks, don't even consider it! Remember what happened to Bettina?"

"I know, I know." Bettina was an eighth grader at Spence who texted her boyfriend a picture of her boobs. Later, when she broke up with him, he forwarded it to his lacrosse team. Within days, every private school kid in New York had seen her topless selfie. I got it from Kiki *and* from Madison. At first, Bettina tried laughing off the whole thing, but now she was transferring to Choate.

"Kiki, you usually seem happier about new boyfriends."

"Think I should write Dear Kate?"

"Maybe. But don't mention me! Or just dump him. He doesn't deserve you."

We turned around and started heading back. "How about you?" Kiki asked. "Any new crushes?"

"Well, last weekend at Kate's, I sort of met a guy."

"Wait. *Kate?* You call her *Kate?!*"

"My dad calls her Katie. I don't call her anything."

"Okay, so you met a guy?"

"I was trying to skip stones, and I was terrible. He came out of nowhere and started teasing me."

"And?"

"And I told him I'd never done it before."

"A virgin in his midst! Did he seem disappointed?"

"More like surprised. I said I was from 'the city,' and he laughed because I guess I'd made it sound like there's only one city in the world—"

"Which there is."

"—and then—"

"You made wild, passionate love?"

"I don't know why I'm even telling you!"

"Oh, c'mon," Kiki said. She and I had been dissecting boy-girl stuff since third grade.

"He showed me how to flick my wrist."

"He showed you how to flick your wrist?!" She stopped in her tracks and made an obscene gesture.

"Keeks, cut it out. You're disgusting. You want me to tell you or not?"

"Sorry. Go on."

"It wasn't like that. It was like…he was sort of holding my hand."

"What's his name?"

"Sam."

"Sam and Sofia," she said. "Sofia and Sam. I like it."

"Me too."

"Hey, can I tell my mom about your dad?"

"No."

"You know, I always really wished they—"

"I know."

We headed up the hillside, and at Eighty-Ninth Street, I pointed out the tree that Dad had had planted months earlier. "It's already grown a little," I said. Kiki stayed quiet. "I dreamed about her last night. I dreamed I was at Kate's with Dad, but Mom was there too, sitting in a chair. She didn't say anything. She wasn't mad or sad or even surprised to be back. She was just there, with us."

"Maybe she is," Kiki offered quietly.

"I'm going to come back tomorrow. For Mother's Day."

Kiki nodded, and before we left, I turned to the tree and whispered, "*Hasta mañana.*"

. . . .

Día de las Madres. When Mom was alive, I never gave much thought to Mother's Day. It came and went unheralded. Sure, I'd give Mom a card or flowers or some no-big-deal gift, and we'd all go out to dinner. But we ate out fairly often, not just on specific occasions. And Mom and I always got along, so who cared what the calendar said? Mother's Day never felt like my birthday or Halloween or Thanksgiving or Christmas—days that could inspire countdowns beforehand and reminiscing afterward.

This time, Mother's Day was different. The relentless advertising wore me down, and the Sunday arrived like a scorpion with a sting.

"It's not too late," blared a pharmacy's in-store announcement, "to show your mom how much you care. You'll find everything you need in aisle six to make your mom's day special."

Wrong. It *was* too late. Way too late! And while a lot of people missed Maria Wolfe, only I missed her as Mom.

That afternoon, I decided to look at old photos and listen to music by Rodrigo and Granados. *Fotos y música española.* That was how I would honor the day.

"Want to go out to dinner tonight?" Dad asked before leaving to do his rounds.

"And watch all the happy families celebrate their beloved mothers?"

"Point taken. Want to order in?"

"How about paella from Café con Leche? Even though Mom thought their chorizo was too salty."

"Sure," Dad said.

I told him I was planning to say hi to Mom's tree, and we agreed to meet at seven.

As I pored through photos in boxes and on my computer, I was struck by how many more recent photos there were of my friends and me than of Mom and me. Why hadn't we taken more of the two of us?

I walked to the park, and it was filled with families, couples, runners, dogs.

When I got to the little dogwood tree—Mom's tree—I sat down on the ground and hugged my knees to my chest. I was silent at first, breathing in the scent of earth and cherry blossoms, feeling the warm sun. I looked around. Some trees had already lost their blossoms. Some were surrounded by a quilt of pink petals.

I hadn't planned to speak out loud, but suddenly, I started talking. Someone passing by might have thought I was talking into a phone or rehearsing lines. Or maybe, if they saw my tears and realized it was the second Sunday in May, they might piece it all together.

"Mom," I said quietly. "I don't know if you can hear me, but it feels a tiny bit like I'm talking to you." My eyes began to burn. "I know you wouldn't want me to show up and cry all the time, so I don't.

"But part of me wants to. This is my *second* Mother's Day without you. Someday, it's going to be two years without you. Then five. Then ten. Then twenty-five! I just can't believe you're never coming back. Ever! It doesn't seem possible. Or fair."

I wiped my eyes and looked around. I was sobbing. Officially making a scene.

"Mom, I miss you. That's all I really want to say. I'm living my life. I'm getting good grades and seeing friends and babysitting. But I miss you so much! I get jealous of other girls who have moms—moms who will go to their middle school and high school and college graduations. And their weddings! Moms who will meet their future kids. I can't believe you won't be there for any of it."

I took a breath. "Most people don't get it. At least not the girls with two parents. I know other people go through other stuff, but how can anything be this hard?" My shoulders were shaking. "*Es tan difícil.* And Dad's not always around.

"I'm sorry. I didn't mean to come and water your tree with my stupid tears. And I'm not blaming you. I know you wish you could be here too. You didn't want to leave so soon. I don't mean to complain or make you sad—if you can even hear me. It's just that sometimes, I do feel sad, so sad. And broken inside. Sometimes, I think I'll never be completely happy again.

"But, Mom, I'm trying to be brave. And I want you to know that even though I miss you, I'm being a good girl." I knew that sounded childish. "I've gotten through a whole year without you—a year and a month and a week. And I'm getting better at not being sad and silent all the time. But please don't think I'm forgetting you! I'm not. Not for a minute! I guess I'm just starting to learn how to live without you here."

I wiped my eyes with my sleeve.

"I still love you as much as ever! I have your picture in my wallet and your love in my heart and your genes in my blood."

I went quiet.

"And now I don't know if I should tell you this or not, Mommy, but here goes: I'm never going to get a new mom. *Claro.* You're it for me. Mother's Day, for me, is you. But Daddy has been seeing somebody. And I'm trying to be okay with it because he was so sad for so long! But I'm *not* really okay with it.

"Anyway, if you're ever looking down from above, I mean, if that's how it works, you might start seeing me with another lady. But nobody will ever replace you, Mom. Because I'm never letting you go. You're my mom and you will always be right here inside. *Dentro de mí. Aquí, Mami.*

"Next week, at the moving up ceremony, you'll be with me too, okay? And when we move to another apartment. And someday if I have a daughter, her middle name will be Maria and I'll tell her all about you." I hadn't expected to say that.

"For now, though, I'm just going to keep going because you'd want me to—and because it helps Dad. But no matter what, *te quiero ahora y para siempre.* I love you now and forever."

With that, I stood up.

I looked at the tree and waited to see if the wind would bend it or a flower would bloom or there would be some answer. But no, nothing. The air felt cool, and I rubbed my arms and hugged myself. I couldn't think of a way to say good-bye in English or Spanish, so I blew the tree a kiss.

. . . .

That night, I was surprised to see an email from Dear Kate.

> Hi, Catlover—
> I hardly ever write girls unless I'm writing them back, but I was
> just thinking about you, so I looked up your email in my old
> mail. How are things? I bet today was hard. After my dad died,
> I felt like ripping the Father's Day ads out of all the newspapers
> and magazines! I especially hated ads that said, "Make his
> day special," and contests that said, "Tell us, in 100 words or
> less, why your dad is a great guy." I still don't like Father's Day,
> though I've learned not to let it hurt.
> Anyway, take care of yourself, okay?
> Kate

Wow.

Maybe Alexa didn't give her mom enough credit. Maybe Dear
Kate *did* care about her pen pals. I phoned Kiki and asked, "Do
you think she thought about Catlover99 because she met me? Or
because of Mother's Day?"

"I don't know," Kiki said. "But she wrote me too."

"What?!"

"I wrote her and said I was fourteen and asked: What is the
right age for sex?"

"You did not!"

"I did. And I'm about to read you what she wrote. But listen
up because then I'm pressing Delete!"

"Okay," I said, and Kiki started reading.

Dear Fourteen,

There is no "right age," but fourteen seems way, way, way too young, which is perhaps why you wrote me. Sex too soon is a terrible idea and can lead to disease, pregnancy, and plain old heartbreak. There's no such thing as casual sex because there's no such thing as a casual baby or casual abortion. Please remember that saying no to someone else can mean saying yes to yourself. Many girls (and guys) are virgins all through their teen years. It only seems as if "everybody's doing it."

"Did you write back?"

"Nope. Did you?"

"Yeah."

"Let's hear it," Kiki said.

I hesitated, then read:

Dear Kate,

Thank you for writing me. Things are okay. I miss my mom, but I met my dad's girlfriend and she's very nice. Today was hard, but I visited the tree we planted for my mom.

Catlover

I admitted to Kiki that I'd spent ten minutes trying to decide between "Sincerely," "Yours," "Thank you," and "xo" and ended up just signing Catlover.

I did not tell Kiki that I also sent a quick follow-up email that I thought was clever because it gave me a way to ask for more advice.

Dear Kate,

Sorry, but I do have one more question. When I met my dad's girlfriend, I also met her twin girls. I don't think they like me. Any tips?

Thanks!

C

At first, there was no reply, and I worried Dear Kate might be kicking herself for getting back in touch. But then this came:

Hi again—

These twin sisters, like you, are going through an adjustment. You're worried about sharing your dad; they're worried about sharing their mom. It's natural for them to feel territorial and protective. They may warm up—especially if you can figure out what you all like to do: Bake? Bike? Hike? Do you like the same movies, music, sports, shows, sites, games? If they stay chilly, let this be *their* problem, not *yours*. (Not easy, I know.) Last thought: If your dad and his GF break up, none of this will matter anyway. So no need to overthink things.

K

Break up? I was still getting used to the idea of Dad and Kate going out!

. . . .

"Kiki, want to go to Armonk tomorrow?" We were in her kitchen microwaving Vietnamese dumplings. "I don't know if Sam or Alexa will be there, but Dear Kate will."

"Omigod! I've been *waiting* for you to ask!"

I told her that last time I was there, I'd fallen asleep in Kate's hammock and woken up with a deer a few feet away from my face. At first, I was scared, but then I realized that in Armonk, the deer are about as aggressive as golden retrievers. I also told her that Dad had given me a lecture about how we had to check for tiny deer ticks.

"Lyme disease is like gonorrhea," he'd said, "easy to get, easy to cure, but devastating if left untreated."

"Kind of a buzzkill," Kiki said.

"I think doctors know too much." I said. "Dad's all about being careful."

The next day, Dad was looking at real estate listings, and I told Kiki to come over. I couldn't believe Dad and I really had to leave Teacher Tower. Apparently, after Dad's practice grew, he and Mom had considered moving into a bigger apartment but had decided against it because they loved "the price, location, and neighbors," and because for us, Halsey really was home.

Not for much longer. On August 1, a young teacher and his family, the Gidumals, would be settling into 5C.

Dad and I had gone to look at a few apartments, but his heart wasn't in it. Everything was expensive or dark or small, and when we did see something halfway decent, some other couple (always a couple, never a father and daughter) jumped in and bought the place.

"We can always rent," Dad said, though he didn't like "throwing money away."

As for throwing things away, I was terrible at it. In Spanish, the word for souvenirs and memories is the same: *recuerdos*. And who wants to throw out memories?

Dad had a sentimental side too. I'd told him he should get rid of his Hawaiian shirt with the pineapples on it, and he'd said, "Can't. Mom liked it."

I understood because two of Mom's dresses now hung in my closet on either side of my clothes, like bookends. Sometimes, I'd touch them, smell them. No doubt I'd hang them in our next apartment too, wherever that might be.

. . . .

When we got to Armonk, Kiki shook Kate's hand and started gushing as much as she had on stage back in February. A few minutes later, Alexa joined us in the backyard by the weeping willow. I was glad she'd missed the hero worship. I hadn't seen her since Spicy Soup Day, and I hoped Kiki and Alexa would get along.

"Can that hammock hold all three of us?" Kiki asked.

"Easy." Alexa led the way, and we climbed in.

"This is the life!" Kiki said, looking at the sky through the pine branches. "I can't believe Dear Kate's your mom!"

"She has all the answers," Alexa deadpanned.

"And I can't believe I'm at her house—your house! Sofia, take a picture of me and Alexa."

Alexa smiled, and I could tell she liked Kiki. Everyone did. Alexa might even think I was cooler because Kiki was my best friend. We stretched out to enjoy the warm late-spring sun. I closed my eyes and saw rosy pink.

Kiki studied the deck. "Let's take time-delay pictures of us jumping off the stairs."

If I'd suggested this, Alexa would have dismissed the idea. But she said, "Sure. Why not?" and we spilled out of the hammock. I set my camera on a bench, and we climbed the steps and took photos of ourselves in flight. In one, all three of us were airborne.

Alexa asked, "What would you guys be doing if you were in New York right now?"

Kiki shrugged. "I don't know. Seeing a movie. Shopping. Going to Starbucks. Getting manicures? Studying? Some Saturdays, Sofia makes sandwiches in a soup kitchen, and I help at my mom's restaurant." I knew it bugged Kiki that she had to earn her money, whereas Dad gave me an allowance and, lately, extra handouts.

"My father lives in New York," Alexa said, "but I can't picture myself living there."

"You should hang out with us!" Kiki said.

Or not, I thought.

"Can't. I have finals coming up. I have a Spanish test on Monday."

"Sofia can help you. She *saves* me. You should take advantage of her!"

Alexa gave me a sideways glance, and I managed a nod, though I wasn't sure how I felt about her taking "advantage" of me.

"Lemme get my notebook." Alexa went upstairs, leaving Kiki and me on the deck.

"I thought you said she was a bitch," Kiki whispered.

"I said she could be bitchy. She's a lot nicer with you here."

Kiki leafed through a magazine in the hammock while I helped Alexa with an essay using the *imperativo* and *pretérito* tenses. Afterward, Alexa offered to drive Kiki and me around Armonk. "Not that there's much to see," she added. "Main Street, a gazebo, a duck pond, and *mi escuela*."

"You have a car?" Kiki asked, incredulous.

"It's just a Jetta, and it's used, but it works."

"You're lucky," Kiki said circling it. She laughed at Alexa's bumper stickers: "My honors student can beat up your honors student" and "Make Out Not War."

"I don't know a single Halsey kid who has a car," Kiki said.

"Most seniors don't even drive," I added.

"My *mom* doesn't drive!" Kiki said. "And I probably won't learn till I'm thirty."

Alexa looked shocked. "How do people get to school?"

"Kiki and I walk. Lots of kids take a bus or subway. A few bike or take taxis."

"Rich kids get dropped off. Some days, there are limousine traffic jams at the lower school," Kiki said.

"Around here," Alexa said, "everyone gets their license the minute they can." We got in the car. I let Kiki climb in front, and I sat in the back and put on my seat belt. It was the first time I'd ever been in a car with a teenager at the wheel.

Alexa drove us to Main Street, then up Route 22 and down Tripp Lane. "That's Byram Hills High School," she said. "Seniors park here, but on weekends, everyone parks everywhere." We got out. "My mom went here too."

"Your mom went here?" Kiki asked. "Dear Kate?"

I'd been looking at the oval track and wondering if I might see Sam running. Now I looked at the football field and tried to imagine Dad hanging out with "Katie" and her big sister.

"A few of my teachers taught her!" Alexa added.

"Must be weird having teachers who taught your mom," Kiki said.

"Weird," I ventured, "is having teachers come to your parents' parties and poke their heads into your bedroom."

"Weird," Alexa said, "is when your mom gives talks about boobs and period apps and Love 101. I made her swear *never* to talk to my grade." She looked at me. "Please don't tell me your dad gives vagina monologues."

"He doesn't." I remembered once seeing that *Playbill* in my parents' culture bowl.

"Hey, what's the difference between a genealogist and a gynecologist?" Alexa asked as we walked toward the school entrance.

"What?" Kiki asked.

"A genealogist looks up your family tree, and a gynecologist looks up your family bush!" Alexa said, and Kiki laughed. "Oh crap!" Alexa said. "Door's locked."

I cupped my eyes and peered inside at the empty hallways.

"What's your school like?" Alexa asked as we got back in her car.

"It's over two hundred years old," Kiki began. "And it goes from kindergarten to twelfth. The building goes up instead of out." Kiki turned to me. "I can't believe we're about to be in the upper school. When we were in lower school, the older kids looked like *giants*."

"'Upper school.' 'Lower school.' Sounds so snobby," Alexa said. "When my mom told me how much your tuition was, I thought she was kidding—and that Sofia was going to be totally stuck up."

I wondered what her opinion was of me now.

"They give some scholarships and free rides," Kiki said. "But yeah, we know a lot of rich kids with country houses."

"Country houses?" Alexa asked.

"Weekend places. Like our friend Natalie used to have a penthouse in New York and a beach house in Southampton," Kiki said.

"How many kids in your grade?" Alexa asked.

"We're down to fifty," Kiki said. "And we're about to lose Natalie."

"That's small!" Alexa said. "Our grade has two hundred, which is perfect. Whenever I get sick of one group, I just hang out with other people."

"Our grade is pretty diverse," I offered. Was I feeling defensive of Halsey?

"Diverse?" Kiki laughed. "Sofia, you and I are 'bicultural,' and yeah, there are lots of 'kids of color.' But, c'mon, there are no boys! They call Halsey single-sex. What they mean is 'no sex'!"

"You going out with someone?" Alexa asked.

"I was," Kiki answered.

"Was?" I looked at her.

"Trevor is over. I don't even know who dumped who."

"Happens," Alexa said. "But hey, there's a lot to be said for experience." She flashed Kiki a devious smile. "Since my mom is going to the opera with her dad tonight," she said, "I invited this hot freshman to come over. I told him I was going to Canada this summer so he had to say a proper good-bye. Then I said, 'But not *too* proper!'"

Kiki laughed.

I considered asking if Alexa knew Sam, the lanky guy with the sandy hair and slow smile. But I didn't want Alexa to make fun of me or pronounce Sam geeky or taken or whatever. I wanted to get to know him on my own.

I hoped I wasn't making too much of one stone-skipping lesson. The stones had all ended up at the bottom of the lake after all.

But a few had skipped.

A few had defied gravity.

. . . .

On Memorial Day, Armonk was blooming with irises, peonies, and azaleas, and Windmill Club was open. At the lakeside party, Dad, Kate, Alexa, and I stood with paper plates topped with hot dogs, salad, baked beans, and watermelon. I studied Kate and Alexa, their blue eyes and rosy-blond hair catching the sun, and I scanned the crowd, searching for Sam.

Dad went to join the beach volleyball game, and Kate and Alexa climbed to the top of the tall slide and splashed down into the cold. I followed them, feeling brave, and swam after them to a float in the lake.

"I want to get a tan," Alexa said, adjusting her bikini straps.

"Did you put on sunscreen?" Kate asked.

"Are you kidding me, Mom? The sun isn't even strong yet!"

I stretched out and hoped I wasn't intruding on mother-daughter time.

"Can I tell you girls about an email I got this morning?" Kate asked.

I was about to say *sure* when Alexa answered, "Mom, why would we care?"

"You used to love hearing about my letters."

"Back when I was ten!"

Kate frowned and looked a little hurt. "I beg your pardon."

Neither of them said anything else, and I pretended to be dozing. Finally, Alexa said, "Oh, go ahead and tell us. You're going to anyway." Kate remained quiet. "I'm not gonna beg," Alexa added.

After another silence, I muttered, "Yes, tell us," but so softly I didn't know if Kate even heard.

"Well," Kate said, "a girl wrote to say that at camp, she gets homesick, but at home, she gets campsick. Don't you love that: campsick?"

The tension disappeared, then so did Kate. She dove into the water and swam toward shore. I sat up, dangled my legs over the float, and looked once more for Sam. "Listen," Alexa turned to me. "I know you idolize my mother—"

"I don't idolize her."

"Yeah, you do. Kiki does too. It's fine, whatever. But I can feel you judging me—"

"I'm not judging you."

"Let me finish! What I'm saying, and sorry if this sounds rude, but if your mom were around—"

She is around! I wanted to shout.

"—you two would be at each other's throats too. It's what moms and daughters do. By the time you got to be my age, she'd be driving you insane, guaranteed! If you don't believe me, ask Dear Kate." I didn't respond. "Seriously, who cares about her pen pals and their endless problems? Sometimes, she just likes to hear the sound of her own voice…"

Whoa! *I* was one of her pen pals! And I'd give anything to hear the sound of my mom's voice! And I didn't want to imagine the fights we might have had.

"Think about it," Alexa continued. "Fifth graders *want* their mommies to chaperone their field trips. But by high school, those same girls are praying their moms won't sign up because they need *space*, you know?"

Obviously, I did not know. "I'm going to swim back," I mumbled.

Alexa said, "Fine," then dove in first and passed me doing the butterfly. She scrambled up the shiny ladder, and I emerged behind her. Kate was on the grass in a sundress and straw hat, a shirt draped around her neck.

"Mom, can I have your shirt?" Alexa said.

"Sure." Kate peeled it off. "You may have the shirt off my back."

How could anyone take that kind of love for granted? I thought. Maybe I would ask Dear Kate about mothers and daughters. I could email her from Kiki's screen name.

"Guys, I'm outta here," Alexa said. "I'm going to Amanda's."

Kate looked disappointed, but she and I walked toward the beach where Dad was playing volleyball. Wait. Was that Sam on the other team? Yes! It was! In shorts with no shirt. I looked at his abs and shoulders and tried not to gawk. He was…well, Kiki would have said "ripped." I watched him stretch and crouch, pass and set the ball. I admired how quick he was and how the other guys high-fived him after a spike.

"He's something, isn't he?" Kate said.

I started to blush, then realized Kate was talking about my father, not my crush.

"Want to go closer and watch?" Kate suggested.

"No. No. Here is fine!" I replied too quickly.

Kate walked toward the game, and I went to rinse off in the outside shower. Afterward, I stood at a distance from the beach and gave a shy wave. Dad waved back.

So did Sam.

. . . .

That evening, back in Manhattan, Kiki and I emailed Dear Kate from Kiki's computer, and Kiki showed me some Chinese martial arts movements and made us spiced tea.

"Get it?" she said, looking pleased with herself.

"Get what?"

"Tai chi and chai tea! How funny is that? I was waiting for you to notice."

I rolled my eyes, then heard a ping, which meant an email had landed in her inbox. Kiki looked at her screen. "It's from Kate!"

Kiki's new setup copied the original email on top, so Kiki read the emails aloud: first my question, then Kate's answer:

Dear Kate,

Do teenagers and their moms always drive each other crazy?

Kikiroo

Dear Kikiroo,

Not always. It's normal when they do. It's nice when they don't.

Kate

JUNE

THE SCHOOL YEAR WAS ENDING. Everyone at Halsey was in the final stretch, gearing up for camps or trips or unplanned weeks of sleeping in and hanging out. Even Kiki, who would be putting in long hours at her mom's restaurant, could not wait for summer to start.

I'd missed the previous summer. It had mostly come and gone without me, though I did remember one August weekend in the Hamptons, back when Natalie's family still had their beach house. Natalie and I were bobbing in the Atlantic, and I'd started thinking about how my mom had loved that the ocean linked New York to Spain. Suddenly, a giant wave had knocked me over, and I'd gotten rattled and teary. But Natalie hadn't been able to tell because both of our faces were wet with seawater.

She also showed me how to water-ski. At first, just standing up had seemed impossible. I was too exhausted, too discouraged. But then I was on my feet, whizzing—no, *flying*, across the bay! I'd found my balance! For a moment anyway. Seconds later, I lost it and went under again.

This year, I was looking forward to summer—deep-red

tomatoes and corn on the cob, street fairs in the city and swimming in Armonk, and walking through Central Park with swirly
scoops of Tasti D-Lite or melty sticks of Ben & Jerry's. And all we
had to do was get through our tests and reach the finish line, the
afternoon when the last teacher said, "Pencils down," and the last
girl said, "I blew it" or "I nailed it," and everyone—everyone!—
knew that what really mattered was that it was over. Middle school
was about to be over.

. . . .

"I took the morning off," Dad said, handing me a blueberry-banana
smoothie.

"The first three rows are for the eighth grade parents," I
reminded him. Mom used to be the one to stake out seats at school
events. She'd found moving up day moving even when it starred
other mothers' daughters.

I was wearing a new floral dress and heels. Alone in the elevator, I studied myself in the mirror. My hair had grown long and my
smile was no longer metallic. I'd even put on eyeliner and mascara.
"*Spanish Eyes*," I thought. Mom had loved that song.

Kiki met me in my lobby. Her dress was coral and fitted.
"Happy MUD," Kiki said.

"Mud?"

"Moving up day."

"You are so weird," I said.

We hurried to our homerooms and were soon filing into the

auditorium. So many things had happened in this room! I'd sung in choruses and cabarets, and I'd met Dear Kate here too. Here was also where, just over a year ago, the school had held a memorial service for Mom.

The entire school community had shown up—from Inez, the security guard, to all our teachers and neighbors. I'd felt so wrung out, and the person I'd really needed to talk to was the person who wasn't there.

Mrs. Morris, from 6C, had helped me put together a photo presentation. Look! It's Maria! A baby in Spain! A toddler in a flamenco dress! A girl on a bike! A teen at a dance! A bride! Look! The couple is expecting! And now there's Sofia: infant—toddler—girl—teen!

As background music, we'd picked "Iberia" played by Alicia de Larrocha. It was a parade of happy photos, but everyone had known where it was leading, and it was over all too soon. The last photo was of Mom alone, a close-up of her beautiful face, her Spanish eyes.

The headmaster had spoken, then the chaplain and principal. Dean Isaacson had read excerpts of adoring emails from former students. A surprisingly elegant reception had followed, arranged by the head of the dining hall. I'd hated every minute, but Mom would probably have thought it was nicely done.

Now, my classmates and I were seated toward the back of the room. The lights dimmed, and a different slide show began—this one featuring not my family but the Halsey family of fifty eighth graders, onstage, on courts, on fields, in labs.

Were we really graduating?

We walked down the center aisle to the front of the room in single file. The dean handed each of us a thornless white rose, and we stepped onto the stage clutching our flowers as HSG alumnae had done for two centuries. Principal Milliman told the audience to refrain from clapping until all the names had been called, and then she presented us one by one to the upper school principal.

"Sofia Wolfe," she said when it was my turn. I held the rose in my left hand and shook Principal Milliman's and Principal Kapur's hands with my right. After the last girl (Xia Zhu) stepped onto the stage, the headmistress said, "And now, the moment you've all been waiting for. Rising freshmen, prepare to throw your roses!"

We faced the crowd. I'd never seen so many parents. Kiki's dad had taken a bus up from DC, and even the celebrity parents and grandparents had shown up. There was a famous actor mom, a former mayor of New York, a world-class tennis player. But my own family was so...*tiny*. Was it really just Dad by himself out there? Should we have flown in Abuelito? Or convinced Grandma Pat to leave Florida one more time? Amazing to think that Dad still had *his* mom. For a second, I wished we'd invited Kate. But no. Halsey was Mom's school, and in this room, Kate was Dear Kate. Besides, I still had mixed feelings about Dad and her dating.

The headmistress leaned into the microphone. "On your mark. Get set. Throw!"

I threw my rose. Fifty white roses sailed through the air like arrows in a western. Each family picked up a rose and waved it at their daughter. A lot of moms and dads had tears in their eyes. Looking at them got me choked up too.

Soon, we broke rank, and group hug followed group hug. Everyone went to find her family, and I silently congratulated myself—not because I'd made it through middle school, but because I'd made it through the past fourteen months.

. . . .

"It sucks," Alexa was saying on the phone. "Sofia's all proud of herself because she 'moved up,' whatever that means, while we still have finals and Regents exams." I was in the upstairs bathroom in Armonk and hadn't intended to eavesdrop, but Alexa's complaints were coming through loud and clear behind her closed door. "In English, we finished *Nine Stories*, and I'm supposed to write a tenth! In world history, I have to draw a map of Europe with the names of forty-five countries, including Andorra, Armenia, and Azerbaijan. And when I look out the window, there's Señorita Sofia chilling in the hammock!"

Excuse me? It was my fault that our schools were on different schedules? Her words stung, and I hated that she was talking to her friends about me.

Fortunately, Alexa was about to go on a wilderness adventure in the Canadian Rockies—for six weeks! Dad told me that her father had provided the frequent flier miles.

Well, good. A little distance would be excellent.

A lot of distance, even better.

. . . .

Dad volunteered to make Alexa a farewell dinner and told me he wanted me there. He said Kate was going to drive Alexa to Boston the next day and would meet the program director before the group flew to Calgary.

When we walked into the house, carrying bags loaded with steak, asparagus, and strawberries, Alexa and Kate were in the middle of a fight. "Sorry to be a killjoy," Kate was saying, "but this backpack is *way* too heavy!"

"You *are* a killjoy, Mom! It's your specialty!" Dad and I traded glances and ducked into the kitchen.

"You need pants, shorts, T-shirts, hiking boots, sneakers, a bathing suit, a hat, and sunscreen," Kate said. "You do not need heels or a miniskirt. And they said *no* cell phones because there's no reception in the hinterlands, remember?"

"Mom, you *so* don't get it!" Alexa said, her voice rising. "And nobody says 'hinterlands'!"

"Call your father. Or ask Brian. Their mantra is: 'Less is more.' And what if your luggage gets lost? Don't pack anything you're not willing to lose. Your passport is in your carry-on, right? With a change of underwear?"

"God, Mom! I've traveled before!" Alexa shouted. Coconut, the cat, scurried into the kitchen to join us.

"Well, no one's going to help you lug your luggage," Kate persisted. "And makeup? You're going *hiking*!"

"I get zits, okay?"

"Do you want to take a game with you? I have travel chess."

"That is the most ridiculous thing I have ever heard in my

entire life! You know what? Just forget about dinner. I'm going to Amanda's!" She flew out the door and let it slam behind her.

Two hours later, Kate phoned Alexa's cell and got no response. She texted. Nothing. She phoned Amanda's landline. No one picked up. She texted again, and Alexa finally texted back, "Having pizza. Don't wait up."

So much for our heartwarming farewell dinner.

. . . .

"Shouldn't I be in a summer program?" I asked Dad over scrambled eggs at City Diner. "Mom would have signed me up for art class or piano lessons or jazz dancing or community service or *something*."

"You could be in Panama building homes for Habitat for Humanity," he conceded. "But you already speak Spanish, and I like having you around. Is that selfish?"

"Yeah, but it's okay." Truth was, I didn't mind unstructured days. I knew I wasn't just being lazy. I was healing. If that meant sleeping late, reading, vegging with Kiki, and watching videos, so be it. "Besides, in a few weeks," I reminded Dad, "we'll be seeing Abuelito." Not that I wanted to think about the task that awaited us in Spain.

Dad speared a home fry. "We have to find a new apartment before that."

"We've been doing a lame job looking," I said. Dad liked to spend his free time with Kate, not real estate agents, so when he wasn't on call, we headed north. When he *was* on call, Kate sometimes came to the city. Last weekend, the three of us had eaten lunch at the Boathouse in Central Park, then ridden a gondola on the Great Pond.

In the gondola, I'd snapped a photo of Kate and Dad. She was wearing a mint-green dress and sunglasses and, despite myself, I could see that she and Dad looked good together. Happy. I did not, however, share or edit the image in any way. For now, it was enough to let them be inside my cell phone.

. . . .

Dad bounded up the front steps and rang Kate's doorbell. "Honey, we're home!" he sang. If Alexa had been there, he might not have sounded so exuberant.

"Come in!" She opened the door and gave us both a hug.

"It's such a nice day," I said, "I might head over to the lake." I thought I deserved a gold star for being a good sport, but I had my own reason for giving them some privacy: maybe Sam would be there. Sometimes, I wondered if I was crazy to think about him as much as I did. For all I knew, he had a girlfriend. All we'd done was skip stones and wave once—nothing. But I felt like we had a connection, and I hoped it wasn't just in my head.

"Sign my name at the snack bar!" Kate said.

"Have fun!" Dad added.

I considered saying, "You too!" But no. I had my limits.

At the club, I looked at the menu and thought about ordering a flatbread or "truffled chickpeas." But I wasn't hungry. I saw kids playing cards on the lawn and Marco Polo in the water, and I wondered if there was a way to join in. For a second, I almost wished Alexa were there. Kiki had helped us break the ice, and maybe Alexa and I could get it to keep thawing? The Spanish tutorial had also helped *un poquito*.

Then again, who was I kidding? When I'd last been with Alexa, she'd trash-talked mothers and blown off her own farewell dinner. It was good she was gone. Better to feel a little lonely than get caught in her toxic force field.

I went down the steps, struggled to unfold a red lawn chair decorated with a white windmill, and settled in with *The Princess Bride*, yanking down the hem of my checked sundress. I wanted to look confident, but how do you project confidence while reading?

Someone behind me—a lifeguard?—said, "Excuse me, ma'am? Are you a member?"

Oh no! Should I have signed in? This was the first time I'd come to the club by myself since it had opened. I didn't know the rules.

"I'm the guest of—" I turned around.

Sam was smiling. "I haven't seen you in a while," he said. He was wearing running shorts and no shirt, and I tried to look at his eyes, not his chest. "How's the stone skipping? Been practicing?"

"No. I had finals. But we might start coming out more now."

"Who's we?"

"My dad and me. I think you played volleyball with him once?" I could feel myself blush.

"What about your mom?"

I didn't expect that question and decided to just come out with it: "She died last year—well, a year and two months ago." If this was going to scare him off, better sooner than later.

Died. Dead. Such short words—single syllables, four letters each. But they changed everything. Was there a better way to say it? "She passed away"? "She's gone"? I didn't like the sound of any of it, but I preferred the bitter *D* words to the sugar-coated ones.

I waited for Sam to ask the inevitable "How?" I always resented that question because then my job was to reassure people that aneurysms are rare and they didn't have to worry about *their* moms. *Their* moms would live long past forty-two, maybe to eighty-two or ninety-two or 102!

But Sam said, "Oh, I'm sorry. That must've been really hard."

"Thanks. Still is."

One of the condolence cards Dad and I received after Mom's "tragic death" (they almost all said that) included the words, "Time doesn't heal, but it helps." At first, I'd thought that was trite. Now I knew it was true. It *had* helped that fourteen months had come between that April afternoon and this June one.

In the latest dream I'd had about my mom, she was sitting quietly in my bedroom chair in our apartment. When I'd woken up, the chair was empty. I'd felt a bolt of fresh sorrow and sat upright. I'd wondered, *Is Mom really dead? How can I survive without her?* Then I'd realized I had survived. I *was* surviving.

"My grandpa died last fall," Sam continued. "My mom was a mess."

Sometimes, I objected when people jumped in with stories of their own. I'd think, We're talking about *my mother*. But it was an impossible conversation. There was no ideal response to "My mother died." Nothing anybody could say was right, yet saying nothing was wrong.

"Tell me about your grandpa," I said. "What was he like?"

Was that what I hoped people would ask: "What was she like?" instead of "How did she die?"

"You really want to know?" he asked.

I looked into his sea-green eyes and nodded.

"Let's take a walk." He extended his hand and pulled me up. A jolt of energy surged between us. Did he feel it too? He stopped at a nearby chair, stepped into his flip-flops, lifted his arms, and pulled on a white Tar Heels T-shirt. I was startled to notice the wispy blond hair of his armpits. "Grandpa Fritz was a Southern gentleman," he began, leading me to the path around the lake. "But he moved to New York and built a little beach house." He glanced at me, then away. "Ever been to Fire Island?"

I shook my head. "No."

"It's only a few hours from here, but it's another world. There are no cars, and everyone rides old, rusty bikes. My grandpa used to spend the whole summer in a place called Kismet. We'd go out on the ferry, and he'd meet us with a beat-up red wagon. On Sunday, my parents would go back to work, and he and I would hang out all week. He's the one who taught me to skip stones. We even went clamming. Ever been clamming?"

I shook my head again. I wondered if nervousness was

making him talkative and me silent. Funny how it could have either effect.

"You squish your toes in the bay till you feel a stone, but it's not a stone; it's a clam. We collected buckets and made spaghetti with clam sauce. We went fishing too. We'd use frozen minnows for bait and bamboo rods with corks for bobbers. If the baby bluefish were running, that was dinner. My grandpa showed me how to chop off their heads and tails, and we'd bread the fish and sizzle them. Back then, if my parents served clams or fish, I'd have pushed the plate away, but whatever Grandpa cooked, I ate. You like seafood?"

"I used to spend every August in Spain. Spaniards are big on fish, and I was a pescatarian for a few months when I was twelve. But go on."

"I'm not boring you?"

"Not at all." I smiled and he smiled and more arrows of energy ricocheted between us.

"Well, I kept getting taller, while my grandpa started, like, shrinking. I still went to see him every summer, but instead of him taking care of me, we were taking care of each other." Sam picked up a stray plastic cup and tossed it into a garbage can in the parking lot. "Then last summer, I was mostly taking care of him. But he was still always fixing things—his wooden deck, his outdoor shower, his fence to keep deer out. He even stitched up the holes in his pants because he never liked to buy anything new. We fished together, but he had stopped fishing by himself. So neighbors dropped by and left buckets with their catch. He loved that, and he loved eating for free, living off the land and sea. It's hard to have a garden in Fire Island—ground's too sandy—but somehow, he grew tomatoes, lettuce, and arugula. He was really proud of his arugula." He paused. "Sofia?"

"Yeah?"

"Shut me up."

I laughed. "I don't want to."

"Can I show you something?"

"Sure."

He led me toward the same windmill that Alexa had shown me, and he seemed so pleased with himself that I didn't have the heart to say, *Been here, done this*. Maybe Armonk didn't have many tourist sites? As we climbed the wooden ladder, he said, "I haven't talked about my grandfather this much since his funeral. I usually just think about him."

"I know what you mean."

"What about your mom? Did she look like you?"

"Yeah."

We reached the top of the windmill. "So she had beautiful eyes." He turned away and looked at the lake. We sat on the same wooden bench where I'd sat with Alexa. The blades of the windmill were turning, creaking. The warm sun was streaming in, lighting up specks of dust, and landing in thick broken stripes on Sam's shorts and T-shirt. We sat down and were silent, and I tried not to stare at his thighs.

I could almost hear Kiki and Natalie squealing, "Omigod, Sofia, he is *hot*." I hoped I wasn't looking at him as if he were chocolate cake and I was starving.

I'd felt nervous up here with Alexa and felt even more nervous with Sam. But it was happy nervous, excited nervous, not I-hope-I-don't-say-the-wrong-thing nervous.

"My mom *was* beautiful," I said, "and maybe I will tell you about her sometime." My eyes prickled. "But not now, okay?" Whenever I tried to talk honestly about my mom, I couldn't trust my voice not to go wobbly. "It usually makes me cry, and that's the last thing I want to do right now."

My tears still came too easily. I wondered if they always would. After my mom died, I could have sat and sobbed forever. Since that was not an option, I'd put a lid on my tears. Yet they were always right there, ready at a moment's notice.

Sam slipped his arm around me. "What's the *first* thing you want to do?"

I looked into his eyes and tilted my head. I felt like a heroine in a romantic movie. And then I kissed him—gently and tentatively at first and then, when he kissed back, like I meant it.

I hoped he didn't think I was easy, some fast city kid. Had he kissed a lot of girls? We barely knew each other, although I already knew him much more than Miles or Julian or Daniel.

It was amazing to be kissing Sam, but was I doing it right? Should I have let him make the first move? Should I be placing my hands somewhere? I closed my eyes and tried to banish all thought, and before I knew it, nothing mattered except that we were kissing and his arms were around me. It felt so good to be held.

And kissed! I felt like I was melting into him. His T-shirt smelled like it had just come out of the dryer, and his chest felt solid against mine. I briefly worried that my breasts inside my bra might feel disappointingly small, but I chased away that thought—he didn't seem disappointed.

So this was kissing! No wonder it inspired singers and painters and writers. Kissing! *Kisssing! Kissssssing!* Someday, I hoped I could tell Sam not only about Mom but also about this day. I'd tell him that these afternoon kisses—right now, with him—were my first true kisses, the first ones that counted.

I wanted them to go on forever, so I memorized that June afternoon, holding and being held, kissing and being kissed, feeling the warm, slanting sunrays as the windmill turned and creaked. No matter what happened, I would keep that hour inside me. I knew this because I'd learned how strange time and memory could be.

I'd learned that while most weeks and months whoosh by, there are moments—some good, some horrible—that last forever. Moments that split your life into Before and After.

Maybe these kisses could last forever—but in a good way. I loved feeling his soft lips and strong shoulders, peeking at his closed eyes and long lashes. I wanted time to stretch like taffy and be every bit as sweet. I pictured Sarah Brown in *Guys and Dolls* singing, "I've nevvvver been in love before…"

I must have giggled because Sam asked, "Are you laughing at me?"

"Not laughing," I said. "Just smiling hard."

"Good." We kissed some more. My heart felt so big inside me. I couldn't believe that on the day that I'd gotten my first real kiss, I'd also gotten my next fifty. Was that how it sometimes worked?

Soon, I pulled away to check the time on my cell. Five thirty already? "I'd better go," I said. "I don't want my dad to worry."

"I'll walk with you. Where are you staying?"

"We're not. We're going back to the city tonight."

"When are you coming back?"

"Next week, I think." I liked his eagerness.

"Why not during the week?"

"My dad has to work. He's a doctor."

"What about you? Are you a doctor?"

I laughed. "Maybe I can come back sooner. I hadn't thought of it." We walked by the lake and through the ball field. "This is the house."

"That house? That one?" He looked at it as though it were haunted.

"My dad's going out with Katherine Baird." He fell silent. "You know 'Dear Kate'?"

"Everyone knows everyone around here. But don't say anything, okay? What happens in windmills stays in windmills."

"Of course."

Was he acting weird, or was I imagining it? I wished I could schedule a private session with Dear Kate. I'd ask, "How come the second you kiss a boy, everything gets complicated?" I'd heard other girls say that.

"Give me your number—I don't have my cell," Sam said. I reached into my bag for a pen, noticing with relief that it was a normal one, not one of the freebies Dad sometimes brought home that said "Monistat" or had the name of some vaginal goo for urinary tract infections. I scribbled my number on a piece of paper, then tapped his into my cell phone. I wanted to give him one last kiss, but he was already backing away. "*Adiós*, right? *Adiós?* Sorry. I take French."

"*Adiós* is correct. But *hasta pronto* is better. It means 'see you soon.'"

He took off, and I turned toward the house and ran up the steps. I felt like I was flying. But I couldn't ignore the nagging feeling that something was wrong. Why had Sam been in such a hurry to say good-bye?

. . . .

During dinner on the deck with Kate and Dad, I wanted to say, *Guess where I spent the afternoon. In a windmill, kissing the sweetest, hottest guy in the whole wide world!* Instead, I said, "This may be a lot to ask, but can I stay a little longer next week? Like maybe I could come Wednesday, and Dad could come Friday after work? It's so nice out here, all the fresh air and everything. It's just an idea. I don't want to impose."

Dad looked surprised. Usually, he was the one pushing Armonk. He'd even apologized to me for taking me away from my friends. Not that I minded. Kiki had come out with me twice, and a lot of my other friends were away anyway—at camps or on programs or vacations. Natalie was visiting cousins in New Hampshire. Madison was in China and, according to Kiki, had eaten a starfish.

Dad looked at me approvingly, no doubt thinking his city girl had fallen under the spell of the country. I wasn't going to tell him that it was the spell of Sam.

"Tell you what," he said. "You clear the dishes, and Kate and I will talk."

"Okay." As I walked back and forth to the kitchen with plates and glasses, I heard bits of their conversation: "Impose? Are you kidding? This house is way too quiet without Alexa. I'm flapping around in my empty nest, answering email all day, and the one girl I want to hear from never writes." Dad meanwhile was assuring her that I wouldn't need much supervision.

They called me back, and Kate said she'd be happy to pick me up at North White Plains Station the following Wednesday. "Depending on your schedule, Gregg," she added, "you could come out Friday and leave Sunday."

Dad's eyebrows went up. Were our daytrips going to turn into overnights—just like that? If Dear Kate thought it was okay, maybe Dad figured: Who was he to argue?

But what about Mom? I thought foolishly.

For a second, I wondered where Dad would sleep. Then I knew the answer.

A song by Stephen Sondheim came to me: "Not a Day Goes By." The Halsey Upper School chorus had sung an arrangement of it last fall, and it had gotten stuck in my head, playing over and over and over.

. . . .

I texted Sam that I'd be back on Wednesday. He texted: Excellent! We agreed to meet at 3:00 p.m. at the club for a bike ride.

Wednesday morning, when Dad was at work, I took a long shower, shaving my legs and washing my hair, and I was surprised to hear myself singing. It had been a while since I'd gone through my rusty repertoire—the Beatles, Disney, Spanish ballads.

I got dressed, blow-dried my hair, and took the subway (switching trains alone for the first time) to Grand Central. I'd never taken Metro North before, but Dad gave me instructions and said, "Just act as if you've taken it a million times." At Grand Central, I found the right track, then asked several women, "Does this go to North White Plains?" before getting on the train. Finally, I took a seat and opened the newest *Fifteen*.

The train started moving, and I turned to Dear Kate's column, nervous that one of my questions might show up. None did. Kate had mentioned that writing for a magazine wasn't like writing for a newspaper or blog or website; she had to work months ahead. She said she'd turned in her back-to-school column before summer even started, a fact that struck me as depressing.

On the train, I felt cold and conspicuous. Everyone else was much older.

I remembered the first time I'd taken a taxi by myself, to a bat mitzvah while my parents were at a dinner party. I'd successfully hailed a cab, then got scared and phoned my mom. What if the driver was a kidnapper? Mom talked with me on her cell as if she were air traffic control. "*No te preocupes.*" Don't worry. And she stayed on with me until I arrived safe and sound.

Taking a taxi alone was a rite of passage for city kids. After the first, the rest were easy. I hoped taking a train alone would be like that too.

I took a quiz ("Do You Think For Yourself?") and was reading an article ("The Fine Art of Flirting") when I heard the conductor announce, "White Plains!" I jumped up and hurried off. The train doors hissed shut behind me.

I went to the parking lot and looked around. Where was Kate?

It took me a few minutes to realize I'd made a mistake. I'd gotten off too soon!

I called her cell. "I'm really sorry! I know you said *North White Plains*—"

"It's okay. Stay there. I'll come get you. It'll take me a few minutes."

I thanked her, apologized again, and waited by the curb for what felt like a long time. When Kate arrived, she studied my outfit. "You weren't cold?"

"I didn't think about air-conditioning." I looked down at my tiny pink skirt and white tank top. Underneath, I was wearing a matching pink bra and thong that Kiki had talked me into at Victoria's Secret. "The thong's the thing!" Kiki had said. "Once you get used to them, they're more comfortable than regular underwear." Like an idiot, I had listened. So far, the thong felt like a wedgie.

"I made us dinner reservations at an Indian restaurant at 7:00 p.m.," Kate said. "Your dad said you like chicken fritters and creamed spinach with cheese?"

"Saag paneer! I love Indian food," I said.

"Great. Listen, Sofia, my October column is due in the morning, and I'm still working on it. If you're interested, I'd love for you to take a peek when I'm done, you know, make sure I'm on target."

"I'd love to!" I said. Kiki would faint! But would *this* column include one of my letters? About lying or noticing girls or that stupid personal pimple? At some point, I knew I should either come clean or change my screen name. The longer I waited, the more underhanded it all seemed. I didn't want Dear Kate to find out that I'd chosen to keep silent about our correspondence.

"While I'm working, you can swim or read or just make yourself at home. Sound good?"

"Sounds great. And I might meet a friend for a bike ride."

"Sure. I assume that would be okay with your dad."

"It'd be fine."

"Okay. You can bring her over after."

"Actually, it's a…him."

Kate gave me a glance. "Ah, the plot thickens." She nodded, almost to herself. I hoped Kate didn't feel tricked—or used. Should I have mentioned the "him" part earlier?

"I'd feel better if we ran this by your dad. Do you mind? Why don't you call him? No biggie, but let's keep everything in the open, all right? You'll find I'm very reasonable if you keep me in the loop."

I pressed DAD, a pit gathering in my stomach. "He's not picking up." I left a message: "Dad, I'm with Kate, and I'm going to meet a boy at Windmill Club. He's really nice and not a bad influence or anything. We're going for a bike ride, and then Kate and I are going out for dinner at seven. Call us back. Or meet us! Love you."

"Good," Kate said.

"Is it okay that I said he could meet us?"

"Of course. But it's also okay if it's just us."

I felt bad about missing my stop, being sneaky about Sam, inviting Dad on our girls' night out, and withholding the truth about Catlover and Dear Kate. "I'll make sure you meet the Mystery Boy," I said, immediately regretting those words. Hadn't I referred to *her* as the "Mystery Woman" back when we were emailing? "I don't know why I didn't mention him before."

"Oh, I do. Kids don't tell adults everything. But I'd like us to be as up front as possible, especially while I'm, you know, taking care of you. Okay?"

"Okay," I said, tempted to tell her about Sam. No doubt Catlover would have written about him at length to Dear Kate. But now that I knew the real Kate, it was more complicated. I couldn't exactly tell her that I'd made out in a windmill with a boy I barely knew.

"After your bike ride, why don't you bring him over to say hello?"

"Okay."

I looked at her and wondered if I *should* spill all—well, almost all—about Sam and about Catlover. I was thinking about where to start when Kate said, "Oh! Look!" and pointed to a large, reddish-brown deer with velvety antlers. "A buck. Isn't he magnificent? We rarely see the males!" Kate rambled on about deer, and then we pulled into her driveway, my confession unspoken.

Maybe over dinner I'd find a way to open up—especially if it was just the two of us.

. . . .

Sam was waiting for me at the club. "Kate wants to meet you later," I told him. I didn't want him to think I was overprotected or that I'd rushed to announce that we were a couple. But what choice did I have?

"Actually, there's something I want to tell you." Sam looked troubled, and I thought, *He wants to break up with me already? We aren't even going out!* But then his expression changed, and he asked, "Where's your bike?"

"My bike?"

"It's customary to have a bike when you go on a bike ride."

I laughed, embarrassed. "You think Kate has one I can use?"

"I know she does." We walked his bike back to Kate's. He didn't say what was on his mind, and I didn't prod. We looked in the garage, and Sam went to a far corner and pulled out Alexa's bike from behind a sled.

"It's a little big, but it's okay," I said.

"Put on this helmet."

"Oh, come on." Was he serious?

"I'm serious," Sam said.

"I don't want to wear a helmet."

"You have to."

So much for my blow-dried hair! He helped me strap on the helmet, and our faces were inches apart. His fingers brushed my cheek as he fastened the strap under my chin and snapped the clasp. In the musty cool of the garage, he gave me a quick kiss, and the sound and feel and surprise of that kiss made up for the fact that I'd have helmet hair all afternoon.

Sam waited by the bikes while I went back inside and called up, "We'll be back soon. I'm borrowing Alexa's bike."

"Have a good time!" Kate called down. I appreciated that she was treating me like a trustworthy teenager. I didn't want to ruin that.

Sam and I set off—out the driveway, onto the street, past a few houses, and whoa! That was quite a hill! Talk about steep! We weren't really going to go down it, were we?

I pedaled ahead, hoping I looked cute from behind and that my skirt wasn't blowing too much. All I had on underneath was that tiny, pink thong. Why had I listened to Kiki? What had I been thinking? I looked behind me. Sam looked even hotter than he had last weekend, which was saying a lot. I turned toward the hill, then back to Sam, smiling while trying to hold down my skirt. One hand on the bike, one on the skirt. The wind whipped through my hair and I started going faster, faster. It was exciting but also scary and…

. . . .

Dirt, pebbles, rocks.

My knees. My shoulder. My head.

Someone was moaning.

Whoa, whoa. Was *I* moaning? Were those moans coming from *me*?

What was going on?

Someone was cradling my head, saying, "It's okay, it's okay, it's okay." Kate's voice? She was stroking my hair, but her fingertips felt wet. Why were her fingertips wet? "Has someone called 911?"

"An ambulance is on the way."

"Can somebody call her father?" Kate's voice again.

"What's his number?"

"I don't have my cell. 917—917—917—He works at Mount Sinai. Gregg Wolfe. Can someone get ahold of him?" Kate sounded so upset.

I wanted to tell them my father's number and tried to say it out loud. But no words came. Just "Ow, ow, ow."

Everything hurt. I opened my eyes, closed them, opened them again. A woman was hugging Sam. Sam! I forgot about Sam! Who was hugging Sam?

A siren. Louder, closer.

A streak of blurry red.

The smell of burning rubber. An ambulance?

Two men rushed toward me. It was like on TV. Who were they? Parachuters? Paramedics?

"What happened?"

"We were biking." Sam's voice! "She must have hit a patch of gravel. Or maybe she used the wrong brake? She went flying over the handlebars. When she hit the ground, she started shaking." Sam's voice was shaking.

"Where's the girl's mother?" a man asked. I wanted to tell him about my mother. And I tried…but ow, ow, no words.

A person above me was attaching something plastic to my neck.

"Her mother died last year," Kate said. This was true, but I wanted to shout, "She did not!" Or at least say something *else* about my mother. Didn't anyone ever want to know anything about my mother besides that she died?

Was I dying too? Was this what it felt like? A fuzzy, quiet fading away?

"I'm dating her father," Kate said, her voice strange and high. "Is she going to be okay?"

Who, *me*? Why wouldn't I be okay?

"We'll do everything we can." Two people lifted me onto a stretcher, strapped me down.

"Be careful!" Kate's voice.

"Ma'am, step away! Let us do our job." They slid me into their ambulance as if I were a loaf of bread going into an oven.

Another man's voice: "Okay, come with us, quick! Get in front!"

A door slammed, sirens blared. A woman—a nurse?—was next to me.

A man was talking. The driver? "Valhalla isn't the closest hospital, but it's the best place for head trauma."

Valhalla? Like in mythology? Wasn't that where heroes went when they died?

Kate's voice but husky. "Sofia, I'm with you. I'm up front. You had a bike accident, but you're going to be okay."

An accident?

"Oh no! Is the bike okay?" Hey, that sounded like *my* voice!

"Sweetheart!" Kate sounded so relieved. "Yes! It's fine! And you'll be fine too!"

The same words popped out. "Oh no! Is the bike okay?" Alexa would kill me if I wrecked her bike!

"It's fine. How do *you* feel?" Kate's voice.

"Oh no!" My voice again. "Is the bike okay?"

"Yes, it's fine. No worries." Now *Kate* sounded worried. Why did she sound worried?

"Keep her talking," a person next to me said. "Keep her awake. I have the IV ready in case she needs antiseizure meds."

I was so tired, sooo tired. I'd never been so tired.

Kate kept talking to me, and the driver started talking—on a phone? He sounded far away, very far away. "Fourteen-year-old girl…possible brain injury…contact seizure…bicycle accident…brief loss of consciousness…convulsions…cuts and abrasions on head, shoulder, elbow, knees…"

Kate's voice again: "I remember his number!" Then, softly, "Gregg, listen, Sofia was in a bike accident. We're in an ambulance going to the Westchester Medical Center. She's…talking. Meet us there. Drive carefully—or get a cab. I don't have my cell with me, but I'll call again as soon as I know anything."

Oh, I get it! Kate was calling my *dad*. She should call my mom too. Oh, wait, my mom, my mom…

I closed my eyes again.

I wanted to sleep, needed to sleep, sleep, sleep.

. . . .

The back door of the ambulance flew open and daylight poured in. People lifted me, brought me inside. They set me on a table in a too-bright emergency room. It *was* like TV. Doctors in white and green were talking about a "chest, pelvis, and cervical spine x-ray." They were also taking off the plastic collar. And cutting off my skirt. Wait, were they snipping the elastic of my *thong*?

Whoa there! Just a second! Was I *naked*? In front of all these people?! This was so embarrassing! I heard my voice. A question was burbling up, popping out: "Oh no! Is the bike okay?"

Everyone ignored me, but the words surfaced again: "Oh no! Is the bike okay?"

"We want to make sure *you* are okay," a female doctor answered. I saw a lady lean against a wall, crumple. Who was that? Kate?

"Do you know how you got hurt?" a male doctor asked.

"Diving board?" I replied.

Kate said. "A bike accident. It was a very steep hill."

"But I'm a good bicyclist," I protested. Kate looked shocked. Why was she so shocked? Did she think I was *not* a good bicyclist? "Oh no! Is the bike okay?" I added.

"Yes. It's fine," Kate said. "We're not worried about the bike."

A nurse with squeaky sneakers rolled me into a hallway. "We're going to do a CAT scan." She handed Kate forms.

Where was my mom? I wanted my mom. Oh…right…

I wished they'd turn off the lights and leave me alone and let me sleep. But wait, first, I had a question: "Oh no! Is the bike okay?"

"It's fine," Kate said so quietly that I wondered if I'd destroyed the bike, completely *totaled* it.

A doctor approached Kate. "Head injuries are weird," he murmured. "Repetition like this is not uncommon. Some patients lose short-term memory and then it comes back."

"Thank you," Kate said.

"No promises. All I'm saying is not to assume the worst."

I felt like I was wrapped in gauze. Everything hurt. Wait, was I in bed? How did I get in bed?

"Kate?" My voice.

"Yes?" Kate leaned over me, eyes wide and expectant.

"Don't go," I said.

"I'm not going anywhere." She squeezed my hand, stroked my palm. "I'm staying right here with you."

I wanted to squeeze back but couldn't. I was too tired. I felt her fingers curling around mine. It was nice, comforting.

"We need to get her prepped for the CT," a nurse said.

I was being wheeled down a long corridor. "Oh no! Is the bike okay?"

The nurse replied jovially, "Darlin', who cares about a silly ol' bike? We're making sure you're okay. Okay?"

And then someone gave me a drug that took away the pain…

. . . .

A small, white room. A hospital? In my arm, an IV. On the wall, a monitor with different-colored zigzagging lines. I opened my eyes and saw Dad and Kate. Side by side in two chairs. She was leaning on him. They looked tense and yellowy.

"Daddy."

"Cupcake!" He jumped up and came to my bedside.

"Am I going to be okay?" I whispered.

"More than okay!" He kissed my forehead, held me. "Tell me what happened."

"I don't know. We were biking. I hope Sam doesn't think I'm a klutz." Kate peered over the bedrail, looking as if I were saying something profound. "I really wanted to go on the bike ride."

"There will be other bike rides," Dad said, looking younger and more himself again.

A doctor appeared. "Sofia?"

"Yes."

"I'm going to say three words, and in a few minutes, I'll ask you to repeat them, all right?"

"All right."

"Cow. Ball. Bottle. I'll be back in two minutes. Mom, Dad, no helping."

It bothered me that the doctor had assumed that Kate and Dad were my parents, and they didn't correct him. But I could see how they could pass for parents, even though Kate didn't look anything like my mom. Kate wasn't small, and she didn't have chocolate hair or Spanish eyes. And she didn't resemble me.

The doctor leaned in and examined my scalp, lifting up pieces of hair. It felt gross, full of gravel and dirt and…dried blood? "As soon as I catch a break, I'll put in some staples," he promised.

Dad thanked him, doctor to doctor.

After he left, Kate said, "I wish he'd just do it now."

"In an emergency room," Dad said, "there's a hierarchy. Trust me, you don't want to be the most popular patient. If you're getting neglected, you should thank your stars."

Kate nodded, then turned to me. "Sofia, it's so good to hear you talking in full sentences again."

"What do you mean?"

"For a while there, you kept repeating the same sentence."

"I did?"

The doctor poked his head in the door. "Okay, princess, what were those words?"

Huh? Words? I had no idea what he was talking about.

"Not to worry," he said, Dr. Casual. "I'll come back later and give you three new words. I'll do those sutures too." He left.

Kate looked anxious, and I sensed that I'd flunked an important quiz. My stomach tightened. "Dad, what am I going to do about my finals?"

"I have good news. You already took them. And you did really well."

"Really? I did?"

"You aced everything except math, and you did okay in math too. Relax. It's summer vacation."

"It is?" It was all so bewildering. I couldn't remember my finals, the accident, or, apparently, even three simple words.

. . . .

More doctors, more words. Hours later, when I finally said, "Car, paper, owl" as if it were no big deal, the doctor high-fived me, Dad acted as if I'd nailed Final Jeopardy, and Kate looked like she might cry. Next, the doctor sat down to clean my head. He gave me a shot and, while talking about his own little boy, used a staple gun to close the gash in my scalp. I thanked him and said that my head ached and I was really thirsty. He said he was sorry but he couldn't give me water or painkillers yet and then was called away.

"She'll have to stay in the hospital overnight," a nurse stated. "For observation."

"Of course," Dad answered.

"We'll move her upstairs as soon as a room becomes ready."

"I'm really thirsty," I said.

I closed my eyes and heard Kate ask, "Why can't she have water?"

"Withholding fluids helps prevent vomiting," Dad replied. "It's also important in case she has a seizure or needs surgery as a result of a subdural hematoma."

"A subdural—?"

"Blood around the brain."

Kate stopped asking questions, and I dozed on and off, propped against pillows in the hospital bed. After a while, I started staring at the medical monitor. I realized I could control one of the lines with my breathing, so I practiced, as if it were a video game, then said, "Dad, watch."

I blew three short breaths followed by three long ones. With each breath, the green middle line on the monitor spiked up, up, up, then down, down, down, making little stair steps.

Dad laughed. "You are a funny little wolf cub. Can you spell wolf cub backward?"

I hesitated but did it: *B-U-C-F-L-O-W*. "Or did you mean like our name? Because I could add the *E*."

Kate hugged us, eyes glistening. Then she excused herself, returning moments later with a clear plastic bag containing my bra, top, and the ripped thong—which was mortifying. "The skirt was too torn to salvage," she said. "The helmet too. It had a crack down the middle."

"Sam made me wear it. I didn't want to mess up my hair."

"Probably saved your life," Dad said.

"Can you tell him I'm okay?"

"It's almost 10:00 p.m., but I bet he's up. What's his last name?"

"Davison," Kate said. "On Fox Ridge Road. In Windmill Farm, everyone knows everyone. It's a little incestuous."

"I'll call him now," Dad said, getting up. "And then, Katie, you can go home and get some sleep. You can take my car."

"I'd rather stay. If that's all right."

"More than all right." He kissed her, and she hugged him, and I heard him whisper, "I love you," and heard her whisper it back.

First I thought, *Wow*.

Then I was surprised to realize that I wasn't more surprised. They were about to spend the night in the hospital with me. They were a couple, in good times and bad.

When Dad left the room to call Sam, he turned off the light.

Kate mumbled, "I'm staying right here, Sofia." I nodded, exhausted, and when Dad came back, we all three tried to sleep. A nurse had wanted to move me out of the ER, but there were no available beds.

. . . .

In the middle of the night, a scream pierced the hallway. I woke with a start. I heard: "*No! No! No! No!*"

I sat up, alarmed. It was dark, but I saw that Dad and Kate were both wide-awake too.

Dad got up and reached for my hand.

The wail continued: "*No! No! No! No!*" What was it? An animal? It was harrowing.

Then I remembered I was in a hospital. And I knew—I just *knew*—that it was the cry of a mother hearing news she could not bear.

I felt sick for her, but her wailing also made me want to leave the hospital. To get out. To get better. To be *alive*.

. . . .

In the morning, a speech pathologist in a white smock arrived with a clipboard. She asked me to touch my nose, blink twice, and name the president.

I did.

"Do you know where you are?"

"A hospital." I looked around and saw that during the night,

I'd been moved to a different room, which meant I must have fallen fast asleep after all.

"Do you know *where*?"

"No."

"She's not from here," Kate interjected. "She doesn't know we're in Valhalla." I appreciated her defending me and noticed that she was wearing the same sweater as the day before. Dad had gone out for coffee.

The woman dismissed Kate with a wave. "What are your favorite foods?" she asked, pencil poised.

I had to think about that. "Paella, tortilla española, gambas al ajillo, shumai, lamb saag, shrimp tikka masala," I began. "Sushi, gyoza, curry tom…"

The speech pathologist looked confused. Kate jumped in again. "She's a city kid. She has a sophisticated palate."

The woman asked, "What about hamburgers, Sofia? You eat hamburgers?"

"Love 'em. Hot dogs too. Hamburgers with ketchup, hot dogs with mustard."

At last, the speech pathologist smiled. "And apple pie?"

"And chocolate cake. In fact, I'm *starving*. When can I get out of here?"

"As soon as the release forms are filled out. You got lucky."

"Lucky?" I inspected my torn-up knees and sore shoulder.

"Lucky," she repeated.

· · · · · · · · · ·

"Well, well." Dad was reading a text on his cell phone. "We're about to have company. Sam's coming by."

I felt a rush of warmth. My knees and shoulder and head hurt, and I was tired, but I could feel myself coming back to life. "When?"

"Now. He's on his way."

Dad showed me on his phone: Please tell Sofia I'll be there at noon. Sam.

"I wish I could wash my hair, and this hospital gown isn't exactly—"

"You look gorgeous," Dad said. Which was sweet. Dad looked awful—rumpled and unshaven. Had he and Kate really spent the whole night with me? I peered at Kate—I'd never seen her so unkempt, and it occurred to me that, in their own way, she and Dad looked a little as if they belonged together. Which was disturbing but also a teeny tiny bit comforting. (Though it was also disturbing to even think that.)

Kate helped me stagger to the bathroom, where I inspected myself in the mirror. "I do look better than I thought," I admitted.

"You look great. It's incredible."

"I feel like *caca*, as my mom would've said. *Caca* is poop in Spanish."

Kate met my eyes in the mirror. "That's the first time you've mentioned your mother to me."

"Actually, it's not." Maybe it was because my guard was down or because of the meds, but I wanted to take advantage of this moment and tell her about Catlover and Dear Kate. I wanted to be honest with her, the way I used to be. And I was just about to when Dad knocked on the door.

"Visitors! Sam and Lori Davison!" he announced. Kate held my arm as I took slow, careful steps back toward my hospital bed.

"Hi!" Sam said uncomfortably.

"Hi!" I smiled. "I think you met my dad, playing volleyball."

Everyone started trying to piece together what had happened. Apparently, moments after saying good-bye to Kate, I'd flipped over the handlebars. Sam called 911 with his cell and also called his mom, Lori, who drove straight to Kate's house where, as Lori put it, she honked "like a crazy woman" until Kate got into her car.

I vaguely remembered Kate and the red blur of an ambulance, but I couldn't remember the accident at all, which was, no doubt, just as well.

Lori handed me a bag. "It's a sundress," she said. "You can wear it home, and Kate can get it back to me anytime."

"And these you can keep," Sam said and handed me a dozen yellow roses. "I'm really sorry."

"They're beautiful. Thank you." I wished I had the nerve to ask the grown-ups to let Sam and me have a moment. One moment and one kiss would have made me feel a whole lot better.

"Sam, thank you," Dad said, "for making Sofia wear a helmet."

"The ER people threw it out because it got cracked," I said. Suddenly, I remembered Alexa's bicycle and said, "Oh no! Is the bike okay?"

Kate made a face, but Sam said, "It's fine. I already put it back in the garage."

. . . .

I woke up groggy and sore, in a queen-size bed with crisp, lavender sheets and a patchwork quilt comforter. Outside, I heard a concert of songbirds and the faint creak of a…windmill?

A flood of memories: a train, a helmet, a bicycle, a hospital.

My eyes rested on a vase of yellow roses on the bed table. I studied their delicate petals and fragile centers. I touched one, then another. I pressed my face into the bouquet, breathed in, and thought, *Sam. Yes. Sam.*

I knew where I was: Dear Kate's guest room. What was nice was that I didn't feel like a guest.

I walked downstairs. Dad and Kate were drinking blue smoothies and doing the *Times* crossword. His assistant must have rescheduled his appointments.

It was rare that Dad missed work (except when Mom died), but he said that every once in a while, even doctors get to call in sick. Besides, his patients were used to last-minute changes. Whenever a woman went into labor, his whole schedule got thrown off. I'd gone with Mom to the opera twice because, as she used to joke, whenever she and Dad had tickets, someone had twins. Dad said it was an occupational hazard of obstetrics: "Dr. Wolfe, at your cervix." "Push, push, push, all day long."

I entered the kitchen, and Dad and Kate made a fuss over my cuts and scrapes. "Who's taking care of Pepito?" I asked.

"He has plenty of kibble and water for a day or two," Dad assured me. "And I asked Mrs. Russell to run up and look in on him. She has the key." On cue, Coconut padded over and wound herself around my legs, her soft, white tail caressing the skin beneath my bandaged knees. I crouched and petted her, massaging the scruff of her neck. Soon, she was purring loudly enough for us all to hear.

"You really are a cat person," Kate said.

"Yeah, I love cats." I studied Kate. "Actually, there's something I need to tell you."

Dad must have noticed my serious tone because he looked up from the newspaper. I hadn't planned to say anything in front of him, but I didn't want to miss this chance—or hold on to my secret any longer. I needed to tell the truth. "I am a cat lover," I stated. "A catlover. I love cats. I could have, like, ninety-nine of them."

Dad looked confused, like, *Did the accident have repercussions after all?*

But Kate's jaw dropped and her eyes went wide. She stood and smiled. "C'mere," she said, opening her arms.

I walked into her embrace and let myself be hugged. Then, without warning, I started to cry. Was it the relief of being honest? The release of the anxiety from the day before? The bittersweet comfort of being in a mother's arms?

"Wow," Kate said softly. "So *I'm* the Mystery Woman?"

I nodded.

"What am I not getting?" Dad asked. Kate's eyes were wet now too. "Could one of you fill me in?"

"Not me," Kate said.

"Dad," I began, "you know how Kate visited HSG, and you started going out with her? Well, I started writing her, and she wrote back, and I told her about Mom and then about you meeting someone new, and we wrote a lot before I found out that…you two were going out."

"What's remarkable," Kate said, "is that with all the mail I get, I really felt for Catlover99. She seemed like a good kid who'd been through a lot." Kate looked at us both, and Dad smiled and seemed a little choked up. "Maria must have been quite a woman." Kate added, "But I'm not sure I remember too many other specifics."

"That's okay!" I said too quickly.

"Of course, I could go through my old mail and reread what you wrote. Would you like me to?"

"*No!*"

She laughed. "Would you prefer I delete them all?"

"*Yes!*"

"Fine. We'll do that together. Right after breakfast."

"There's nothing bad in them. It's just…"

She put up a hand. "I get it. Girls write me because they know whatever they say won't come back to haunt them."

"Thank you," I said, relieved. "Can I still proofread your column?"

"Oh. I'm sorry. I just sent it off to my editor. Next time, okay?"

"Okay."

She refilled Dad's coffee mug and poured me some orange juice. "And now, Sofia, in the spirit of full disclosure, I have something I think I should tell you, though maybe Sam should be the one?"

I looked at her, puzzled.

"Here's the thing. Sam's a good guy. I know because, well…he went out with Alexa."

"Alexa?" I said. "Alexa-Alexa?"

"Sam hasn't been around much lately, but Alexa did mention that he came to say good-bye one evening before she went to Canada. Anyway, last winter they went to the Snow Ball—it's like a prom. So you might just want to ask him where things stand."

I was speechless. No wonder Sam blanched when I pointed out the Bairds' house. No wonder he knew exactly where to find Alexa's bike.

Dad looked surprised too, and when neither of us spoke, he said, "Ladies, any other bombshells?"

"It's *your* turn," Kate replied. "Are *you* harboring any secrets, Dr. Wolfe?"

"Oh, hell," he said, "as long as we're coming clean…"

Kate looked apprehensive, and I braced myself. What had Dad not told us?

"Remember when I first drove here in February? I said I had a meeting and asked you to sign a book for my niece." *Niece?* "Well, I didn't have a meeting or a niece," Dad said. "I had an agenda."

Kate looked at me and smiled. "What do you think, Sofia? Liar, liar, pants on fire?"

I shrugged—which hurt. "Oww."

Kate stroked my back gently and faced Dad. "Tell you what, Gregg, I won't count that as a secret. More like a *strategy*."

"It worked," he said.

"It did," Kate agreed.

I texted Sam to meet me beneath the big maple tree. I needed to know what was going on.

"I'm going to the club," I said, grabbing an apple. "But first, Kate, can we delete all those emails, if you really don't mind?"

Kate led me to her messy office, and I lifted a framed black-and-white portrait of Alexa as a little kid going down the big slide.

"Alexa's father took that picture," she said.

Her phone rang and she checked caller ID. "It's my editor. Give me a minute?"

"Sure." She took her cell into the hallway.

I peeked at a chat on her computer and, feeling slightly guilty, started skimming.

DearKate: It's just all happening so fast. I don't want to be rash.

TheBryans: You are the least rash person on the planet! You're the opposite of rash. What's the opposite of "rash"?

DearKate: Calamine lotion?

TheBryans: Exactly! That's you, soothing and sensible. Which is lovely, truly. But if your heart's trying to tell your brain something, why not shut up for once and listen?

DearKate: You're probably right.

TheBryans: Oh, I'm definitely right. Is Sofia totally okay?

DearKate: Yes. Thank God!

The Bryans: Phew!

DearKate: Have you heard from Alexa?

TheBryans: One call, one postcard.

DearKate: Same. My postcard said, "The Rockies rock."

TheBryans: Ours said, "Can you believe I'm someplace where you've never been?"

DearKate: If she calls again, don't tell her. I need to tell her myself.

TheBryans: Believe me, we're not touching that subject. But go for it. You help kids live their lives. You get to live yours.

Kate came back, and I pretended to be studying the foreign editions of her book, but I was confused. Who were the Bryans? And what subject were they not touching?

"Okay, Catlover99, let's do this," Kate said. She went into her old mail, clicked on Addresses, scrolled down to the *C*'s, and highlighted all my emails. When she pressed Delete, a box asked, "Are you sure you want to delete the selected messages?"

I nodded, Kate clicked, and ta-da! They all disappeared—poof!

I wished it were that easy to delete—no, *transform*—Catlover99 herself. I didn't want to get rid of her. I just wanted her to be bolder and braver. I wanted her to speak up and sing and laugh and be herself again, her best self. She could do that, couldn't she?

. . . .

"Sam!" I waved. I was wearing shorts, a T-shirt, sandals, and regular underwear—*not* a thong.

"Sofia! I can't believe how okay you look."

"*Okay?* After all I've been through?" I pointed to my knees and shoulder.

"Unbelievable. Fantastic. Incredible."

"That's better," I said, then frowned.

"Hey, I feel really bad about what happened. I should've realized you're not used to biking."

"At least you made me wear a helmet. And I'd ridden a little, in Spain. Not that I'm planning to get back on a bike anytime soon."

"I don't blame you. I blame myself. That bike was too big for you."

"Yeah, well"—I looked right at him—"that's because it belongs to Alexa." My heart was pounding. "Sam, I mean, if you're going to feel bad about something…"

He exhaled. "Remember when I walked you home…after the windmill? You told me where you were staying and I—"

"Freaked out and took off?"

"Sofia, I haven't gone out with many girls, but the last one was—"

"I know. Kate told me an hour ago."

"I was going to tell you yesterday."

"Did you two even break up? I once asked Alexa if she had a boyfriend, and she made it sound on again, off again."

"I don't think she ever thought of me as her 'boyfriend.'"

"You went to a prom thing."

"True."

"Do you still like her?"

We walked down the stairs of the club. There were no chairs

stacked up, so Sam entered a shadowy room he called the "lifeguard dungeon" and came out with two red folding chairs. He opened his up as I struggled with mine, and then he opened mine for me. "I… admire her," he continued as we both sat down. "She says what she thinks, no matter how it comes off."

"And that's *good*?" I asked.

"Not always. But she and I go pretty far back."

"Go on."

"We knew each other when we were kids. We were on the swim team; we shot hoops in her driveway; we played Ping-Pong in the Teen Room."

"And then?"

"Last fall, I started high school. I'd grown, like, six inches over the summer, and she started telling me about parties and invited me to the Snow Ball. But if I said hi in the hall, she'd sometimes act like she barely knew me. And if I called her, she never called back. She can be pretty—"

"Bitchy?"

"I was going to say 'unpredictable,'" he replied.

I shrugged.

"She's been through a lot," he said, and I thought: *Yeah, who hasn't?* "I think the stuff with her father really threw her," he added.

"What stuff?"

"You don't know?"

"Know what?"

"Alexa was in sixth grade when her dad came out."

"Wait. Her dad's gay?"

"For a while, it was all anyone talked about. This was before the legalization of gay marriage and stuff. She got picked on. And then she got quiet. And then she got sort of mean."

"I didn't know any of this," I said, wondering what else I was in the dark about. "And the whole time, her mom was Dear Kate?"

"Oh man, I hadn't thought about it that way. Yeah, Mrs. Baird was running around giving advice about bullying and God knows what else"—(*Bras, periods, cliques, crushes*, I thought)—"while her one and only daughter was a holy terror." He shook his head. "I wish I could have stopped people from being mean to Alexa and stopped her from being mean back, but—"

I touched his toes with my toes. "But you were ten."

He laughed. "Good point! I was ten!" I tried to picture Sam as a sandy-haired ten-year-old. "Still, Sofia, I can't pretend I never liked Alexa. She was a friend. And then she was more."

"How much more?" I asked, my stomach twisting.

"Pretty much more." He met my eyes, and I felt as if I'd been punched.

"When I was a freshman, she was a sophomore, and the guys on my team were all like, 'Dude!'"

I crossed my arms and pulled my toes back. Lately, I'd felt like I was moving forward. But now I wondered if life was like Chutes and Ladders—you advance and advance but just as quickly, you can slide backward and lose ground.

"She's the one who showed me the windmill," Sam said.

"She showed me too," I confessed. "I didn't want to say anything."

"She did? Really?" I nodded, and he went quiet, taking that

in. "Hey, Sofia, what if we tried *not* to keep stuff from each other? I never knew what Alexa was thinking, and that sucked actually. Maybe you and I can be more, you know, honest?"

"Okay," I mumbled.

"So now what? Alexa's in Canada, right?"

"Until the end of July." I uncrossed my arms and let my pinkie finger brush the back of his hand.

He stood and pulled me up. "Let's take a walk."

I didn't want to let him off the hook so easily, but he hadn't really done anything wrong, had he? He was allowed to have a past. *Yeah, but did it have to involve Alexa?*

"*Sofia! Sofia!*" he started whisper-singing, "I just met a girl named Sofia!"

I smiled, despite myself, and told him that when I was in seventh grade, my school had put on *West Side Story*, and I was Maria.

"You were the *lead*? I bet you were amazing."

"I kind of was." I smiled.

He put his arm around me, but I winced. "Ouch! My shoulder!"

"Sorry!" We held hands instead, our fingers intertwined.

"My mom's name was Maria," I told him. "She loved that song." My voice caught, and for a second, I felt so open that I told myself to take it slow, to try not to care too much too fast.

I'd gotten hurt careening down that hill. Maybe I should try—at least try—to put on the brakes.

. . . .

I walked back to Kate's house alone, and when I got to the edge of her yard, I could see Dad and her in the hammock. I was about to say hi when I overheard Kate say, "Gregg, maybe I do have another bombshell." I slowed down behind the weeping willow and listened, half-hidden.

"*You* are the bombshell," Dad teased. Kate must have looked serious because he added, "Wait. Should I be nervous?"

"I don't know."

"You two have to move, right?" Kate began. "You're about to be evicted and you still haven't found a new place to live."

"You're making it sound dire. We can always rent."

"I love my house," she continued. "I did as a girl and I do now. But it's really…big. Look, I know I need to talk to Alexa about this, but on the other hand, Alexa is going to be leaving soon one way or the other."

I stayed completely still, like one of those rabbits at dusk that, when observed, turns into a miniature lawn statue. I didn't like that spying had become my new specialty, but I couldn't resist.

"What I mean," Kate continued, "is that there's room in my house for you and Sofia and even your cat. At least for a while." She paused. "Or longer?"

"You *do* need to talk to Alexa, and I need to talk to Sofia," Dad began, "but if you're saying what I hope you're saying, well, it's an idea worth considering."

My mouth fell open. This wasn't small talk; this was big talk! Giant talk! And whoa—weren't they taking things way too fast?

"We aren't just in a honeymoon phase, are we?" Kate asked.

"No, we're good together. Of course, *you're* the relationship expert, Katie. I just know what I feel."

"Which is?"

"Happy when I'm with you," Dad said. "And at home when I'm here. And like I've hit the jackpot because if I'm going to add a mother figure to Sofia's life, it's pretty great that I found an expert with girls."

They kissed and I thought, *I don't need a mother figure!* Then I wondered if that was true.

"How about you?" Dad asked. "How do you feel?"

"Happy when I'm with you," Kate replied. "And at home with you here. And a little anxious because Alexa already has two father figures and is *not* looking for a third. And also, for once, a little selfish because I want what's best for me, which is you."

"What would Dear Kate say?" Dad asked.

"Little Miss Know-It-All would say we're getting ahead of ourselves."

I wanted to chime in, *She'd have a point!*

"Well, I'd say she's jealous," Dad said.

"Yeah, what does she know about adults anyway?"

They laughed, then fell silent. More kissing? No way could I show myself now! I backtracked and did another lap around the lake—this time in a daze.

Was I glad the two of them had found each other?

Or was I sorry I'd ever encouraged Dad to go hear Dear Kate's talk?

. . . .

"I'm back!" I shouted and let the door bang behind me.

Dad came over with an I-have-something-important-to-tell-you expression. "Come, let's sit on the porch." I shrugged and followed, and we sat in the rocking chairs. "How you feeling, cupcake? No headaches?"

"I'm okay," I said, waiting.

"You know we have to move..." He didn't have to say any more; I'd heard it all anyway. I knew what was coming. And I knew that everything kept going, ready or not. Real life wasn't like watching a movie on a laptop. You couldn't press Pause or Rewind or Skip or Start Over. Life barely skipped a beat for Death. The planet never slowed down to let people absorb a shock or play catch-up. It just kept spinning and spinning.

"I was thinking," Dad continued, "Kate and I were thinking—"

I looked out at the lush lawn. Why make him even say it out loud? "Here?" I mumbled. "Temporarily?"

"Maybe. But I hope...Katie and I hope..."

I put my hand up to stop his words. I liked Kate and was happy for Dad and, well, both of them. But if they moved in together, that would be it—the very last nail in the coffin.

"Does Alexa know?"

"Not yet. Katie's been trying to reach her in Canada."

I felt so heavy, it was as if I might never be able to get up from the chair. "Will you keep working at Mount Sinai?"

"I'll commute. I might hate it in winter, but I'll get audiobooks or you'll make me playlists or whatever. And we can drive in together if you stay at Halsey. I already paid your deposit. Or you can go to Byram Hills. Your choice."

My choice? What a concept.

Did I want to commute to the small, all-girls' private school where I had gone for nine years and had lots of friends? Or did I want to be the new girl at a medium-size coed public school where I knew only Sam and Alexa?

"Can I think about it?"

"Of course. But if you stay at Halsey, I need to send them a tuition check. And if you switch, we need to get you registered."

"Okay," I said, though none of this was really okay. "Hey, Dad," I said, "what'd you do with that book you got signed for your 'niece' anyway?"

"Put it in my waiting room," he said sheepishly.

. . . .

Fireflies twinkled in the backyard. Dad and Kate were sitting on the porch swing. I found my cell phone and started texting Kiki.

Catlover99: you there?

kikiroo: yep. right here.

Catlover99: the thong didn't make it but i did

kikiroo: huh?

Catlover99: i had an accident

kikiroo: #1 or #2? hehe

Catlover99: no. for real

Catlover99: a bike accident…i spent the night before last in the hospital!

kikiroo: OMG!!!

kikiroo: are u ok???

Catlover99: mostly. but that's not the big news

kikiroo: huh? whats the big news???

Catlover99: if i tell you in person, i'll cry

Catlover99: which is why i'm writing it

kikiroo: k…

Catlover99: we're moving!

kikiroo: WHAT???!!!!!!!!

Catlover99: kate invited us to move in

Catlover99: to her house

kikiroo: im in shock. no.

kikiroo: im depressed.

kikiroo: no. im jealous!!!

Catlover99: i'm in shock. and i'm always jealous of you

kikiroo: youll still go to HSG, right?

Catlover99: maybe… or maybe to that school we saw?

kikiroo: u cant!!!!

kikiroo: no no no NO NOOOOOOO

Catlover99: i don't know yet

kikiroo: you can't leave! i'm serious!

Catlover99: either way, you can come out a lot

Catlover99: alexa likes you more than me…

Catlover99: you can pretend it's your country house

kikiroo: i can't believe this…

Catlover99: i mean it. you can help decorate my room

kikiroo: do u have to share with alexa??

Catlover99: omg!! no!! can you imagine? alexa would never want to share a room with me.

Catlover99: and she is NOT going to be thrilled to have me as a sister!!

kikiroo: i would be.

Catlover99: awww thanks

kikiroo: ok if i call?

Catlover99: yes but reception can be spotty. call the landline, k?

The phone rang. I picked up, and Kiki, without even waiting for "hi," said, "Start from the beginning. You were in the *hospital*?"

PART TWO

JULY

PACK RAT. I HATED THAT term. Yes, I was sentimental and I was a saver, but no, I wasn't a rodent, and my father shouldn't call me one.

"Take it back."

"What?"

"You said I was a pack rat. Take it back."

"Sofia, aren't you getting a little too old to—?" I must have looked near tears because he said, "Fine. I take it back. You're not a pack rat. You're a wolf cub who's not very good at throwing things out."

"I never said I was." Fact is, I felt defeated by my room: full drawers, stuffed closet, overflowing armoire.

Last April, I'd set aside a lot of Mom's things—lipsticks, purses, cards from students, even a "World's Greatest Mom" mug I'd given her one Mother's Day. Now I realized I couldn't keep it all. One thing I would treasure forever was a pair of earrings—pearl studs—that Abuelo had given Mom when she was my age.

Dad was undaunted by the tasks at hand. Just as he had made us put away Christmas on January 1, he would, no doubt, have our worldly possessions boxed up before August 1. Right on schedule, we'd move to Armonk, then fly to Spain.

I still had so many decisions to make. Stubby pencils? Out. Dried-up markers? Out. Unused address labels? Out. But what about that frayed valentine that said "Sweet Open Fun Interesting Awesome"? And the cards and fortune-tellers Kiki had made me? As for letters from Mom, I was keeping every one, no questions asked.

I wished I had a recent photo of my family. On moving up day, everyone had posed with their parents, and I'd been slammed again by the unfairness of it all. Girls often grumbled "My parents this" and "My parents that" without even realizing how…

Oh well, I knew better than to go down that path.

I reached for the ceramic sneakers I'd made in art class right before Mom died. I'd told Mom about them, but by the time the shoes emerged from the kiln, Mom was dead. No. Worse: cremated. Reduced to ashes.

Cremains. That was my least favorite word. Far worse than *pack rat*! I couldn't bear to think about it, yet my parents had "discussed" what they "wanted," and my vote didn't count. Dad had put the "crematory container" in his closet over a year ago, and it was a subject I avoided. I'd told him I didn't see why we had to do anything right away. What was the urgency?

Back to my ceramic sneakers. In or out? I remembered showing them to Dad and how he'd complimented me and said, "The shoelaces even have aglets!" explaining that aglets were the plastic tips that keep laces from unraveling.

As he praised my work, however, I mostly heard the booming

silence of my mother's absence. I put the shoes on the windowsill by my ceramic turtles and wished I could hear *her* praise: "*¡Qué maravilla! ¡Me encantan! ¡Qué dotada eres!*"

I wished *I* had aglets to keep me from unraveling.

It was terrible to crave a double dose of parental love knowing I'd never get it.

At least missing Mom came in waves now. Sometimes, I missed her a lot, sometimes…less. Which was a relief but unsettling in a new way.

I had moved up. I was moving out. Was I beginning to move on?

I fell back onto my pink canopy bed and thought about writing Dear Kate.

Dear Kate,

It's me, Catlover. I know I should be grateful that I'm in one piece, and believe me, I am. But I'm also messed up and mixed up. As you know, we're moving into your house. And I love your house. But I love *my* apartment too and I don't want to leave— not that I have a choice.

I *do* have a choice about schools. I can go from the girl whose mother died to the new girl. Which might be better, except I'm not ready to accept that for the rest of my life, all the people I meet won't know my mom. Here, everyone knew her. There, and everywhere else from now on, no one will.

I just wish someone could promise me that it's safe to come out of my shell. Is that why I like turtles? Because they're good at staying safe?

And what about Alexa? She's going to be sooo pissed when she comes back from Canada camp and finds Dad and me in your house—*her* house! She's going to want to kill me—or you! Have you even told her yet? And what about when she finds out about Sam?

I did not press Send. This was a pretend letter. All in my head. I was becoming a head case.

I opened my bottom desk drawer and looked at the emails from Dear Kate and reread the one that had ended with the promise "Things will get easier."

Would they?

I phoned Kiki. "Can you come over? I'm packing and I need you to be ruthless."

"Ruthless?"

"Hard-hearted. Unfeeling. Merciless."

"I thought I was kind, imaginative, knowledgeable—"

"Just come over. Please?"

She said okay, and while I waited, the sky darkened and raindrops pecked at the air conditioner outside my window.

Kiki arrived, and I greeted her holding the ceramic sneakers. "In or out?"

"In! That's a no-brainer!"

I wrapped them in newspaper and placed them into a box marked "S's Bedroom." "What about my Magic 8 Ball?"

Kiki picked it up. "My sources say no."

"And this sweater?"

"It went out of style two years ago. Which is why you haven't been wearing it."

"But it looked good in sixth grade, right?"

"You were quite the hottie! Except you hadn't hit puberty, so you were quite the warmie."

I hugged Kiki. "I couldn't face this alone." I held up a T-shirt covered with signatures from our classmates in fourth grade.

"Irreplaceable!"

I reached for another shirt and flinched.

"Your shoulder still hurts?" Kiki asked.

"It's getting better, but I'll have a scar. At least I got the staples out of my head."

"Scars are okay."

"I guess. What about my dress-up clothes?"

"Are you kidding?! Think of Alexa!"

"I can't *stop* thinking of Alexa." I frowned. "What about my turtle collection?"

"Sorry. Can't be ruthless about your turtles. They're small— take 'em all."

"And my stuffies? Will I find them good homes?" I laughed but my voice caught.

"Keep Panther and Tigger-Tiger and Yertle. Wash the rest and give them to Goodwill. God, Sof, what would you do without me?"

"What *am* I going to do without you?"

"How do you think I feel? I'm having abandonment issues, and you and Natalie haven't even left yet! At least *you're* staying at Halsey, right?"

I hesitated.

"Sofia, you *have* to! What if your dad and Dear Kate break up?"

"I don't think they're going to. Maybe it's because we have to move anyway, but everything's in fast-forward." I sat down. "Kiki, I never saw my dad this happy with my mom."

"You weren't there for that part. Your parents had a good marriage—I know because my parents had a sucky one." Kiki made a face. "And by the way, you're not allowed to dump me no matter how great it is in the boring 'burbs."

"You can't dump me either."

"No way," Kiki said, but then I heard a ping as she got a text. "Oh! Gotta go. Madison just got back from China, and I said I'd meet her at the Met. Wanna come?"

"Yeah, but—" I looked at the stuff of my life, strewn across my bedroom.

"Aren't you almost done?"

"No. Look under my bed."

Kiki kneeled on the floor. "You never threw out Secret Admirer?!" She pulled out the torn box, opened it, and held the plastic purple phone to her ear. The game board showed the faces of two dozen boys. "Think of the hours we spent on this phone!"

"Hours?! Try *years!*"

"Look at this! David, Jamal, Liam. I had such a thing for Christopher."

"I was in love with Scott!" I laughed. "Was there a Sam?"

Kiki studied the board. "No, no Sam. No Jeremy either. I met him two days ago when I was on the Great Lawn, getting a tan. He said he likes my sense of humor."

"If you were working on your tan, he likes more than that," I pointed out. "But see? Now you get it. How can I throw this out?"

"Watch and learn." Kiki closed the box, stood up, and carried Secret Admirer out the door and down the hall to the communal garbage can by the service elevator. She lifted the box high in the air and dropped it in. "Bye-bye, boys!" She dusted off her palms.

I had an urge to dive in and rescue the game—as well as David, Jamal, Liam, Christopher, and Scott. But I resisted. "It's the end of an era," I said.

"It is," Kiki agreed. "Now we have real boys to call."

. . . .

Every time Kate's phone rang—cell or landline—she rushed to answer, hoping it was Alexa. This time, it was.

"It's so good to hear your voice!" Kate said, glowing. "Oh, that's wonderful!" "That's great!" "I love you!"

"How's Alexa?" I asked when she hung up.

"She sounds *so* happy. Her group stopped in some small town to get supplies and there was a pay phone. She said that instead of mountains, they were seeing mountain *ranges*. And that last night, the Milky Way was crystal clear. They even saw the aurora borealis! She said it was 'sick.'" Kate laughed. "She said the food is 'lame,' but they get so hungry from hiking that nobody minds. Oh, and she's practicing Spanish with a girl named Victoria who also lives near here, in Westchester. She also said I shouldn't worry."

I wanted to say, *Did you tell her* she *should worry?* But I said, "Did you mention…?"

"I should have, but it was a short conversation." Kate went back to arranging the hydrangea and lilies from her fenced-in garden.

"Kate, I just think that if she gets home and it's all a done deal, Alexa might"—*hack me to pieces*—"be really surprised."

"I intend to tell her," Kate said. "But she's been impossible to reach, and just now, she barely let me get a word in—as you could hear." Kate met my eyes. "And I want her to *enjoy* her vacation. At the airport, the coordinator kept saying that these trips are about *disconnecting*."

I wondered if Kate's neglecting to spill the beans was due to kindness, cowardice, or some kindness/cowardice combo. It occurred to me that Kate herself was on vacation—she was in girl-friend mode instead of mom mode. And while she didn't want to burst Alexa's bubble, maybe she didn't want Alexa to burst hers either. Kate liked feeling summery and carefree. And yes, I got that, but I was also realizing that Dear Kate wasn't perfect. She was a good person, yes, but she had flaws like everyone else.

The question was: Where did this leave me?

. . . .

Ten days till moving day. Kate's house had a basement and a garage, but she'd said we shouldn't store things that we should "let go of" or that didn't "spark joy." Sure, okay, but how could I "let go" of my mom's big oval mirror or the wooden "Lemonade 50 cents" sign I made with Abuelo or even my Halsey concert programs? As for framed photos, they sparked both joy and bittersweet feelings. (Did Dad still have framed photos of Mom in his office? Did he have one of Kate now too?)

I made index cards with descriptions of all the objects we no longer needed—lamp, desk, dresser, bed, chairs, television, sofa—and posted them in the mail room.

Selling to neighbors felt more personal than putting stuff on eBay or Craigslist. Teachers also bought odds and ends from a card table I'd set up in front of our building. Dad had said I could keep that money, and by 2:00 p.m., I'd pocketed almost $170.

"If I'd known you'd make that much," he said, "I'd have asked for a percentage."

I was glad for the cash, but our bigger transactions made my insides curdle. My pink canopy bed? A teacher bought it for her daughter. The sleigh bed Mom and Dad had slept in for nineteen years? The Russells bought it for Mason. They said it would be his "big-boy bed."

. . . .

In late July, I went out a lot with Kiki, Natalie, Madison, and other friends—I'd never felt so popular. But every get-together was tinged with sadness. It was as though I'd already started missing them.

One evening, everyone met at Natalie's, and Sam came in by train. I told him to take the shuttle from Grand Central to Penn Station and then the 2 or 3 subway up to Ninety-Sixth and that I'd meet him at the Starbucks on Ninety-Third and Broadway. I got there first and liked watching him walk in and look for me, liked how he kissed me in public.

At the party, I could tell that everyone liked Sam. They were all laughing and joking (but not flirting), and when Sam went to the bathroom, Natalie whispered, "Sofia, he's great."

"I know."

"I still can't believe he used to go out with Alexa!" Kiki said.

"I know."

"Omigod, they didn't *do it*, did they?" Madison asked.

"I don't know! And I don't know if I want to know!"

All three nodded.

"I don't *think* so," I added, mostly for my own benefit.

Dad, meantime, had been telling all our neighbors to visit us in Armonk—"I'll fire up the grill!" But would any of them come? Were some of our "close friends" close simply because they lived close by? I hoped real friendship meant more than that.

Dad also notified the super; arranged for the gas and electricity to be shut off; stopped delivery of *The New York Times*; contacted the post office, phone, bank, and credit card companies; hired a moving van…and complained that his to-do list was out of control.

"Once we move," he said, "I hope Mom will stop getting credit card offers. It's nuts how much junk mail she still gets."

I hated hearing him talk about that—and hated that banks still wanted Mom as a customer. "Speaking of mail," Dad continued, "am I sending Halsey a check? It's a lot of money, so I want you to be sure. And if you're not going, they need to offer the slot to a girl on the waitlist."

Halsey School for Girls or Byram Hills High School? I couldn't make up my mind. Kiki suggested I toss a coin—and then, when it was in the air, figure out which school I was hoping for.

I tried: Heads for Halsey. Tails for BHHS.

But it didn't help.

. . . .

Kiki begged me to stay at Halsey, but Sam had a different opinion. One day, he came by after work at his parents' stationery store in Mount Kisco where his job was to deal with inventory and customers. ("Pens, paper, and Post-its," he joked.)

"The teachers at HSG have known me forever," I explained. We started walking up Evergreen Row, and he showed me the foundation of an old stone mansion that had burned to the ground decades earlier. "So if I stay, I wouldn't have to prove myself. And I'd be the copresident of the Spanish Club, which is cool as a freshman. And if you do all thirteen years, K through twelve, you get to be a Survivor. There's even a Survivor page in the yearbook."

"A Survivor? Is that, like, a badge of honor?" he asked, and I realized how silly it sounded. Then again, sometimes surviving was harder than people realized.

"At least consider Byram Hills," Sam said. "You probably think I'm saying that for all the wrong reasons." He pulled me closer.

"Windmill afternoons?" I said. *Windmill afternoons.* It sounded like the first line of a haiku. I slipped two fingers into his belt loop. "You're not getting impatient with me?" I couldn't believe I said that aloud, but he knew what I meant: so far, all we'd done was make out.

"No. Not that I—" I kissed him to stop him from finishing the sentence, and we went back to the original subject.

"Sofia, with the school thing, don't you *want* a change?"

I shrugged. "Maybe change is overrated."

"Maybe comfort is too. Don't get offended—I know Halsey is the god of private schools." When I'd told him it was up there with Trinity, Exeter, Sidwell, and Harvard-Westlake, he looked perplexed and said he hadn't really heard of those schools either. "I just mean," he continued, "is being a 'Survivor' enough for you? Thirteen years at the same place with the same people?"

"Surviving isn't nothing," I said. "And it's *not* all the same people. New girls come, and some leave when it's not a good fit."

"If you switch, you get to reinvent yourself," Sam said.

"I don't want to reinvent myself," I said, then wondered if that was one hundred percent true. "I don't mind myself."

"I don't mind you either." He smiled. "I'm not saying this right. Can I tell you a story?"

"You can and you may."

"Two summers ago, my grandfather—"

"Grandpa Fritz, the Southern gentleman?"

He nodded, pleased that I'd remembered. I liked that Sam and I had real conversations, full of teasing and references. In middle school, my circle of friends didn't include boys, so whenever I met one, it had been hard to relax. Now, Sam and I were heading back to "our windmill," holding hands and pointing out chipmunks.

"Once, when Grandpa Fritz took me fishing," he continued, "he asked what I was thinking, and I was like: 'Nothing.' So he said, 'What do you see?' and I was like, 'I dunno. Water?' He sounded disappointed and said, 'Don't just look down, Sam. Look *around*. Use your five senses! That way you'll always appreciate fishing no matter what you catch.' Well, that may sound stupid, but...like, right now, it's a beautiful day, and I'm with a beautiful girl, and I'm *here* for it, you know?"

I knew. I too wanted this feeling to last. It was good to feel happy again. "In sixth grade," I said, "I was a total geek—"

"A girls' school geek in desperate need of corruption."

"You would've hated me."

"I would've corrupted you!"

I laughed. "We were watching some old movie in history, and I got out my spiral notebook and raised my hand and was like, 'Will this be on the test?' After class, the teacher—who was also, of course, one of my neighbors—took me aside and said, 'Sofia, you're eleven. Don't worry about your permanent record. It's a privilege just to be a sponge in a school like this.'"

"You could be a sponge at Byram Hills," Sam said, squeezing me. "We win Intel science prizes and stuff. What does your dad think?"

"He's forcing me to move, so he doesn't want to force any other decisions." I sighed. "If I go to Byram Hills, I'd save him thousands. Maybe that's reason enough, especially since we don't have Mom's salary."

"Unless your dad *likes* having his girl at an all-girls' school. Does Dr. Wolfe thinks all boys are wolves?"

"Would he be right?" I gave him a shove.

"Maybe. You know what, Sof? You have to decide for yourself. Don't think about your dad or your friends or even me."

"It's hard not to." I held his hand tighter.

We reached the windmill, Sam jiggled the rusty latch, and we slipped inside. I paused to take in the cool, musty stillness. Sight, touch, smell, sound. My fifth sense was taste, and before we even climbed the steps, I kissed Sam right there, holding his face in my hands. I moved my fingertips to the nape of his neck and tugged delicately on his long hair. I made a little mmm sound. Like yummm. Or Sammm.

When we broke off, he howled. "OWWwooooo."

"What are you doing?" I giggled.

"Howling. No, *ululating*. You scared to be alone with a wolf?"

"I'm a Wolfe too, remember?"

He laughed. Being alone with Sam didn't scare me. It made me feel fizzy and excited, like a soda bottle that's been shaken. What scared me was how much I was letting myself care.

. . . .

Dad, Kate, and I were drying dishes when Alexa phoned again. At first, Kate sounded thrilled to hear from her. But her tone quickly changed.

"Robbed? Oh, honey! I'm so sorry… Are you okay… Look, it's just money. If you're okay… I'll cancel the card. I'll take care of it. You take care of yourself… All right… I'm so sorry… Okay, okay, okay, see you in eight days. Love you."

Kate hung up and told us that Alexa was at a hostel taking her "first hot shower in a month" when someone stole her wallet.

"Poor kid," Dad said. "That's a terrible feeling."

"It is!" Kate said, reaching for her purse. "I'm glad her credit card has its own separate number. Last year, Alexa left her purse in a cab, and I had to change my info on E-ZPass, PayPal, Netflix, everywhere."

Dad nodded, but I knew he was thinking what I was thinking.

Kate looked up. "I know! I know! But how could I when she was already so upset?"

She handed us a postcard from her bag. It was a close-up of a moose's snout. On the back, Alexa had written: "Hi, Mom. I saw a herd of meese. It was epic! Are you keeping Teen America out of trouble? How are things with Gyno Guy?"

"You need to tell her," Dad said gently. "Doctor's orders."

. . . .

After dinner, I joined Dad on the porch swing and told him I was going to Byram Hills. I said I loved Halsey but couldn't see making the commute twice a day, and it would probably be good for me to "get out of my comfort zone" and go to a school where everything didn't remind me of Mom. He nodded and said if I kept my grades up, Halsey's doors would always be open.

Nice to know that while some changes were permanent, others were reversible.

I considered unloading my worries: What if I miss my friends? What if Dad and Kate break up? What if Sam and I break up? What if the teachers don't think I'm smart? What if Alexa turns people against me?

Instead, I stayed quiet—and Dad opened up.

"When I was a boy, we had a porch swing like this," he began. "Sometimes, after dinner, I'd look out and see a little red light. That red light was my green light, because it meant my dad was outside smoking a cigar, so I'd go sit with him. Father and son."

It was good to be sitting with my dad, father and daughter. He always spoke fondly of his father; he too had been a doctor, a general practitioner in Katonah. I was sorry I never got to meet him.

I wondered how Dad had managed to accept his dad's death, how so many people manage, generation after generation.

But I knew the answer: You can't mourn forever. When you're alive, you have to live.

. . . .

Kate pointed to a hamper in the upstairs bathroom. "Dirty clothes go here."

"Really?"

She laughed. "Really."

I'd been doing my own laundry for fifteen months. Mine and Dad's. Mrs. Morris in 6C had explained how to operate the basement machines and had told me to "hoard quarters." She'd said to separate lights from darks, put in towels and heavy items first, and empty all pockets. "No pens, no makeup, no gum."

It was only after Mom died that Dad and I understood how many jobs Mom did besides teaching. At first, neighbors brought food, but before long, our fridge and pantry grew bare. Pepper ran out of cat food. The printer ran out of paper. The shower ran out of shampoo. Only the laundry basket got fuller and fuller.

When Dad and I finally realized that elves weren't going to pick up where Mom had left off, I volunteered to be in charge of laundry, and Dad said he'd vacuum and grocery shop.

Now Kate was offering to do our laundry? Score! I felt guilty and giddy. "I like to fold," I said. "I used to help my mom when I was little." I told her that Mom and I would take opposite ends of the sheets, fluff them, then step toward each other, meeting in the middle to match up corners. "It was like a dance."

"It *is* like a dance!" Kate agreed. "I used to help my mother with sheets too, right in this very house. I always thought of 'London Bridge.'"

"Do you have any clothes that need folding?" I offered.

"I bet I do," Kate said.

As we headed to her laundry room, I asked, "Have you talked to Alexa yet?"

"No, but I called again, and the coordinator got back to me.

He said the hikers are deep in the woods, 'unreachable and far from civilization,' and that I should let her enjoy her independence. He said that Alexa had told the group leader that she was getting a ride home from Logan with Victoria's dad."

"That saves you a trip to Boston."

"Yeah, but I was looking forward to the one-on-one," she admitted. "The coordinator also went on and on about some high-maintenance mom who flew in on a private plane to bring her daughter acne pills. He said his program wasn't 'a coddling American camp' with camp cams and daily blog posts for helicopter parents." She looked at me. "He doesn't like me, and I don't like him."

"He can't lecture you about parenting! Doesn't he know you're an expert?"

"A wimp too." She frowned. "But I do have a plan."

. . . .

Dad and I were driving back to the city, and I said, "Dad, you've got to talk to Kate. In three days, we're moving in! In five, Alexa comes back! She's going to blow a gasket when she finds my tooth-brush in her bathroom."

"Common sense is an uncommon gift, and Katie has it in spades. But right now, she's being remiss."

Remiss? Try moronic! "That's putting it mildly," I said, frustrated with both of them. Then I added, "But she did say she has a plan."

"She told me she 'took action.'" Dad said that Kate asked the main office to ask Alexa to call home. "She said she didn't want to alarm her, so she told them not to use the word 'emergency.'"

"That's taking action?"

"No, but last night, she said, 'I'm a writer, for God's sakes,' and then she spent hours composing a letter. She sent it to the main office and asked them to forward it to Alexa's group leader."

"It's about time."

"True."

"Dad, you know her dad's gay, right?"

"Katie told me."

"Sam told me. I had no idea. What'd she say?"

"That she and Bryan are better as friends than spouses, and that theirs was a 'happy marriage' but not a 'real marriage.' She said I'd like him. His partner is also named Brian, but with an *I*, so everyone calls them the Bryans. Oh, and they're engaged. Katie said that at first Alexa did *not* like the extra attention from her peers, but she adores Brian—the partner—and sometimes refers to him as her 'fairy godfather.'" He shook his head. "She's a pistol, that kid."

"Where do they live?"

"Chelsea. He's a freelance videographer. Katie said he does weddings as well as sports and theater videos for schools. They also do travel assignments."

"Sounds cool."

"Yeah, well, apparently, when Alexa learned what *I* do, she told her mom, 'So Dad couldn't deal with women's bodies and this guy can't get enough of them?'"

"Signature Alexa."

"She also said she was the only person she knew whose parents *both* had boyfriends."

I had to laugh. "What'd Kate say?"

"That you never know about people's private lives."

"Remember what Mom used to say? '*Cada familia es un mundo.*'"

"'Every family is a world'?" Dad ventured.

"Yeah. I'm not sure I ever got it before, how complicated everything is."

"Well, your mom did. At parent-teacher conferences, she saw a lot of families from the inside, even high-profile ones."

I nodded.

"I've been reading Katie's columns," Dad continued. "Maybe there's no such thing as 'a normal childhood.'"

"Maybe not."

We drove under the George Washington Bridge, and I was amazed at how fast the trip had gone. Had Dad and I really been talking the entire way home?

"Alexa's childhood couldn't have been easy," he added.

"No," I agreed. "And right now, she's a happy camper who's in for a shock."

. . . .

Pepper was *not* a happy camper. He was meowing more than ever, asking about his favorite blankets and cushions.

On moving day, he paced. He still had his kibble, water, and litter box as well as the occasional fly to chase. But he kept looking at me as if to ask, *What's going on?*

"Come here, scaredy cat." I picked him up, then sat with him on the floor in a diamond of sunlight. I petted him until he started to purr. He was shedding up a storm.

"It's going to be okay," I said. "In your new home, there's a fat old cat named Coconut, and you two are going to get along great, you'll see. You've been a city kitty, and your world is about to get a whole lot bigger."

Pepper purred, clueless.

I hoped he could handle the transition. Halsey Tower was the only home he'd ever known, and he'd never even tried to sneak out the front door.

"The end of one chapter," I told him, "is the beginning of the next." Dad had said those very words to me that morning, our last in my childhood home. He'd placed a pound of coffee and a welcome note on the counter for the young family who was about to take our place in 5C.

I still couldn't believe we were really doing it—moving. In our apartment, I had grown used to Mom's absence, but I could feel her presence too, in the rooms, the photos, the air. What would it be like to step away from these memories?

The buzzer sounded, and Pepper arched his back and jumped sideways. Dad pressed the button, and soon, three burly men wearing matching black Movers Not Shakers T-shirts entered our apartment. Pepper puffed himself up like a Halloween cat, but the movers, unfazed, started packing up the remaining furniture. Pepper hightailed it to my bedroom.

Too late. My canopy bed was already gone. There was no place to hide.

AUGUST

KIKI AND SAM HELPED ME turn Kate's guest room into my bed-room. We unpacked boxes, shelved books, hung my mom's oval mirror, and lined up photos on my bureau. One was of my parents standing back-to-back when Dad was very skinny and Mom was very pregnant. (Dad says you can't be "very pregnant"—you either are or you're not.) Another was of Kiki, Alexa, and me jumping off the deck in May, knees up, arms outstretched. Kate had it framed, probably hoping we'd morph into the three musketeers.

"When does Alexa get here?" Kiki asked.

"Tomorrow around four thirty." I couldn't believe Alexa was going to show up and find an insta-sister who'd moved in on her mom, house, and sort-of ex.

I'd enjoyed the peacefulness of the last six weeks. Dad and Kate and I had dined on the deck and watched movies on TV. Sam and I had taken evening walks, serenaded by crickets, and gone to the club after 7:00 p.m., when the lifeguards went off duty and we could swim beyond the lanes to the gazebo in the middle of the lake.

One evening, Sam had suggested we go down the giant slide

playing Categories. When I climbed to the top and pushed off, he called, "A Founding Fathers musical!"

I shouted, "*Hamilton*," seconds before splashing into the water. When he climbed up and pushed off, I shouted, "A Nobel Peace Prize winner!"

He shouted, "Mandela!" before being submerged and "Malala!" when he came up for air. "Winged insect!" he shouted to me.

"Firefly!" I said. "Another winged insect!" I shouted to him.

"Dragonfly!" he replied. When I climbed up a third time, he shouted, "Hottest girl in Windmill!" I said nothing but smiled underwater.

Of course, I still thought of my mom. But I was remembering how to have fun again. I was picking raspberries and baking pies and…coming back to life.

Kate invited both Kiki and Sam to stay for dinner the night of our move, and afterward, the five of us played Boggle. Kiki shook the set, put it down, looked it over, and proclaimed, "Too many vowels. Let me shake again."

"No!" I protested. "I already found a seven!"

"That's impossible," Sam said.

I pointed to *tapioca* snaking around the cubes.

"Wow," Kate said, impressed. "You'll have to teach Alexa."

So not gonna happen, I thought, and wished that Kate would accept that we were *not* about to turn into one big, happy family.

"Kate, you must be so excited that Alexa is coming home," Kiki said. I knew Kiki was still excited to be on a first-name basis with her idol.

"Oh, I am!" Kate replied. "But I wish she'd answered my last email, the one about—" She gestured to Dad and me.

"Maybe she didn't know what to say," Kiki said.

"Maybe," Kate answered.

. . . .

"You like your new room?" Dad stood in my doorway in Armonk. I was proud I'd emptied the boxes and found places for everything, even my turtles, which were in a huddle on my bedside table.

"I do," I said, looking up from a Spanish novel I was reading.

"Shouldn't you go to sleep?" Dad said. "It's after midnight."

"I will. One sec."

A few minutes later, he came back. "Can I turn out the light?"

"One sec," I said and kept reading.

Five minutes later, Dad was back again. "Cupcake, I'm turning off the light."

"One sec!" I said.

"You've had lots of secs!"

Lots of…*sex*?! We stared at each other.

"*Seconds!*" Dad said. "I mean *seconds!*"

He turned off my light, and I tried to turn off my mind. I was thinking about Sam and how "hooking up" and "love" meant different things to different people. A lot of girls said "I love you" to other girls, but I still couldn't imagine saying it to a boy. Yet I did love being with Sam, and I hoped Alexa wasn't going to mess that up.

I looked at the ceiling and missed my pink canopy. Funny

thing to miss. I told myself that canopies were for little girls and princesses, then imagined Alexa cackling, *And you aren't a princess anymore—you're a wicked stepsister.*

I drew up the sheets and listened to the quiet.

Was it possible that I missed the hum of traffic? The sirens and honking and car radios? The people on the sidewalk who laughed and argued at all hours, sometimes drunkenly?

When I used to look out my old bedroom window, I'd see lights in other people's apartments. I'd peer out during the day too. Adults would hurry by with briefcases, strollers, shopping bags. Kids would be going to or from school. Doormen, dog walkers, delivery people, bicycle messengers—someone was always there.

Did I miss the city now that I lived in the "country"? Kate thought it was funny that we called Armonk the country. She said, "It's pretty here, but don't kid yourself. It's the suburbs."

The door opened. Dad again? No. Pepper. He'd found me. He didn't join me in bed—not his style—but he leaped onto my soft desk chair and settled in for the night.

· · · · · · · · · ·

Dad and I made shish kebabs and a tomato-mozzarella-basil salad for Alexa's return. I suggested dousing everything with hot sauce.

"Don't you dare!" Dad said.

We heard the crunch of gravel, and I looked out the kitchen window. A silver Mercedes pulled up, and Alexa emerged, tanned and toned. *Here we go*, I thought. *Let the games begin.*

"Alexa's home!" I called. Kate went flying out the door so fast, I was afraid she might trip.

"Think we should say hi?" I asked Dad.

"Let's give them a minute."

"No argument here." I brought forks and knives to the deck where we'd set the table with a red-checked tablecloth, red napkins, and a bouquet of just-picked day lilies and black-eyed Susans. Two tall candles stood inside hurricane lamps. I walked behind the porch swing and peeked toward the driveway. Once again, I was spying in broad daylight.

Kate and Alexa gave each other a long hug (I felt the sting of jealousy), and Kate invited Victoria and her father in for lemonade. "Thank you," the man said with an Argentinian accent. "Victoria's mother is anxious for us to get home."

"Believe me, I understand," Kate said. She thanked him, and soon, it was just mother and daughter in the driveway.

"You look great!" Kate said, beaming.

"I'm in unbelievable shape! Feel my bicep." Alexa flexed her arm. "And have you ever seen me so tan? Check out my feet! I have a flip-flop tan!"

Kate laughed, eating her daughter up. "So how was it?"

"So perfect! The group was great—well, except for a few idiots. The rest of us became, like, best friends. We did everything together! I'm really looking forward to lazing around the house alone—just us."

Kate lowered her voice, and I couldn't make out what she said.

"Mom, I was in the *boonies*. I haven't been online in, like, six weeks! Our tents weren't exactly wireless, and there are no Internet cafés on the mountaintops. Besides, the director kept saying this was our opportunity to 'cut the electronic umbilical cord' and 'face the world without Facebook and Instagram.'"

Kate said something I couldn't decode.

"Yeah, he mentioned you wanted to get in touch but said it wasn't an emergency. I was going to call from the airport, but everyone started taking pictures, and I knew I was about to see you…"

"Oh Lord," Kate said.

"What?"

"You don't know?"

"What?"

"I wrote you a long email."

"What did it say?"

"It's not something I wanted to summarize."

"Mom, you're scaring me! Is Dad okay?"

"He's fine."

"Brian?"

"Fine."

"Then…?"

"Honey—" Kate's voice got quiet again and then I heard:

"Are you *kidding* me? Mom, you just met him!"

Kate mumbled something. She was trying to keep the volume down, but there were no birds or crickets or lawnmowers or airplanes to drown out their conversation.

"What? He must've been shocked out of his mind!"

Mumble, mumble, mumble.

"Mom, how well do you even know him?"

Mumble, mumble. "I know *myself.*"

"Oh, *spare* me. So what did he say?" Alexa sounded shrill.

Mumble, mumble.

"*WHAT?!*" Alexa's voice rose an octave. "What do you mean '*moved in*'?"

Mumble, mumble. "Sofia—"

"Sofia? *Sofia!* I practically forgot about that little brat! Please tell me she's not moving in too!"

Mumble, mumble. "…*his daughter.*"

"Yeah, well, I'm *your DAUGHTER!*"

Dad stepped onto the deck. I shushed him and pointed. Their voices wafted over loud and clear, and he got sucked in too.

"I *wanted* to tell you!" Kate said. "But the first time you called, you were ecstatic, and the second time, you were distraught, and there was no third time. Honey, I spent *hours* writing you that email. I revised it over and over—"

"Oh, thank God, because a typo would've sent me over the edge! Tell you what, Mom. I'll print it out and you can sign it with one of your rose-colored calligraphy pens. And I'll get it framed! Ooooo, a letter from Dear Kate! God, Mom, I can't leave you alone!"

Dad and I looked at each other, eyes wide.

"Excuse me, Alexa, but you *do* leave me alone! As well you should. You're getting older, and soon, you'll be off to college, and you're going to leave me alone more and more."

Now they were both hollering. The neighbors were probably

having a field day. I hoped nobody was going to walk by with a cell and press Record. "I have to start looking out for myself for a change," Kate was saying. "Which will work out for you in the long run because you won't wind up feeling responsible."

"Who said anything about feeling responsible?" Alexa shot back. "And how do you know he's not using you for a place to live!"

"He has savings! He's contributing! This isn't a free ride for him. We've done some math."

"How do you know he's not just on the rebound?"

Mumble, mumble. "…over a year since his wife died…judge of character…discussed it at length…faculty housing"—*mumble, mumble*—"…evicted…"

"Wow, so you figured you'd roll out the welcome mat? I hope this is temporary?"

Kate lowered her voice then said, "I hope it isn't."

Dad and I stood frozen, partners in crime.

"Mom, they could have rented! You could've had your stupid little romance—"

"Dammit, Alexandra!" Uh-oh, Kate was ticked. "Do I strike you as a woman of 'stupid little romances'? I made a mistake of sorts—well, honey, not a mistake. Of course not a mistake—thank heavens I married Bryan and had you. But when we didn't work out as a couple, I took myself right off the playing field. I became an umpire for everyone else's romances. This time, I want in. Gregg is a great guy. And I'm not twenty-something. I'm forty-six! So I'm going for it. Yes, he's lucky he found me. I'm a catch. But he is too."

I looked at Dad; he was rapt. "He's kind; he likes his work; he's attractive; he's healthy; he's…straight! And he's a doctor, for God's sake! And he loves me. So I feel lucky too. Really lucky! Because I love him."

Dad gave me a thumbs-up, and I was happy for him even though a part of me still wished…

"What about me?" Alexa asked, suddenly sounding like a hurt little kid.

"Darling, I adore you. You're my number one. You know that." *Mumble, mumble.* Kate's voice was quieter now. "But let's go in. Gregg and Sofia made you a welcome dinner. And there's something else I should probably tell you."

"My home has two new people in it, and there's something *else* you should probably tell me? Mom, my head's going to explode. What? What is it?" Alexa flew into another rage.

"It's nothing big…" Kate said. I leaned against the house, my heart beating a mile a minute. I was still processing Kate's "you're my number one." Was Kate going to tell Alexa about Sam? *Please don't tell Alexa about Sam!*

"You know Sam?" Kate asked.

"What? In the biblical sense?" Alexa replied. Kate winced, and Alexa added, "What about him? And why would I care?"

"Good. Then never mind."

"No. What? Is he okay?"

"He's fine," Kate said.

"Are we adopting him too?"

"No." Kate paused. "But…" She hesitated. "He and Sofia met

at the lake, and they went on a bike ride. She borrowed your bike and had a spill and wound up in the hospital." Dad put his arm around me.

"Oh no, is my bike okay?" Alexa asked.

Bitch! Then again, I vaguely remembered having that very same worry.

"It's fine. Your helmet got trashed, but Gregg already replaced it with a more expensive one."

"Good. I should hope so."

Somehow, this felt like reality TV. Dad and I never watched TV together anymore because he ruined it with his commentary. During doctor shows, he'd point out that neonatal specialists do not strut in heels or hook up in supply rooms. During sitcoms, he'd point out that people in their twenties can't afford spacious apartments.

But here, he and I were both transfixed.

"Look, Alexa, they're going to Spain tomorrow night," Kate said. "They'll be gone a whole week. And I really appreciate your trying to be on board with all this."

"Mom, are you in la-la land? I'm not on board with *any* of it!" She headed toward the front steps.

Dad and I dashed inside, and he raced to open the front door. "Alexa! Welcome back!"

"Hey," she replied. I remained in the background, and she and I exchanged a quiet hi.

"Sofia and I made dinner in your honor," Dad said.

"I'll be down soon," she said and raced upstairs—probably to call Amanda to say there were Wolfes at the door.

· · · · · · · · · · ·

When Alexa came down, both cats wandered over. "Coconut!" she said, picking up her old, white cat. "I missed you!" She kissed him between the ears.

I scooped up Pepper, and it felt as if Alexa and I were both armed. Pepper, as in pepper spray?

"I see your cat has moved in too," she said.

"Yes, this is Pepper." I lifted his paw as though to shake Alexa's hand. *What was I, three?* Alexa kept both her hands on Coconut, so I let Pepper's paw drop. "The cats are mostly staying out of each other's way," I informed her, "though Coco has hissed a few times. Pepper gets nervous around her, and he's also scared to go out. He likes the great indoors. We rescued him from a shelter, and he's always been skittish." *Stop babbling!* I told myself but then wondered if babbling was better than going mute.

Alexa reached over and scratched his ears. "He's right to be nervous. Coco's used to being the boss around here."

"Dinner's ready!" Dad called with impeccable timing.

We sat down, and Kate asked, "How was the trip?"

"I got here, didn't I?" Alexa glowered.

"Do you like the dinner Gregg and Sofia made?" Kate tried again. "Shish kebabs, caprese salad, and corn on the cob!"

"It's okay."

Dad said, "So tell us about the Canadian Rockies. See any animals?"

Alexa finally took the bait and started talking about moose,

elk, eagles, and loons. "You got my moose postcard, right?" Kate
nodded. "I took tons of photos with the camera Dad gave me."

I considered saying, "I'd love to see them!" But I didn't want
Alexa to bite my head off.

Kate's cell rang, and she picked up. "Yes! Just now…" She
handed the phone to Alexa and said, "It's the Bryans, in their
car. They have you on speaker." I wondered if "the Bryans" often
called together, and if so, whether Alexa ever wanted to talk just
to her dad.

"Hi, Dad! Hi, Brian!" She walked down the steps of the deck
and toward the field, though we could still hear every word.

For distraction purposes, Kate chimed, "Dinner was delicious!
Gregg, how'd you make the lamb so tender?"

"No, no, perfect timing…" Alexa was saying. She lowered her
voice and asked accusingly, "Did you guys know?"

Alexa came back and handed Kate her cell. "Mom, I'm going
into the city tomorrow," she said. "Brian's making angel food cake
and devil's food cake for my homecoming."

"But Gregg and Sofia are *leaving* tomorrow," Kate protested.
"I was looking forward to a little mother-daughter time." Alexa was
silent. "A little girl time," Kate added.

"Yeah, well, I was too," Alexa shot back, then added, "And by
the way, Mom, you're not a *girl.*" Kate looked hurt, and Alexa added,
"You realize I could live with the Bryans if I wanted to, right?" She
let that land, then turned to Dad. "Hey, Gregg, Brian—not Bryan
my dad, the other Brian—once asked me to ask you something.
You know they're gay, right?"

"Right," Dad answered warily.

"He wanted to know if there are any gay male gynecologists."

"Uh, I've never seen any statistics…"

She shrugged. "He's pretty crazy."

"Who isn't?" Dad said.

"Kate's not," I said, then wondered why in God's name that had popped out of my mouth.

Maybe because I was almost feeling sorry for her?

Alexa stared at me, disgusted. "Don't kid yourself, Sofia." She got up and said, "Mom, don't wake me tomorrow until, like, two. Our plane left really early, so I didn't even *try* to sleep last night."

Kate nodded, pained.

I'd been worried Alexa might strain things between Sam and me. Now I was worried she might strain things for all of us.

. . . .

I woke up early to the sound of birdcalls and got busy packing.

When Alexa got up, around noon, she came into the kitchen with an overnight bag. "Did anyone make coffee?" she asked, then told her mom she was going to Amanda's and that Amanda would drive her to the train station.

Alexa barely acknowledged me, but as she left, I said, "Say hi to New York for me." She stared at me like that was the lamest thing anyone could have possibly said.

Maybe it was. Alexa brought out my stupid side.

. . . .

Dad's and my flight to Madrid left after dinner. Almost immediately, the captain said, "We are experiencing some turbulence…" and that there would be "more bumps ahead." I tried not to take that as a sign.

Somehow, I dozed off, and then, in what felt like seconds, the flight attendants woke us for breakfast, hungry or not. Soon, they were asking us to lock our tray tables, fasten our seat belts, and "prepare for landing." Was I prepared for what Dad and I had to do?

A recorded voice told us in Spanish and English to be careful taking down our carry-on bags because "contents may have shifted during flight." I was all too aware of what was in Dad's carry-on: the "crematory container" with Mom's ashes. Had the ashes shifted? Did it matter?

At the Barajas arrivals area, my checked luggage said MAD for Madrid. But I was SAD, not MAD. I tried not to stare as mothers hugged their children—and children hugged their mothers. I also tried not to feel the echoes of long-ago hellos and good-byes, *bienvenidas y despedidas*.

Dad and I took a train to Chamartín, boarded the AVE train to Segovia, then found seats on the number eleven bus to the ancient aqueduct. Even though I was fighting sleep, I've always loved the aqueduct with its tall stone pillars and arches, so I got out my cell phone and took a selfie to send to Sam and Kiki. Then Dad and I took a taxi (they're white in Spain) to my grandfather's. On the way, I pointed out two pairs of storks on top of roofs and church towers and told

Dad what Abuelo had told me: that stork pairs usually return to their nests every year from early February to early August. Dad joked, "And storks bring babies." I said, "With a little help from obstetricians."

We got to Abuelo's in time for a late Spanish lunch. He was so happy to see us; he'd prepared *tortilla española*, salad, shrimp with their heads on, and fresh peaches.

His home looked about the same, though he'd framed two more photos of Mom: one of her as a teen and one of her with him and her own mother, my *abuelita*.

We sat down and Abuelo said grace, and I had seconds of the potato omelet and shrimp.

Afterward, Abuelo peeled his peach artfully, removing the skin in one spiral. When I was little, he used to peel my oranges for me, and afterward, I'd reconstruct the peels so they looked like real oranges even though they were fragile, empty rinds. I'd offer them back to my parents and they'd play along. I never fooled anyone, yet from a distance, a real orange and an empty rind *did* look about the same—like a confident girl and one who's shell-shocked.

Sixteen months ago, had I looked about the same on April 8 as I had on April 6, even though the floor beneath me had completely given way?

After lunch, Abuelo, Dad, and I each made a distinctive knot in our cloth napkins so we'd know whose napkin was whose at the next meal. We put all three in a terracotta bowl that said "*Salud, Amor, Dinero—y Tiempo Para Gozarlos.*"

I'd seen that bowl many times but had never given much

thought to the words. *Health, Love, Money—and Time to Enjoy Them.* Now it seemed like they represented a great truth.

Dad and I retreated for a siesta, and when we woke up, we went for a walk—as did the rest of the town. The weekend paseo was a local ritual. Everyone spilled into the streets and strolled in the same direction, many arm in arm.

Abuelo's neighbors couldn't get over how much I'd grown. Several said I was *guapa* (pretty) and that I looked like my mother. They asked, "*¿Cuánto tiempo te quedas?*" and "*¿Qué haces por aquí?*" The first question was easy: a week. The second was harder. I didn't want to tell them about Mom's ashes.

Ever since my grandmother, Abuelita Carmen, died a decade earlier, when I was four, Abuelo's neighbors had been referring to him as *el viudo*—the widower. Odd to think that Dad was also a *viudo*. Strange how the word "*viudo*," unlike "widower," brought a quick new stab. Dad said his grief group had talked about "grief bursts," unpredictable bursts of sorrow that could be triggered from a sight or song—or word.

That afternoon, my grandfather and father both relied on me to translate, so when Abuelo looked at Dad and said, "*Hijo mío,*" I looked at Dad and said, "My son…"

Dad still didn't ask me to translate anything about Kate. Not that I blamed him. *Mañana, mañana.* Tomorrow, tomorrow. There was plenty of time—all the time in the world. If Dad got the tone and timing right and I got the translation right, someday, Abuelo might even wish his son-in-law well.

Then again, maybe not. Dad could get a new girlfriend, but

Abuelo could not get a new daughter any more than I could get a new mom.

Dad and Abuelo did ask me to help them plan the next morning. We were going to walk to the Catedral de Santa María, climb the winding path through the Sierra de Guadarrama hills, and there, above the aqueduct and the rivers, near the fairy-tale castle, the one Abuelo said had inspired Walt Disney, scatter Mom's ashes.

I relayed the words in Spanish and English, hating the sound of them in both languages.

I had thought about saving some ashes to place by Mom's tree in New York, but I wasn't sure I had it in me to scatter my mother twice, and last year, whenever Dad had wanted to talk about the ashes, I'd cut him off. It was too late to ask about saving some now, wasn't it? Besides, I didn't really believe Mom was in these ashes. And she had loved these hills. Abuelo said that when she was a little girl, *una nenita*, she'd liked to talk to shepherds and suggest names for their newborn lambs.

After the scattering, our plan was to go to Mesón de Cándido, a restaurant where Mom had celebrated many childhood birthdays. Once, Chubby Chef Cándido himself stopped by in his tall, white chef's hat to wish her a *feliz cumpleaños* as she ate Baked Alaska, his signature dessert.

Years later, Mom had been known for her Baked Alaska. I used to help her mold the ice cream, bake the cake, whip the meringue, slide the dessert into the oven, remove it, sprinkle it with brandy, and set it on fire. We always brought it to the lobby on New Year's Day.

I couldn't imagine making that dessert without her.

But then, I couldn't imagine doing what we had to do now either.

. . . .

The Spanish hillside smelled of rich, damp earth. A flock of soft sheep grazed nearby, bleating rhythmically. A pair of storks circled overhead. Below, the waters of the Eresma and Clamores Rivers flowed endlessly onward. My father and grandfather and I stood in the gentle breeze.

"*Es hora*," Abuelo said. It's time.

Dad had already opened the white container and removed the plastic bag of ashes. Now Abuelo extended his palm and Dad tipped some of the contents first into my grandfather's palm, then mine, then his own. Abuelo's hand, I noticed, was trembling. I flinched but accepted my handful of the dark gray "cremains."

I had a memory of being at the petting zoo in Central Park years earlier. Mom bought pellets from what looked like a gum-ball dispenser and spilled them into my palm. Nervous, I offered the pellets to the baby goats and tried to stand still as they licked my small hand with their muscular tongues.

This time, the wind licked my open palm. I wanted to say something, to slow the moment down, but the wind was too quick. The "*maldito viento*," damn wind, as Abuelo put it, did the initial scattering for us. The ashes disappeared like puffs of smoke—here, then gone.

Dad spilled a little more into each of our hands, and this time, I crouched and sprinkled them onto the grass by my feet, as if scattering seeds.

We took a third and fourth grim turn, and then the bag was empty.

Just as Mom's life had ended in an instant, our ceremony was over almost before it had begun.

Abuelo pointed at my shirt. A gust had blown some ashes back onto my shoulder. I stared, almost spellbound and didn't want to brush them off. But what else could I do?

I patted at the dark dust—and my face contorted as I brushed away the last physical remains of my mother.

Abuelo reached for my hand and grasped it, and we stood in silence, our long, linked shadows stretching across the Castilian countryside. He was comforting me, but I knew my hand was a comfort to him as well.

I wondered if he would come back to this spot after Dad and I returned to America. I imagined he would.

Finally Abuelo said, "*¿Nos vamos?*"

I couldn't answer—there was still a lump in my throat—but we three turned and began the walk back to town.

We'd done what we'd come to do: we'd brought my mother home.

. . . .

At Mesón de Cándido, Dad made us wash our hands, and then we sat at an outside table next to the aqueduct the Romans had built two thousand years earlier. Abuelo ordered a Spanish lunch with bread, salad, suckling pig (*cochinillo asado*), local wine for them, and grape juice (*mosto*) for me.

He lifted his glass. "*A María.*"

We toasted, but tears filled my eyes. "It all happened so fast," I said, referring both to her death and the scattering of ashes. "I wanted to say good-bye." I turned to Abuelo and translated. "*Quería decir adiós.*"

"You didn't need to," Dad said. "Nothing was left unsaid."

"I wanted to say," my voice wobbled, "that I was proud to be her daughter."

Dad reached across the table and took my hand. "She knew that."

Abuelo nodded. He understood it all.

A band of singers dressed as medieval troubadours swept by. My mother had often told me about the *tuna*, student minstrel groups who sang traditional songs for love and money and had once serenaded her in college.

The troubadours formed a circle around *our* table. Eight young men in black doublets with capes and bright sashes studded with ribbons and badges were playing guitar, mandolin, tambourine, and lute.

"*¡Clavelitos, clavelitos, clavelitos de mi corazón!*" they began.

I knew that song! It was about flowers. Little carnations of my heart. Mom sometimes sang it when she said good night, her silhouette etched in my doorway.

The lead singer had dark hair, thick lashes, and a closely

trimmed beard. He was handsome, and he knelt on one knee in front of me and sang in a full baritone voice, "*¡Clavelitos!*" He was looking into my eyes, inviting me to sing along.

"*¡Clavelitos!*" I sang back. "*¡Colorados igual que el fresón!*" Carnations as pink as a strawberry. I could feel myself turning pink, but I was singing! Singing!

When was the last time I'd sung in public? People at other tables were smiling, and the lead singer looked pleased as I belted out the next verse and the next. I even did one in harmony.

"*Qué bien cantas,*" he said.

"*Gracias.*" I thanked him, and my eyes burned. Mom would have loved listening to the musicians serenading me, loved hearing me join in, loved pulling up a chair at the famous tavern.

It almost felt as if she were with us.

"*Si algún día, clavelitos, no logrará poderte traer, no te creas que ya no te quiero, es que no te los pude traer.*"

Had I ever really thought about those odd final lyrics? "If someday I can't bring you flowers, don't think it's because I don't love you. It's that I couldn't bring them to you."

Even way back when, the person who wrote the song knew that what mattered wasn't the flowers; it was the love.

It had been so hard for me to accept that Mom would never be with me again except "in spirit." At first, I had thought, *In spirit? Small comfort!*

And yet it *was* a small comfort. Perhaps, in spirit, Mom would *always* be with me. Nothing could keep her away now—not rush hour or faculty meetings or a stack of quizzes to grade. I didn't have to say good-bye because in spirit, my mother could be with me every moment, invisible and invincible.

. . . .

As soon as our plane landed at JFK, I turned on my cell phone. There was a text from Sam. He said I'd been gone too long and would I please get my cute butt back ASAP?

we just landed i'm on the runway! I typed.

about time! meet me at the club tmw after im done with work?

look for the girl in the yellow bikini, I wrote.

look for the wolf.

Three gray dots showed that he was still typing, and I waited, my heart beating.

or listen for him: OWWWooooooo

Dad caught my smile. "Sam?"

"Sam," I confirmed.

"I don't have to talk to you about the birds and the bees, do I? You're way too young."

"Daaaad!" I protested, and he dropped the subject. Mom would have persisted.

Dad phoned Kate from the runway, and I wondered if she had gone ahead and told her daughter I was seeing Sam. Maybe not. After all, she wanted to stay on Alexa's good side.

. . . .

It was a blue-sky day, and on my way to Windmill Club, I walked through the parking lot. In New York City, I never paid attention to cars (except to avoid getting hit by them), and it amazed me that Sam had his learner's permit and was practicing for his road test. His plan was to get a secondhand Jeep. Soon, even *I* would be taking driver's ed! How could that be possible?

"Sofia!" Sam spotted me. "*Ho-la!*"

I laughed. "The *H* is silent."

"Ohhh-la!" he said and gave me a kiss. "Want to go swimming?"

"*Sí.*"

"First, taste this." He handed me a plum with a bite missing. "How good is that? Mother Nature is a genius!"

"That *is* good." I met his eyes. "Race you to the slide?"

"I'll win. I ran fifty miles this week. Punch me right here."

"I don't want to punch you," I said.

"Go ahead. Unless you're worried you'll hurt your hand…"

I punched his stomach. "Whoa, Sam! You're ripped."

"That's all I did while you were away. Worked, worked out, and went for runs."

We raced to the giant water slide, and I took off my cover-up and climbed the tall ladder. I could feel Sam's eyes on me, and when I got to the top, I smiled and sailed down. Splash! He was right behind me. Splash! We treaded water, our hair wet, shoulders shining.

"Race you to the float!" he said. We were there in seconds.

"Ever play underwater footsie?" I asked.

"How about underwater grab ass?" He pinched me, and I shrieked and splashed him with both hands. He splashed back, and we kept splashing until the lifeguard blew his whistle.

. . . .

"Shh! Listen!" I whispered to Sam. We'd shared a quick kiss in the outdoor shower and now were at the top of the windmill. "You hear something?"

"No."

"I heard a noise—or maybe a person? Is this *illegal*?"

"Kissing or trespassing?" he teased, but then he heard the creaking too.

"Um, hello?" I called down, my voice a little shaky. "Hello? Excuse me? We're up here?"

"Omigod, I do *not* believe this!"

"Alexa?" I recognized her voice.

"Sofia?! What are you doing here?"

"Uh…" Did she expect me to spell it out?

"God, Sofa." *Did she really just call me Sofa?* "I show you this place and now I have to make a reservation? You expect me to get in line, take a number?"

"No…" I began. Sam grasped my hand and looked down at Alexa and the guy standing next to her. Evan was my guess. This morning in the kitchen, her cell rang and it said EVAN. "We can leave," I offered.

"We don't have to leave," Sam murmured.

"Yes, you do!" Alexa called up.

"No, we don't," Sam called down surprisingly calmly. *Easy for him to say! He didn't have to live with her!* "Alexa, give us a break."

"Omigod, Sam, is that you? Give *me* a break!" she spat back. "I mean, it wasn't that long ago that you and I—"

Evan spoke up. "Lex, chill. We'll come back another time. No big deal."

"It *is too* a big deal," she said, raising her voice. "It's not enough that Sofa Bed moves into my house. She has to take over...the windmill too?"

Sofa Bed? Now my name was Sofa Bed?

"Relax, Lex," Evan said. "We can go somewhere else."

"Yeah, and she can go straight to hell!"

They left, and we heard Evan say, "Oh, c'mon. It's actually kinda funny, isn't it? The Windmill of Sin!"

"No, Evan, it is not funny," Alexa retorted. "It is not remotely funny!"

SEPTEMBER

FIRSTS ARE MEMORABLE. FIRST DAY with braces. First day without. First kiss. First real kiss. First graduation. First memorial service.

I knew the first day at my new high school would stay with me, and I tried to ignore the tightness in my stomach.

On the first day of kindergarten and maybe boarding school, everyone is eager to make friends. But at Byram Hills, there were only a handful of brand-new ninth graders. Most of the other kids had been going to the same schools together for years: Coman Hill, Wampus, Crittenden. I knew I was going to stick out.

Of course, I was used to life without camouflage. Teachers often cornered me to ask how I was doing. When I went to the nurse's office, Mrs. Abrahams encouraged me to lie down while shooing other girls back to class with just a Tums or Tylenol. And once, when I had a borderline grade in history, the teacher rounded my A- to an A—a tribute, I suspected, to my mom, her fallen friend.

I appreciated the support of the community. But I always knew the day would come when I would no longer be marked "handle with care."

The first day at Byram Hills High School might be that day.

. . . .

"Is it too late to change your mind?" Kiki asked on the phone.

"Yes. School starts in two days. I'm pretty nervous actually." I'd spent my entire life on the same Upper West Side block, and while I liked the idea of spreading my wings, that didn't mean I was ready to fly.

"Nervous is normal. Remember the first day of middle school? We were worried about having more than one teacher. And you were worried about getting lost."

"I'm still worried about getting lost."

"If you get lost, you'll have an excuse to talk to random hot guys."

"What are *you* worried about?" I asked.

"Massive assignments. I'm not exactly the queen of time man-agement. And I hear lunch is crazy short. Wait, you have to pay for lunch now, right?"

"Pay?"

"Aisha went to public school before she came to Halsey, and she said she always had to start eating while she was still in line because otherwise she'd run out of time. She said she'd pull up to the lunch lady with her wallet and, like, three crumbs on her plate and an empty milk carton."

"I hope that's an urban myth."

"Or suburban one?" Kiki lowered her voice. "I'm also worried about going to school without my Spanish tutor."

"I can help you on the *teléfono*. And you'll do fine without me." Just saying this made my throat close up.

"Remember our middle school uniforms and how Principal Milliman made me do the fingertips test?" That drove Kiki crazy. The longer your arms, the longer your skirt had to be. Kiki complained that she was penalized for having long arms. "Now we can wear whatever we want—except sweatpants or words on our butts. But that means it'll take *forever* to get dressed every day! I'll have to get up at dawn."

"I still haven't decided what to wear. It's anything goes—even words on your butt. Not that I'm going to show up in shorts that say, 'Juicy.'"

"Speaking of, how is Sam?"

"You are gross, you know that?"

"Yep. Gross and proud of it! Answer the question."

"He's fine. I met some of the guys on his track team. They started preseason."

"Do they all wear short shorts?"

"One shaves his legs." I didn't tell her that Peter, a pole-vaulter, seemed nice, but Jayden, the leg shaver, was obsessed with his "core" and big on making lewd comments about cheerleaders.

"Don't let Sam shave his legs!" Kiki said.

"I won't! He wouldn't!"

"So did you ever talk to Alexa about Sam?"

"You kidding? Alexa and I barely talk about *anything*."

I told her about Alexa finding us at the windmill, and I must have turned it into a funny story because Kiki couldn't stop laughing. But it didn't feel funny to me. It was hard living with a girl who pretended I wasn't even there—especially since, for so many months, it had felt as if I wasn't.

. . . .

I needed advice. Was there some unofficial Byram Hills dress code—an ideal top, right kind of jeans? What about earrings? Hoop, dangly, stud?

Alexa was in the kitchen, making a peanut butter–banana sandwich, so I asked, "Do you remember your first day of high school?"

She acted as if I were a mosquito she could hear but couldn't see. I waited, and she finally said, "Yeah. The principal said, 'From now on, your grades count,' which was bad. But a lot of guys got hot over the summer, which was good. For me, though, it was same kids, new building. For you, it's more complicated. Obviously."

I wanted her to say, "Don't worry. It'll be fine," or "Byram Hills is cool. You'll see." Something. Anything.

Instead, she picked up her sandwich and started to walk away. Then she turned and added, "If you have any other questions, just ask your boyfriend."

It was the first time Alexa had called Sam my boyfriend. Lately, his name hadn't been coming up because he hadn't been coming over. Not that I blamed him. Awkward! We saw each other mostly at the club or his house or…the windmill.

"Alexa, Sam and I—"

"Save your stories for someone who gives a crap, okay, Sofa?"

"Okay," I said and watched as she headed off to varsity volley-ball practice.

That night at dinner, Dad asked Alexa which she liked better:

basketball or volleyball. She acted as though she were doing him a giant favor by answering and said she liked the volleyball uniform better but was more "invested" in basketball.

"Volleyball is all about team play," she explained. "As a setter, my job is to make hitters look good, which means I can play a perfect game and barely get noticed. In basketball, as point guard, it's much easier to stand out. And who doesn't want to stand out?"

I thought, *I don't*.

. . . .

"I sent you an email before dinner," I mumbled to Kate the next day as I stacked plates in the dishwasher.

"I answered it." She smiled as she pushed through the swinging door with a bowl of sliced mangoes and blackberries.

I'd written:

Dear Kate,

I hope you don't think this is dumb because I realize I could ask you directly, but do you have any advice on getting through the first weeks of a new school? On a 1 to 10 scale of nervousness, I'm about a 7. I wish I could be invisible tomorrow.

I also want to say thank you for everything. I keep wanting to say it in person, but it never comes out, partly because I don't want to seem like a suck-up in front of Alexa and partly because it's easier to write stuff than say it. Anyway, thank you for everything!

Oh, and I don't think of you as "Dear Kate" or "my father's

girlfriend" anymore. I think of you as my friend, and that feels really good.

Your fan and friend,

"Catlover"

After dinner, I read her reply.

Dear "Catlover,"

Thank you for everything too: your email, your sweet presence in our home, and all you've done to welcome me into your life. These things go both ways, you know.

I feel blessed that your dad is a "package deal" and that falling in love with him meant I'd have the privilege of becoming your friend. And I'm your fan too. (I mean that.)

As for general advice:

1. Be kind and friendly, and stay open-minded.

2. Give yourself a few days to figure out which kids you want to get to know and which kids to keep at a distance.

3. Speak up in class and do the homework. Some teachers decide right away who is or isn't a good student.

4. Join activities—yearbook, theater, sports, student council, etc.

5. When asked about your old school, don't go on and on about how great it was.

6. Have confidence that the qualities that helped you make friends in the past will serve you well again. They will.

7. Since you're going from all-girl to coed, don't be too shy…but don't be a flirt. ;-)

8. Stay in touch with old friends. A few will be friends forever.
(Like Kiki!)

Gotta go because I'm making dinner. (Red pepper lasagna! Can
you smell it?)

Oh, and you *can* talk to me anytime, anywhere, online or in
person, okay?

Your friend and fan,

Kate

PS There's no such thing as an Instant Family, but even Coco and
Pepper seem to be moving in the right direction, don't you think?

It was good to read her words, and I appreciated the long response.

But was she right about the cats? Pepper was younger and more playful than Coconut and had taken to hiding around corners. When Old Coco came plodding along, Pepper's little butt would quiver in anticipation, and he'd leap out and pounce in a surprise attack. Coco would hiss, they'd have a cat spat, and Pepito would scamper off to plot his next ambush. It wasn't fierce, but they weren't exactly curling up for catnaps.

I guess pepper and coconut weren't a natural mix either.

Did Kate think Alexa and I were getting along better than we were too?

. . . .

The night before school started, I heard Alexa on the phone with Amanda. Amanda was a senior, so she was allowed to park her car at school and was offering Alexa a ride. Alexa's door was closed, but I could hear every word, and I'll admit, I was taking my time getting a towel from the closet.

"They help themselves to the towels," Alexa was saying, "they turn lights on and off, and they eat whatever's in the fridge. I swear I'm gonna start labeling my yogurt. Or I should just hand the girl a map—she has *no* concept of boundaries! She puts her hands all over *everything*. Literally. Even Sam!"

Amanda must have laughed because Alexa kept going. "My dad used to obsess about deer-proofing the garden. Well, he should have *wolf-proofed* the house! Gregg keeps rearranging everything. The kitchen drawers? Yesterday, it took me *ten minutes* to find a spatula. I'm, like, *dying* here."

I tiptoed into the bathroom clutching a fluffy Baird towel because we had given all of ours to Goodwill. What did Alexa expect me to do? Drip dry? And yes, Dad could be a neat freak. Would it be better if he were a slob?

I wished I had the guts to barge in and yell at her. She had no idea what it was like to lose a parent!

I got in my pajamas and found Pepper. It still took forever to fall asleep.

The next day, I put on a black tank top, jeans, leather boots, and my mom's pearl stud earrings. Amanda picked up Alexa, and I crossed the street to wait for the big yellow school bus. It all felt sort of familiar because of TV and movies but foreign too. And surreal. And lonely.

Two older girls were at the stop, discussing their schedules and not looking at me. When the bus came, I took a seat toward the back next to an older girl who didn't acknowledge me except to move one inch closer to the window.

The bus ride was mercifully short, and at 8:00 a.m., I attended an assembly about regulations, lockers, clubs, and advisors. I didn't see Sam, so I just sat down and tried to blend in. Who were these hundreds of kids? The boys looked so big. The girls all greeted each other with shrieks and hugs.

A bell rang, and I went to my first class: English. During attendance, the teacher, Mr. Greer, said, "Wolfe? Many authors are 'wolves': Thomas, Tom, Tobias, Virginia, Naomi. It's a fine literary name." I appreciated that but wished he'd said it to me alone. Calling attention to my name was not going to help me stay beneath the radar.

In bio and algebra, heads also turned, and I tried to look harmless as kids whispered, "She's the new girl."

Was I new? I didn't feel new. Sometimes, I felt *old*.

Lunch was burgers topped with small, slimy blobs of gray goo. It made me miss the food at Halsey, but at least I'd remembered to bring money. Still, it was hard walking into the crowded cafeteria not knowing where to sit. The tables were all full, and as I carried my plate and water glass, I wished I could spot Kiki and Natalie and Madison.

Was my outfit okay? I was the only girl wearing boots.

A group of loud girls beckoned me over, and I sat with them, grateful. One took out her retainer, wrapped it in a napkin, and placed it on her lunch tray. I remembered when Kiki threw hers out by accident. She and a janitor had had to go through two garbage cans to find it.

The girls quizzed me about New York and Broadway shows, and one asked if I ever ran into famous people. "Sometimes, at my old school during drop off and pick up," I replied, then downplayed this and hoped it hadn't sounded like boasting.

One girl started talking about her cousin's birthday the previous weekend. She'd invited seven friends to a restaurant but wanted only six to sleep over. So she asked the chosen six to drop their sleeping bags off early and *not* to tell the seventh except—surprise, surprise—she found out!

Everyone laughed, and I tried to smile, but it wasn't funny, was it? Who were these girls anyway? By having lunch with them, did it seem like I wanted to join their clique? Or were *they* auditioning me?

The two girls across from me were identical twins. Their auburn hair matched their eyes, and I couldn't see how anyone could possibly tell them apart. "I just got the new *Fifteen*," Twin One said. "Sofia, don't you like, *live*, in Dear Kate's house?"

"Yes..."

"Guys, guys, you *have* to hear this!" She jumped up and started reading: "'Dear Kate, I've been noticing how beautiful a lot of my friends are, and since no guys ever like me, I was wondering if there's a chance I might be bi or lesbian.'"

Twin Two shrieked, grabbed the magazine, and pretended to read the response. "Dear Lesbo, If your BFF is your dream date, you should start sexting her right away!"

Everyone cracked up, and my face was burning. *My letter got published? Oh God, just kill me now.*

"What'd she *really* answer?" another girl asked.

"Something boring, I'm sure. The questions are the best part," Twin One replied.

I knew what Dear Kate had answered. When I'd read her words in February, they'd been a comfort. But I never expected my letter to become a read-aloud.

"You think she makes up the questions?"

"Probably. What's she like anyway?"

"Yeah, tell us," Twin One said. "I mean, Dear Kate gives out all this advice, but her own kid's a piece of work!" She laughed.

"Shut up. You're talking about Sofia's sister," said Twin Two.

"Not her *blood* sister."

I mumbled that I liked Kate. A girl next to me got up, and a good-looking guy sat in her seat. He had black, tousled hair and curly, dark eyelashes. "Hi," he said. The twins seemed excited by his presence. "I'm Zack."

Wait, wait, was he addressing me? Since when did good-looking guys talk to me?

He kept smiling, and I felt embarrassed and confused. Was it possible I'd gone from ugly duckling to decent-looking swan without any notification? Then again, if he was talking to me, did it have anything to do with *me*—or just my newness and New York–ness?

"I'm Zack," he repeated. He was wearing a white button-down shirt, and I was surprised to notice that he had little curls of black chest hair. "This is the part where you say your name," he prompted, "which, I hear, is Sofia."

"Sorry. I'm Sofia." I must have been pink.

"By the way, I've been there."

"New York?"

"Sofia. The capital of Bulgaria. You know what Bulgarians do? They shake their heads side to side when they say yes instead of nodding." He shook his head, and the girls at the table laughed appreciatively.

Was I supposed to shake? Nod? Laugh?

I looked up, and there, across the lunchroom, was Sam. My heart lurched, and I gave a discreet wave. He waved back, and I wished he'd come over. I wished *he* were sitting next to me!

How were things going to change for us now that we were in the fish bowl of high school? It was one thing to hold hands in sunlight and moonlight, but what about fluorescent light?

I liked that with Sam, I didn't feel like the girl whose mother died or the girl from New York City or the girl who lived at Dear Kate's. I just felt like myself.

The bell rang, and everyone headed off to class. In history, a girl behind me whispered, "Yeah, she lives in Alexa Baird's house. You know, that bitchy basketball player?" I wanted to say something, but what? That it was my house too? (Was it?) That Alexa was a sweetie pie? (She wasn't.)

My last class was Spanish. I'd placed out of freshman and sophomore Spanish and was put into AP Spanish with ten seniors and two juniors. One was Alexa. It was the first time I'd seen her at school, and I wasn't sure if that was normal (Byram Hills was bigger than Halsey) or if Alexa had spent the day avoiding me.

The seats formed a semicircle. Alexa sat at one end between Amanda and Mackenzie, and I sat at the other. They were all three wearing pastel tops, jeans, and sandals. In a clear Colombian accent, the teacher, Señor Muñoz, said we were going to focus on short stories by Cervantes, Borges, Quiroga, Cortázar, Rulfo, and García Márquez. But first he wanted us to get acquainted: "*Vamos a tomar unos minutitos para hablar de lo que han hecho ustedes este verano. Empezamos con usted, por favor.*"

Cool. The classic what-I-did-this-summer assignment except out loud and in Spanish. It might even help me get to know everyone. I was glad I was at the end of the semicircle and would go last.

Around we went. Most kids started by saying their Spanish had gotten rusty, but everyone came up with something. When Alexa spoke about her six weeks in *las montañas de Canada*, Señor Muñoz congratulated her on keeping up her language skills. He looked pleased, and Alexa did too.

More kids took their turn, and then the teacher turned to me. "*Y ahora usted. Su nombre, por favor.*"

I gave my name and said I'd moved from Manhattan to Armonk. I did not mention kissing in a windmill, falling off a bike, moving in with Alexa, or taking Mom's ashes to Spain. I did say I was *contenta*, happy, at Byram Hills and that everyone seemed *muy majo*—very nice.

"*Pero no entiendo. ¿Cómo se hace que usted habla español tan bien? ¿Usted es española?"* The teacher wasn't curious about my city-to-suburb move. He wanted to know if I was Spanish.

"*Yo, no, pero mi mamá, sí era.*" I'm not. But my mom was.

Past tense. Oh no! I'd done exactly what I'd hoped to avoid: I'd announced that my mother was dead.

Nobody picked up on it. All they noticed was that the new girl was fluent (something everyone at Halsey already knew) and that while the teacher was impressed with Alexa's Spanish, he was blown away by mine.

"*¡Pues, bienvenida! ¡Va a ser un gran placer tenerle en clase!*" he said, welcoming me and telling me that it would be a great pleasure having me in class.

Alexa shot me a dirty look as if my being bilingual were some show-off-y stunt I'd just pulled to put her down.

Once again, I seemed to have accidentally trampled all over her turf. When the bell rang, she knocked into me on her way out, as if I were invisible.

And this made me realize that I'd been wrong. I did *not* want to be invisible.

But what did I want?

. . . .

That evening, Kate, Alexa, Dad, and I drove to La Manda, a nearby Italian restaurant. We settled into a booth, and Alexa went to wash her hands. "Order for me, Mom," she said. "You know what I like."

Kate nodded, and I noticed that she looked exhausted.

I was tired too. I'd been on all day, and Alexa's offhanded request set off feelings of hurt and envy. I didn't want to fall into the quicksand of wishing I had a mom who knew what I liked and would do her best to get it for me. *Don't go there*, I told myself. *Alexa wasn't being insensitive—I was being oversensitive.*

The waitress took our order, Alexa returned, and Dad asked, "So, girls, how was school? Sofia, you first?"

"Good." I studied the place mat: a map of Italy. "I didn't get lost, and I met a lot of people." I didn't mention that I'd felt lonely at the bus stop, awkward at assembly, and mortified at lunch. And I didn't say that lunch was mystery meat and tater tots (which made me miss Halsey's grass-fed beef and organic vegetables). I also didn't say that even though I'd forgotten to bring a change of clothes for kickball, gym was still less excruciating than it had been in middle school. Dad was waiting for more. "Oh, and my world history teacher, Mr. C, is ridiculously cute." I looked at Alexa, hoping we could at least agree on that. Alexa's face stayed blank.

"How about you, Alexa?" Dad asked.

Alexa gave a rundown of her classes and said she might want to do her junior author paper on William Golding since *Lord of the Flies* was one of her favorite books.

Lord of the Flies? Did she think of herself as Jack?

"Oh, and let's see," Alexa continued, "in AP Spanish, there's a new kid, a freshman, whose Spanish is *perfecto*. It's kind of an unfair advantage actually."

Alexa looked at me.

My spine tingled. "Señor Muñoz was very impressed with Alexa's Spanish too," I offered.

Alexa gave me a withering look.

"When does volleyball start?" Kate asked, changing the subject.

"First game is next week. A home game against Dobbs Ferry."

Kate turned to me. "Are you trying out for a sport, Sofia?"

"No." I was glad there was zero chance of my outshining the family athlete, especially at a school where sports seemed to reign supreme. At HSG, being involved in sports or theater or orchestra or Model UN or newspaper or yearbook all offered about the same cachet. At Byram Hills, I sensed that being a jock or cheerleader conferred extra coolness points.

Kate asked if any activities appealed to me. "At some point, I might do parliament," I replied. "But for now, maybe chorus?" I looked down at the paper map because just saying this out loud was a big step. "I'll also join the Spanish club. If people want to go to the city to see a movie in Spanish, I can arrange that."

"*No problema*, right?" Alexa sneered.

The waitress appeared with a pizza. "Watch out!" she said. "Don't burn yourselves!"

. . . .

I phoned Sam at 10:00 p.m., and he said, "Bottom of the ninth. Can I call you right back?"

"Not tonight." I laughed. "I'm going to sleep. But I'll stop by tomorrow after your practice, okay?"

At 5:15 the next day, Sam opened his front door. "You made it through the first two days!"

"More or less," I said. "But I never see you."

"It's a pretty big school." He kissed me. "Sorry. Do I smell? I just ran ten miles and was about to shower. You can shower with me," he said with a sly smile.

I pushed him. "Hey, Sam, how come you didn't come over at lunch yesterday?" I had *not* meant to bring that up so soon.

"I wanted to give you some space. And you had Zack breathing all over you. I could see you blushing from across the room."

"Zack?!" I was blushing because a girl had read my humiliating email out loud. "I could care less about Zack!"

"Good, because he only cares about himself."

"I wanted to talk to *you*. That's why I waved."

"I waved back. Sofia, it goes both ways. You could've walked over."

"I walked over just now. That goes both ways too."

He nodded. "I'm sorry. I know I haven't been to your house since Alexa got back. It's just—it still feels like *her* house, you know?"

"Believe me, I know."

We headed up to his room. "So you're at a school with real live boys. How's it feel?"

"They're everywhere!" I laughed. "They're, like, two lockers away! And they travel in packs." I almost mentioned a boy on the bus whose T-shirt said, "Beneath this shirt, I'm naked." Instead, I said, "My math teacher is hard of hearing and—"

"Mrs. K? She should've retired ages ago!"

"Well, the boys all sit in the back and make fun of her. I was shocked. Halsey girls are well behaved. You know, straight out of *Madeline*."

We sat on his unmade bed. His room was so different from mine—my new one or old one. I studied his sound system, Yankee license plate, *Rolling Stone* magazines, fish tank, heaps of dirty clothes. On his shelf were cross-country medals and plaques and team photos. On the wall, a *South Park* calendar was still open to August. Was this a "man cave"?

"I joined chorus," I said. "And one girl was really friendly. Gracie?"

"Yeah. Gracie's nice. Dresses a little funny."

"She's in your grade, right?"

He nodded. "What about the work?" he asked. "Challenging enough for you?"

"What's hard is learning everyone's names."

"I can help you there." He got out a yearbook, *The Arch*, and we snuggled close.

Smack! What was that? We both heard it. Something had hit his window. A rock? A baseball?

We ran outside and spotted an injured blue jay lying on its side.

"Poor thing!" I said. It had flown straight into the living room picture window—just beneath Sam's bedroom.

"Happens. Birds around here are pretty dumb. They get dazed and confused. I think this one's still alive though. I bet it'll make it."

We stood a few yards away from the bird and watched as it slowly blinked, twitched, and righted itself. Soon it began to hop and flutter its wings. All at once, it flew off.

I was absurdly relieved.

. . . .

I wanted to make things better between Alexa and me, so I figured I'd go to her next home game.

When I got to the gym, I saw Kate in the bleachers. I sat down next to her and was surprised when she apologized for Alexa's recent "prickliness." *Recent?* Alexa had been a cactus from the start.

But this week, I found myself worrying about Kate. She seemed so worn down. Was living with two feuding teens taking its toll?

Kate had on a baggy T-shirt that said "BHHS 25." She said she'd gotten it as a prize for having traveled the shortest distance to her twenty-fifth reunion. "The person who traveled the farthest got the same prize—and he came all the way from Brazil!"

"That's not really fair," I pointed out.

"Life isn't," she replied. "But that's not news, right?"

"I guess not." I looked around the gym. "I can't picture myself going to a twenty-fifth reunion."

"You might end up going to two of them."

"Two?"

"Halsey and Byram Hills. Private schools do their best not to lose alumni. They never know who'll become a big donor."

"But I'm not at Halsey anymore. I'm not a Survivor."

"Oh yes you are, Sofia." Kate looked right at me. "You really are."

I nodded, pensive. Was I? In science that day, Dr. Pavlica had mentioned the speed of light, and I'd heard "the speed of *life*." While he was going on about $E = mc^2$, I was thinking again about how crazy it is that life just speeds along, sunrise after sunrise, season after season. Whether you're totally miserable or insanely happy, the months keep coming, crashing like waves. There are no do-overs, no backsies, and bad stuff happens. But then I thought, *Wait. Good stuff happens too. And sometimes, even a kiss can slow time down.* I gave myself credit for that tiny epiphany. And for realizing that I wasn't a closed-down middle school kid anymore. I was in high school. High school!

The ref blew his whistle, and the game began. Kate started cheering as the Bobcats took the lead. I did too.

"Got it!" Alexa set the ball, and the hitter spiked it to the other side, unreturnable.

"Got it!" Alexa took charge on defense, and the coach nodded in approval.

"Got it!" Alexa tipped the ball right over a blocker's out-stretched hands.

Eventually, the whistle blew for the final point. Byram Hills won, and at the net there was handshaking and high-fiving and bouncing ponytails.

Kate stood up. "Ouch. My back."

"You all right?" I asked and told her I could show her a few yoga stretches I'd learned at HSG.

She thanked me, and we walked over to congratulate Alexa.

"You played great," I said.

Alexa eyed me dismissively.

"Really great," I repeated.

She made a face. "You have no idea." She was right that I was no expert, but couldn't she ever cut me some slack?

Kate drove Alexa and me home. It was hard to fake a civil conversation, and I sat in the back, sorry I'd even tried to show support. For all I knew, Alexa was mad that I'd infiltrated her last refuge.

"Seventeen!" Kate suddenly chimed. "Alexa, in two days, it's your birthday!"

Alexa said nothing.

"We can go out," Kate added. "Shall I make a reservation at the Moderne Barn? Or North? Or Truck? Wherever you want."

Alexa stayed quiet. Was she imagining the horror of being trapped as a foursome from appetizers till flaming cake? "I made plans with my friends," she announced, digging out her cell and texting furiously.

Kate sighed and turned on the radio, so I took out my phone and started texting too. I wrote a group text to Kiki and Natalie and Madison: "Miss you guys." I added a frowny face.

Natalie replied right away: "Miss you too." Then she sent a text just to me that said, "It's not easy starting a new school."

"No, it's not," I replied, choosing another frowny, and we texted back and forth, both glad, no doubt, that we could admit this honestly.

. . . .

Alexa and I were brushing our teeth side by side. She was wearing a faded, oversize T-shirt that said *Calgary*, and I was wearing my creamy pajamas with Siamese cats on them. "Look, tomorrow's my birthday," Alexa began, "and I just want to say one thing: 9/11 is a sucky birthday. Even *I* don't think of September 11 as my birthday. I think of it as a national day of mourning, same as everyone else. I rarely even have a party because, you know, tacky, tacky."

I wasn't sure what to say, and I heard myself answer, "My birthday's December 21, which is way too close to Christmas. My mom used to give me presents wrapped in pink, then, four days later, presents wrapped in green and red. But even she sort of gave up." Alexa stayed quiet. "I never felt like I had my own special day because there are so many random parties around Christmas. Last year, I had a Latin midterm on my birthday."

"Boo hoo," Alexa said and spat into the sink. "I win. 9/11 is worse. Instead of a happy birthday, it's a *crappy* birthday. Even the flags are at half-mast. The year Dad left, I baked my own cake. Back then, I was into baking. Now I'm not, but Mom still expects me to do it. Oh well, who cares? Doesn't matter. Brian will bake me an amazing cake this weekend. Maybe two."

Alexa snapped off a piece of green floss. "Anyway, and I don't know why I'm even saying this, but I realize I can act like a jerk sometimes. My birthday sucks, my parents are divorced, and when people meet me, they don't see me. They see my advice columnist mom, my gay dad, and now my 'sister,' the 'hot new freshman.' A

couple of junior guys are bugging me to introduce you to them."
She spat again.

"I'm sorry. I don't even get it. Kiki's hot. I'm…invisible."

"Hot can happen in a hurry, Sofia, and right now, you're the opposite of invisible. Which works both ways. A few girls think my 'sister' acts stuck-up and like she's God's gift to the suburbs because her old school is chock-full of celebs."

What?! "I'm not stuck-up. And I'm not hot."

"And you're not my sister." Alexa snorted.

Our eyes met in the mirror. "I never said I was," I replied, fighting the urge to go mute.

"Look, all I'm saying is that I was an only child—not a lonely child. I was fine."

"Me too. In Spanish, they don't even say only child; they say '*hijo único*,' which is how I felt. When people asked my mom why she didn't have another kid, she'd say, 'We got it right the first time.'" Actually, I knew my parents *had* tried to have another kid, but I still liked Mom's explanation.

"Well, my mom never had to explain anything. Gay husband—spoke for itself. I'm lucky I got born."

I looked at Alexa's blue-jean eyes in the mirror. "Happy Almost Birthday."

"Thanks." She opened the medicine cabinet, got out tweezers, and began to pluck her brows. "So *do* you want to meet some juniors?"

"I don't know. Maybe. But, well, Sam—"

She cut me off. "Spare me, okay? Just never mind."

"Okay," I mumbled. For a second, it had seemed like we were connecting.

"Tell you what. I'll introduce you to two guys who aren't dicks. And steer clear of Zack. He's with someone named Zoe anyway, and believe me, Zack and Zoe deserve each other. Here's some more free advice: if things ever go too fast with any guy, just say you have your period. Totally freaks 'em out."

"Good to know." I tried not to recoil. "Hey, Alexa?"

"Yeah?"

"Thanks for not hating me."

"Who says I don't hate you?" She put the tweezers down and gave me the tiniest trace of a smile. "To tell you the truth, I've been trying to figure out why I *don't* hate you. I mean, the Sam thing is like a bad joke, especially since—" She interrupted herself. "But I can't say I'm brokenhearted. Of course, it's possible that my heart got petrified when I was a kid. Like, maybe I have a rock instead of a heart?" She glanced at me in the mirror. "Even my name got, you know, usurped. 'Alexa, play the Lumineers.' 'Alexa, play Rihanna.'" She looked at me. "Sorry. I get weird before my birthday. And seventeen is...*old*."

"Number one," I began, "seventeen is not old. Number two, you have a heart. And number three, I didn't set out to be a trespasser in your life. I didn't ask for any of this either."

She shrugged. "Well, next time I'm a bitch, take it as a compliment. I'm only bitchy to people I'm comfortable with."

"You were bitchy to my dad when you first met him," I said, surprised to hear myself contradicting her.

She laughed. "True. But that was different. I was trying to scare him away."

"Didn't work."

"No. It didn't, did it?"

Pepper leaped into the bathtub, perched himself beneath the faucet, and stared up at me.

"What is your cat doing?"

"He wants me to turn it on."

"You're joking."

"He thinks he's a bobcat." I turned on the faucet, and Pepper batted at the stream of water with his paw, tilted his head, then licked with his quick, pink tongue. Alexa laughed, and Pepper, startled, bolted.

"A Byram Hills bobcat," she said. "That's our mascot."

I turned off the tap. "Well, 'night. Don't let the bedbugs bite."

"Aren't bedbugs a disgusting city thing?"

"We never had them, thank God. But okay, don't let the deer ticks bite."

"I won't." She walked out then turned around. "You neither."

I smiled. That was about the nicest thing Alexa had ever said to me.

. . . .

Right before bed, an idea came to me, so I set my alarm an hour and a half earlier than usual. I couldn't imagine making Baked Alaska, but I knew how to make a box cake.

The next morning, I preheated the oven, combined eggs, vegetable oil, and chocolate cake powder, and poured the batter into two round pans. I let the cakes bake and cool, then iced them with a tub of French vanilla frosting Kate had in the pantry. Ta-da! I spelled out *Happy Birthday Alexa* with chocolate chips and added seventeen candles and one "to grow on." Then I woke Dad and Kate.

Minutes before Alexa's alarm was set to go off, Dad, Kate, and I stood outside her bedroom. We lit the candles, knocked on her door, and nudged it open while singing.

Alexa looked shocked, confused, and then—no denying it—pleased.

"Wow," she said, rubbing her eyes. "Sweet."

OCTOBER

WISHED I HADN'T SEEN IT. I would have loved not to have seen it. I was finally getting used to my new routine: bus ride, assembly, lunch, classes, rehearsals. My life was beginning to feel normal-ish again. I was no longer the kid whose mom died or the brand-new kid, and that was fine. I didn't want trauma or drama. If someone asked, "What's up?" I just wanted to say, "Not much. You?"

But I *did* see it. In the wastepaper basket in the downstairs bathroom. I'd thrown away a bottle of Peach Snapple, then fished it out for recycling. And there it was—the pregnancy stick. I'd never seen one up close, but being a high school freshman and a gynecologist's daughter, I knew what it was. Besides, the white plastic wand had a window with a digital readout, and even from above, I could read the result. The letters spelled one word, and that word was "PREGNANT."

I'd figured Alexa was not a virgin. But *pregnant*?! She didn't even have a boyfriend, did she? Guy friends, yes, lots! But someone she cared about? Evan maybe. Had Alexa and Evan *already* done it? How many guys had Alexa been with?

Two days earlier, Sam and I were on his back porch watching

a flock of four wild turkeys pecking at the grass. I asked if he'd ever seen so many wild turkeys, and he said, "Once. A year ago with Alexa." I should have left it at that, but I took that as an opening and made him tell me more about their relationship. He resisted, I insisted, and he finally said, "Sofia, it all happened really fast." He said that at a party in Whippoorwill last Halloween, "Alexa had done some shots and…"

"And what?" I asked.

"She…Sofia, c'mon, a gentleman doesn't kiss and tell."

"Sam, you have to tell me. You *have* to. Are you saying Alexa, like, date-raped you?" I hoped I was making too much of things. Maybe all they'd done was kiss?

"No, nothing happened that was against my will," he admitted. "It was just, she was in a big hurry, and I wasn't."

"Wait. Sam, I don't understand—" My voice was cracking. "You guys actually… Whoa. You…? Sam, I have to know."

He bit his lip.

"I'm sorry," I continued, "but it's just too weird if other people know stuff I don't know. Starting with Alexa! And you wanted us to be honest."

"Sofia, maybe I should've said no to Alexa then or maybe I should be lying to you now, but there was one time—"

Tears were rolling down my face. I didn't like picturing Sam and Alexa together. "You're right. I *don't* want to know. I wish I didn't know!"

"So you're mad if I don't tell you and mad if I do?"

I nodded.

"That's not exactly fair, you know," he said.

"I know." It came out like a squeak.

"Sofia, I don't want to hurt you, and I don't want us to have secrets."

I nodded, and he stroked my hair. "Look, it would be really different with someone who didn't toss back tequila first. Alexa rushed me, and I'm not going to rush you. But I'm not saying I'm not hopeful."

"That's a double negative," I mumbled.

"Well, I'm hopeful-hopeful that someday-someday in the distant-distant future…"

I pushed him away. It was crazy: I could be angry at him and charmed by him all at the same time. God, I loved him! No, I didn't! Did I? Love Sam? Wasn't *love* way too big a word?

Thinking about Sam and Alexa and sex and love was making me dizzy. Meanwhile, I was still staring at a stick that was screaming *Pregnant*. Should I talk to Alexa? Or Kate? She'd stand by her daughter no matter what, wouldn't she?

If I spoke to Kate, would that be betraying Alexa?

If I said nothing, would that be betraying Kate?

I had an urge to bury the stick deeper and pretend I never saw it. Yet maybe I should confront Alexa. We'd finally started talking, hadn't we? Where was she anyway? Not home. Was she playing volleyball—*pregnant*? I considered texting—but no, no way.

And where was Kate? Oh, right, in the city, addressing parents of teens. She was speaking at Dalton at 8:15 a.m. ("Getting Through the Tricky Years") and Nightingale at 6:00 p.m. ("Raising

Confident Daughters"). That morning, she'd driven to the train station before the rest of us had even gotten up.

No Alexa. No Kate. Should I call Dad at work? Dad was a pregnancy pro. But that didn't feel right either.

I decided to stop thinking about the stupid stick and hunker down with my English homework. We'd finished *The Glass Menagerie* and were about to start *Old School* (which was by one of those wolfy authors).

Tonight's homework was to write a page defending the daughter or mother in the Tennessee Williams play. Defending? It would have been easier to criticize them! I mean, sure, I could defend Laura, but I wanted to shake her for being too scared to live her life. As for her mother, Amanda Wingfield, she was all denial with a smile.

Fear. Denial. I couldn't stop thinking about what I was trying not to think about! I had to do *something*—so I decided to do what I used to do when I was upset: email Dear Kate. How could I keep her in the dark when she'd treated me with nothing but respect from the start and when she was an expert in, as she put it, the "minefield of adolescence"?

At Subject, I hesitated. I didn't want to write "URGENT!!!" because Kate complained that girls always wrote "URGENT!!!" whether their houses were burning down or their crushes were ignoring them. Then again, this situation *was* serious.

My fingers took over.

Subject: Serious
Dear Kate,

Alexa and I have been getting along better, and I don't want to ruin that, so I feel bad saying anything, but I'd feel worse saying nothing. Maybe you already know this, but I just found out. Anyway, here goes: Alexa is pregnant. I don't know how many months or who the boy is, but I saw the pregnancy test, and I didn't feel I should keep it to myself. I hope it's okay to tell you. To tell you the truth, none of this feels okay. But I'm pretty sure you shouldn't be the last to know, especially since you're Dear Kate.

Love,

Sofia

I wanted to press Send, but would that be responsible or make me a tattletale? Good daughter or bad sister? Maybe I should write something more oblique? I could say, for instance, that Kiki needed advice for her newspaper column. Or that I had an HSG friend who was in trouble…

I called Kiki. No answer. I sent a text: Call me!!! URGENT!!!

My cell buzzed: KEEKS. "What? I'm on the subway platform. Talk fast and loud."

"Alexa's pregnant."

"*Seriously?*"

"She did a home pregnancy test. I saw it!"

"Hang on. How do you know it's right?"

"It's not a dot or a line or a cross. It's a word. It says, '*Pregnant.*'" I walked to the bathroom, leaned over, and read it again. "Kiki, she's pregnant. You want me to send a picture?"

"No, no. I get the picture without a picture."

"So what do I do? I'm alone and I'm going crazy here!"

"*You?* How do you think Alexa feels?"

"I haven't talked to her yet. I just found the thing."

"Well, how do you know it's not one of her friends?"

"Because—" How *did* I know? Maybe Amanda was pregnant! Or Mackenzie? Or Nevada? Maybe Alexa forgot that her mom was going to the city and so she brought a friend over for free advice. No, that didn't sound like Alexa. "I'm practically positive."

"So talk to her!"

"She's not here! Neither is Kate. I was thinking of emailing her."

"*Emailing Kate? Are you insane?!*"

I looked at the open email on my laptop. "She knows a lot and—"

"Sofia, if Alexa is pregnant and you tell her mom, Alexa will never ever forgive you. Case closed. My mom would disown me. I thought you and Alexa were starting to talk."

"We were—are—a little."

"So don't blow it! You called for my advice, and I'm giving it to you. And I'm 'Ask Kiki' now. My first column is in the next *Halsey Herald*."

"Congratulations! I mean, that's really *great*, but—"

"No buts. Do *not* email 'Dear Kate' and that's final—unless Alexa threatens to jump out of that Windmill of Sin."

"Keeks!"

"Just talk to her first. Dear Kate would back me up on this. She doesn't like when girls squeal. In her last column, this one girl smoked outside school, and this other girl reported her, and the smoker got suspended—but now everyone hates the loudmouth."

I heard a distant noise. "Okay, okay, I won't write an email." I didn't confess that I already had.

"Good, because once you press Send, it's Sent, and you're toast."

"Okay." I pressed Delete and could hear the roar of an approaching subway.

"Gotta go!" Kiki shouted.

"I just wish Alexa would come home," I said, a first. But the connection was already lost.

. . . .

Alexa came home. The front door slammed, and I heard her make a beeline to the bathroom. I tried to figure out what to say.

Suddenly, she was tromping through the house, barreling up the stairs two at a time, and storming into my room.

"*What is wrong with you?*" she shouted. Pepper ran under the bed. "Listen, *señorita*, don't even try to pull your sweet, innocent number on me. I'm sick of being the bad girl in this so-called family. At least I'm smart enough to use birth control! And yeah, sorry to yell at you in your time of need, but how the *hell* could you let this happen? Does my mom know? 'Cause if you don't wanna wreck your wholesome image, I can drive you to Planned Parenthood, which, I have to say, is an extremely generous offer."

"Wait! Wait! What?"

"If I'd known you were so naive, I would've talked to you!

Why didn't you come to me? I've got condoms in my desk drawer. I'm surprised Sam didn't—"

"Whoa, whoa, whoa," I said, putting my hand up. "I thought *you* were pregnant!"

"*Me!* Are you crazy? I'm not a virgin, but I'm not a moron. When I was eleven, Mom started making me proofread the sex chapters in the new editions of *Girls' Guide*."

"Well, then, is it Amanda?"

"Amanda?" Alexa looked at me like I had two heads. "Why would it be Amanda?? She—Omigod."

"What?"

"Omigod!"

"What??"

"*Omigod!*"

"*What?*"

"It's Mom!" Alexa said.

"*Your* mom?" I asked.

"Well obviously not *your* mom!" She looked at me. "Oh. Crap. Sorry." She sat down on my bed. "Yes. My mom. Your Dear Kate."

"But how—?"

"The old-fashioned way, I assume. Your dad probably had something to do with it." She shook her head. "But that doesn't even make sense. Your dad's a gyno, and my mom has a million jokes about the 'urge to merge' and the 'sperm of the moment' and the importance of 'weenie beanies.' It's part of her spiel. She thinks she's hilarious."

The phone rang. It wasn't in its cradle in the hall, so Alexa and

I went hunting for it. She found it under her pillow and held it in the air. "It's Mom. You want to talk to her?"

"No. I wouldn't know what to say."

The phone kept ringing. "Me neither."

Kate's disembodied voice drifted upstairs. "*Hello there! You've reached our questioning machine, and we have three questions: Who are you, what do you want, and how can we reach you?*"

"You're not going to answer?" I said.

"Nope."

"*Your words may be recorded for quality assurance,*" Kate's cheery stage voice concluded. We heard the beep and then Kate's normal voice: "Girls, you there? Pick up! Alexa? Sofia? Did you go out to eat? All right, listen, Gregg and I are about to have dinner at Gennaro's, so we'll be back late. Tomorrow, I'd like us to have a family meeting at six thirty. Okay? Well, see you later tonight—or early tomorrow."

"What should we do?" I asked.

"I should do some physics problems. I have a test tomorrow."

"I'll make us a potato omelet."

"I'll make a salad, and I'll text Mom so she doesn't worry. I'll say we were walking around the lake, taking in the fall colors."

"Good call."

"I would *call*, but then I'd have to talk to her." Alexa followed me to the kitchen.

I put an onion on the cutting board. "Now I get why she's seemed so tired lately," I said. "Yesterday, she took a nap in the hammock. I'd never seen her do that, not even in the summer."

"She told me her back's been hurting," Alexa said. "She even asked if I thought we should get fluffier cushions for the kitchen chairs. I was like, 'Whatev,' but didn't think any more about it."

My eyes got watery. "It's the onions, not the news," I said, though the news *was* disorienting. Every time I began to feel like I knew where I was, it was as if the signposts got switched.

"Well, it makes me want to yell at both of them," Alexa said. "For starters, I'd say: 'You two are too old to make a mistake like this!'"

"What if it *wasn't* a mistake?"

Raindrops tapped against the window.

"Sofia, don't even put that in the universe!" Alexa filled a bowl with triple-washed baby romaine and tossed in crumbled feta, walnuts, and cranberries. "I can't imagine my mom getting pregnant on purpose."

"Yeah, but a year ago, could you have imagined us making dinner? Or having a family meeting?"

Thunder rumbled in the distance, and wind rustled the trees. Alexa leaned on the kitchen island, looking marooned. Was there such a thing as a midteen crisis? And if so, were we both having one?

. . . .

During the night, a storm knocked down a bunch of honey locust branches and scattered them all over the backyard. After school, I went around picking up the branches and dragging them to the edge of the woods by the ball field. It felt good to clear away the mess. And it took my mind off the mess Dad and Kate were in.

I got so involved in carting off fallen branches that I didn't see Dad appear on the deck. "Be careful," he said.

Be careful? Why hadn't *he* been careful?

"I know what I'm doing," I replied.

"Something the matter?"

"Just gathering sticks." I didn't mention the stick I'd found.

Dad came down and helped me carry off some heavy branches. "I've been thinking about Mom lately," he said. "This time fifteen years ago, she was out to here." He put his right hand in front of his belly. "She loved being pregnant."

I used to love hearing the Sofia Story. It had taken my parents a long time to conceive, and my mom liked telling her students that the Spanish word for pregnant was *embarazada*, which was a "false cognate." Mom said she had been the opposite of embarrassed— she'd been thrilled.

"When you were born," Dad said, "Mom was over the moon. We took you everywhere and spoiled you rotten."

"Not rotten," I said, and he knew he had me.

"No, not rotten. I used to carry you piggyback to the Hippo Park. I'd hold on to your little sandaled feet. I remember our very first conversation."

He knew I was always hungry for these stories. And I knew they were not coming out of the blue.

"You were perched behind me," Dad continued, "and I said, 'What does a doggy say?'"

"And I answered, 'Woof.'" How could I stay mad at Dad? It was almost unfair.

"Then I said, 'What does a sheep say?'"

"And I said, 'Baa.'" I felt so turned around. I was fourteen and two at the same time.

"Listen, sweetie," Dad said, his tone more serious, "by now, Mom would've taken you aside and talked to you about contraception—"

"Dad! I'm taking Health and Wellness at Byram Hills! And I took Life Skills at Halsey!"

"I see so many women in my practice who are unexpectedly expecting, and I want you to know that you can come to me for information and, uh, in the future even, uh, for supplies—"

"Dad! It's not like that!" Why was everyone offering me condoms?!

"Good. Good." He wiped his hands on his pants. "My parents never told me anything. And in high school, my girlfriend's father used to give me the hairy eyeball as if I were 'only after one thing,' which I resented. But, Sofia, you do know that some boys—"

"Dad! Enough!"

"Okay. Sam seems like a nice kid…"

I threw my armful of sticks to the ground and marched inside.

Dad shouted, "And he'd better not break your heart!"

. . . .

"Ready for the big meeting?" Alexa flopped down on my bed.

"I guess."

She spotted my copy of *The Catcher in the Rye* and said, "Eww! I couldn't stand Holden. He was so preppy and whiny and depressed. He should've just taken meds!"

"I liked him," I said. "His little brother died, and it messed him up for a while."

Alexa considered this, and it occurred to me that Dear Kate was like a catcher in the rye. Her job, some days, was to stand on the edge of a cliff and catch kids who were about to go over.

"I've never been to a family meeting," I said.

"Me neither." Alexa looked at the photo of Kiki and her and me in flight. "Unless you count the breakfast when I was eleven. That's when my mom and dad sat down next to me and said that Daddy would always love me but that Daddy was out the door."

I felt a pang for Little Alexa. "What did you say?"

"I just stared at my cereal. I always used to eat my Trix in order: first red, then orange, then yellow. When it came to Trix, I was, like, totally OCD. Anyway, Mom kept talking in this upbeat way about Daddy and his 'new friend,' and I did *not* get it. All I wanted was for Mommy and Daddy to keep being Mommy and Daddy. My dad barely said anything, and later, when I looked down, I saw that my milk had turned pink, and my puffs had turned soggy, and I threw the whole thing out. Pretty stupid story, right?"

"No, Alexa. Not at all stupid."

. . . .

Kate and Dad were waiting for us in the living room. They were sitting on the sofa by the fireplace, the cats on either side of them like sphinxes.

"This looks cozy," Alexa said. "Maybe we should toast marshmallows."

"Not before dinner," Kate said. "Listen, we have some news." I sat down. Alexa stayed standing. "We could have kept it to ourselves, but we thought it would be better to be honest, and you two are big girls now."

"Big girls?" Alexa smirked.

"Listen, I'll get to the point. I've been feeling slow and achy lately. I thought it might be early menopause. But yesterday, just to rule it out, I did a home pregnancy test—"

"Mom," Alexa interjected. "We could act shocked, *shocked*. But I'm a lousy actress, and you might as well save your breath. Still, yeah, we *were* pretty shocked. Weren't we? Sof?"

I shot her a look that said, *Keep me out of this.*

"If you really want to know," Alexa continued, "Sofia saw the plastic thingy first, and then I did, and last night while you were enjoying seafood risotto, we basically started accusing each other of being nasty hos. I'm not kidding. You missed quite the scene. We invented a whole new sport called jumping to conclusions."

"Oh, that's terrible!" Kate said aghast. "I should have buried it! But I was just so stunned! And then I had to race for the train to give my talks about how to be…a responsible parent!" The cats both stared at her.

"Katie's nine weeks along," Dad said. "She came into my office yesterday. We did a sonogram." I remembered how Kiki used to joke that whoever dated Dad would get free gyno appointments for life.

"And by the way," Kate said, "it's not like we threw caution to the wind. You know that contraception is never one hundred percent—"

"Mom, please, stop! TMI! We *don't* want to know!"

I sat there all keyed up, the way I sometimes got in class when I had something to say but wasn't quite ready to raise my hand.

"Mom, aren't you way too old to have a baby?" Alexa asked. "I mean, are you getting this taken care of?"

My jaw dropped. Somehow, I hadn't thought about what would happen next. Kate was pregnant—that's as far as I'd gotten.

I looked at Dad and saw a sadness in his face that I hadn't seen for many months.

Alexa pressed. "Gregg, do you handle this?"

"We've been talking about it," Kate said. "And we scheduled an appointment for next week," Kate added quietly. "But—"

"Why even wait?"

Dad turned toward her and sternly said, "Because, Alexa, you can't terminate a pregnancy and then change your mind. Teenagers think the big worry is parents finding out. Adults know there's a lot more at stake."

I remembered that Dad and Mom had always said I was their miracle baby, their *milagro*.

"We weren't even certain we were going to tell you—" Kate began.

"Well, we found out anyway," Alexa said.

Kate sighed. "Sometimes, life ends when you don't want it to, and sometimes, it starts when you don't want it to. Girls, I'd appreciate it if you didn't spread the word. Let's keep this to ourselves, okay?"

"Actually, Mom, for American History, I'm supposed to write

about how a social policy has affected me personally, and this could work. I mean, so many people are pro-choice, but hardly anyone ever admits—"

"*No!*" Kate shouted. "You may *not* write about me for wrinkly, old Mr. Bagwell. He was my teacher too, remember?" Coco and Pepper both jumped off the sofa and fled.

"Okay, okay. Sorry!" Alexa said huffily. "Whatever," she added. "End of story."

Kate rubbed the small of her back and stood up. "End of family meeting anyway."

. . . .

Dinner was beyond awkward, and afterward, Dad and Kate went upstairs. Alexa and I washed the dishes.

"Sorry if I made you squirm in there." Alexa handed me a bowl to dry, and I thought about the times she'd *deliberately* made me squirm. "But, Sofia, you don't get it. In your dad's eyes, my mom is young. In your dad's *field*, she's ancient. And what if they had a special needs baby?"

"They'd love it specially?"

Alexa rolled her eyes. "Oh, please!"

"They would! Besides, my dad could run tests. Lots of couples have healthy late-in-life babies."

"And lots and lots don't. My mom is forty-six! That's not a good age to have a kid."

I dropped the bowl I was drying, and it shattered.

Alexa got out a broom and dustpan. "Don't worry. It was already chipped. But I think my mom needs to put this all behind her and keep it under wraps. Especially since she's, you know, Dear Kate. I mean, she's probably embarrassed on top of everything else."

Embarrassed about being *embarazada*.

"Fertility is a such crapshoot," Alexa continued. "Mother Nature can be a sweetheart or a bitch. Anyway, I'm not going to write about this or tell anyone. When people found out about my dad, I was the hot topic of conversation for months, and I do *not* need that again. Even when I got used to the whole dad thing, I still didn't like that some people thought I should be a poster child for gay dads. So do me a solid and do *not* tell Sam or Kiki or that new girl I've seen you with, Grace, okay? The one who dresses weird. And I won't tell anyone either."

"Gracie," I said. I didn't add that her dream was to go to FIT, the Fashion Institute of Technology.

"Whatever. I just mean, it's Mom's secret."

"Okay."

"I'm serious." She looked right at me. "You swear, Sofia?"

"I swear."

"All right then." She wiped the stovetop and said, "Speaking of Sam, has he talked to you about me?"

"Um, he told me you were on the swim team together."

"Good times! The other teams all practiced in pools, so whenever we had meets at Windmill, I'd say, 'Watch out for the snapping turtles!' just to mess with their heads. And it worked!" She laughed. "But that's not what I meant. You know that he and I—"

"Yeah, I know." I took a breath.

"Well, I wanted to say that Sam's a great guy. I like him—I don't mean that way. He's all yours. Too young for me anyway."

I continued putting away the pots and pans. Was there more? Were we finally having this conversation?

"I guess I do want to say one other thing."

"So say it!"

"Well, for what it's worth, I was the one who bumped up the friendship. Not that Sam objected. But looking back, I was rocked by what happened with my parents, and I guess I needed to make sure the guys I liked were straight, you know?" I didn't answer. "So I might have pressured Sam more than I should have. A couple of other guys too, though not as many as people think. I'm not a skank."

"I know."

"I just wanted to tell you that."

"What about Evan?"

"What about him? I like him." She sponged off the counter. "He's into indie bands, and he collects vinyl and he always says stuff I don't expect. He can also calm me down, which is pretty impressive, considering."

"So go for it," I said, "but, you know, let it mean something."

"Maybe." She hung up her dish towel. "Hey," she said as if she'd just thought of it. "Amanda's having a Halloween party tomorrow night. She said you can come if you want."

. . . .

"So who was it?" Kiki said on the phone. "Alexa? Amanda? Montana?"

"None of the above! And it's *Nevada*, not Montana." I changed the subject. "Kiki, what are you doing for Halloween?"

"I'm still deciding. You?"

"I'm going to a party at Amanda's with Alexa."

"Amanda's? Isn't she a senior?"

"Yeah. But it won't feel like Halloween without you!" I said. Kiki and I used to have a tradition of getting dressed together, taking the elevator to the top of Halsey Tower, and wending our way down the stairwell on foot, ringing dozens of doorbells.

"Remember when I was a Wolfe in sheep's clothing and nobody got it? Everyone thought I was a regular ol' sheep."

She laughed. "I remember when you were a giant ice cream cone."

"Mom and I made it with a beach ball and papier-mâché." Mom had loved Halloween. They didn't have it in Spain.

"I can't believe I don't have a costume picked out," Kiki said.

"This morning, my dad gave us a lecture about how he hates when guys dress up as lecherous doctors and girls dress up as naughty nurses."

"Hey! I can be a naughty nurse! A naughty night nurse! An NNN!"

I laughed. "Out here, if you have a great costume, you either freeze to death or you have to cover it with a coat. And how many houses can you even hit in two hours?"

"So come to the city! We'll be NNNs together! We won't tell your dad!"

"Maybe next year—unless we're too old for trick-or-treating."

"Take it back!" Kiki said, though that was usually my line.

"I take it back."

"Hey, Sof, you should come see Madison in the fall musical."

"Maybe. I guess."

"Actually, forget Madison! How about coming in this Sunday to see *me*?"

"Done," I said, surprising us both.

"We'll go to the Museum of Modern Art. I have student passes."

"Great," I said, already looking forward to it.

. . . .

"Three! Two! One!" Alexa hurled her basketball from the corner of the driveway, and it swooshed through the net. "Hey, Sofia, Amanda said you can invite Sam to her party if you want. You two are still together, right?"

"Right." Her question seemed odd. I hadn't talked to Sam much that week, and truth be told maybe I was sort of avoiding him. I hadn't even returned his texts or calls because I was afraid I'd be tempted to tell him everything.

She bounced the ball. "Good, because I think this annoying sophomore, Tifini, wants to get her hands on him. She sat next to him at lunch today."

"Thanks for the heads-up." *Tifini? Tifini of the long bangs and big boobs?*

"You know her, right? She's got tits out to here, and she's besties with this girl Suzy who spells her name *S-I-O-U-X-Z*." Alexa made another basket. "So what are you going to be tonight?"

"I don't know." I didn't want to say that lately I'd been giving myself credit for being able to be myself.

"I have some outfits: cave girl, French maid, witch with stick-on warts..."

"I don't want to be a warty witch!"

"Come take a look." Alexa tucked the ball beneath her arm and led me up to her room, a first for us. I'd snooped a little when she was in Canada, so I'd seen her sports trophies, posters (the Knicks, the Stones, *The Scream* by Munch), even a photo of Sam and her at last year's Snow Ball. But I'd never been *invited* in.

The Snow Ball photo was gone, and Alexa had put up new posters of indie bands. Her bulletin board was covered with sports articles from *The Oracle* and fortunes from Chinese cookies: "You will experience new things," "The time is right to make new friends," "If you continually give, you will continually have." Alexa had scribbled "*in bed*" at the end of each fortune.

She saw me eye the giant book on her desk, *Fiske Guide to Colleges*. "So far, I'm thinking about applying to Oberlin and Carleton and Occidental," she said. "But nowhere nearby. If Mom knew I was applying to St Andrews, in Scotland, she'd die." She looked at me. "Sorry! I don't mean 'die.' I mean 'flip out,' 'have a cow,' 'go ballistic.'"

"It's okay," I said, struck by her sudden sensitivity. In eighth grade, Kiki had often said things like, "I could kill my mother!" and then apologized. But I didn't expect Alexa to ever consider my reaction to specific words.

She reached into her closet and pulled out a box of costumes.

A dress-up box? Ha! Who'd have guessed? I'd have to report this to Kiki.

Alexa started rifling through her outfits, then announced, "I'm a genius! You can be Dorothy from *The Wizard of Oz*—but hot!" She handed me a blue-and-white gingham dress; a poofy, white blouse; ruby-red slippers; and blue ribbons to wear with pigtails.

I tried on the outfit and checked Alexa's mirror. Not bad. Yet what I liked most was the way Alexa and I looked in the mirror— not like sisters, no, but not like archenemies either.

. . . .

I finally texted Sam and told him to meet me at Amanda's. The music was loud, and the floor was sticky. There were about forty kids there, mostly juniors and seniors. At first, Sam and I hung out with Alexa and Evan, which meant Dorothy and a pirate (with an eye patch) hung out with a devil girl and John Lennon. (Evan was wearing a Beatles wig, granny glasses, and a peace necklace.)

Amanda said, "Sofia! I made Spanish food!" and pointed to a bowl of chili and guacamole. I decided not to tell her that Mexican food and Spanish food are *not* the same.

It was hard to hear each other, so Sam and I started dancing. But no sooner did I put my arms on his shoulders than my gingham dress ripped down one seam. I looked at Alexa and started apologizing profusely, but she shouted, "Relax. It's not like I'm planning on wearing it again."

"Besides," Sam said, "It's sexy. You look like Dorothy *after* the tornado."

He pulled me down a hallway and into Amanda's room. "Sofia, can we talk?" he said. "I called and texted you a lot this week. Did you, like, lose your phone or something?"

"No, I…" We were sitting on Amanda's bed, and I was trying not to think about Sam and Alexa hooking up at that Halloween party exactly a year ago. But I was also thinking that I was sorry that I'd sworn to keep my mouth shut about Kate. I was afraid that if I opened up to Sam, everything would come tumbling out.

"I missed you," he said.

"Can't we just kiss?" I said.

Sam studied me, with a look I'd never seen before. "Sofia, what's going on?"

"I…I don't know." I put my arms around him and kissed him, hoping we could feel closer, but this time, he pulled my arms off and said, "There's something you're not telling me. And we said, 'No more secrets,' remember?"

Alexa barged into the room.

"Oh, whoops!" she said, though I doubted she'd walked in by mistake. "I came to get my phone. I left it here, charging." She grabbed her phone from Amanda's bureau and shot me a look of warning before going back into the party.

"Sofia," Sam said when Alexa was out of earshot, "you know, you're acting kind of like her. And I don't get it."

"I'm sorry, Sam," I said, and he waited for me to say something else. I didn't.

Finally, he said, "Well, I'm sorry too." He sounded both disappointed and annoyed.

"Let's just dance, okay?" I said.

"No, Sofia. Not okay. It doesn't work that way." I was torn between staying mute and telling him everything. I wish I hadn't sworn to Alexa that I would keep Kate's news to myself. Sam got up. "I just thought you and I had something better." He walked toward the door.

Had? Had?

"Sam, wait! We do!" I started to say, but he didn't turn around, and then it was too late. He was back in the middle of the loud, sticky party, and I was watching from the hallway. Tifini and Suzy—no, *Siouxz*—trotted toward Sam in their matching vampire costumes. They were pulling him into the living room and everyone was dancing.

And just like that, I was alone.

Alone in a crowd.

Where was Alexa? Oh, in the den on Evan's lap, flanked by two juniors from her volleyball team in Batgirl outfits. Zack and Zoe were dressed as a plug and a socket, which I thought was a little gross.

Nevada saw me. "You okay?" I tried to look more okay than I felt, and she handed me a can of beer. I was about to say *no thanks*, but I took it. It was bitter and cold. Why did everyone love beer so much? I drank a sip and started to feel a little clammy when a girl ran past me to go outside and…puke?

I stood there, beer in hand, feeling uncool and off balance. I wished I were in the city, trick-or-treating with Kiki. Then I realized that Kiki was in high school now too, maybe at a party like this one. She wasn't trick-or-treating; she was probably dancing or playing Truth or Dare or who-knows-what.

I headed to the bathroom and knocked. After a moment, a boy and girl came out, and I went inside, glad for the moment of privacy.

But I couldn't escape my own thoughts.

I remembered that party in the city when Miles wanted to kiss me, and I'd pushed him away. Now I'd wanted to kiss Sam, and he had pushed me away.

Were Sam and I having a fight? Breaking up? Was it all my fault?

I could feel the tears forming, and I hated myself for being a baby and a crybaby. Dear Kate had promised that things would get easier. But nothing was easy, and I wished I could ask my own mom for advice.

I looked in the mirror and was startled to see Dorothy staring back. I splashed my face, fixed my hair ribbons, smoothed my dress, and wished I could click my ruby slippers together and go— not just home but all the way back to childhood.

You can't! the mirror chided. *You're not in Kansas anymore!*

NOVEMBER

IT WAS FRIDAY AFTER A long week of school, and I climbed into the hammock. It swayed, then slowed, and I looked through the ropey parallelograms at the leaves and pinecones. My new home, which had been shimmery green in the spring and summer and bright orange and yellow weeks ago was fading to brown. And night was falling earlier and earlier.

Dad's weekend plans were to clean the gutters and store things away for the winter—the picnic table, the lawn chairs, the hammock. He'd also started pulling down an "invasive" woody vine called bittersweet that he said was "choking" some trees. I pointed out its pretty, red berries and asked if I could cut a few sprigs for decoration. He handed me shears, and I arranged the sprigs in a vase and put them in the living room. I liked them even if they were invasive. And I liked their name: *bittersweet*.

Kate's "procedure" was still set for Tuesday. She was on her way back from Providence, Rhode Island, where she'd spoken at a girls' school.

Alexa was driving up the driveway, so I tipped myself out of the hammock and joined her in the kitchen. We nuked some apple cider, and her laptop rang like an old-fashioned telephone, which meant her dad was Skyping in. Suddenly, Alexa and Bryan were face-to-face. She walked around holding her laptop as if carrying his head on a tray. He was a handsome middle-aged man with messy, salt-and-pepper hair and stubble. Funny that I still hadn't met him in person.

"Hi, Dad!" Alexa said. She tilted the screen toward me so I could give Bryan a quick wave. "How's Barbados?"

"Good weather and good birding. Get this: the hotel café has a ceiling fan, and a hummingbird built a nest *right under* one of the blades."

"What a birdbrain!" Alexa joked.

"Turns out all the guests want to protect the mama bird, so the staff taped a sign over the switch that says 'Do not touch.'"

I wondered if Alexa was going to tell him about Kate's pregnancy.

"How's Brian?" Alexa asked.

"Fine. He can't decide whether to write that the water is 'jade' or 'emerald' or 'turquoise.'"

"Tell him 'azure'!"

"You'd love it here. The hotel guests and Bajans all splash around together."

"So take me next time."

"I will—if you're not in school."

Alexa picked up Coconut and wiggled her paw in front of the screen. "Coco says hi."

It was surprising to see Alexa's little-girl side. She usually kept it hidden. They talked for a few more minutes and then he said, "Listen, Lexi, I'd better scoot. If I don't rescue Brian, he'll get a ferocious sunburn."

After the swooshing noise that meant the call was over, Alexa looked at me. "It's like he's in some alternate universe."

Coco meowed and weaved between Alexa's ankles. Poor cat was too old to smell her food anymore, so Alexa added a tablespoon of water and stirred. Coco rubbed Alexa's shin in gratitude, looked both ways for predators, then dug into her newly discovered chow.

"Does your dad know your mom's pregnant?"

"I don't think so," Alexa replied. "He would have said something."

"I still think they should consider having the baby." I added quietly.

Alexa put her hands up and sighed. "You live in a dream world, Sofia."

I gave her a tiny nod. Maybe she was right. Maybe I did live in a dream world.

. . . .

An hour later, Alexa dribbled her basketball right into the dining room. "Watch!" she said. She bounced the ball at a sharp angle and flipped on the light switch in one try. "Astonishing, right?"

I had to agree. And I was glad we could disagree one minute and be friendly the next.

Dad called to say he was going to be working late, so Alexa made pesto pasta, and I set the table for three. I checked my cell to see if Sam had called—but no. No missed calls. No texts. I pressed SAM but then put my phone back down. I hated that I didn't even know what to write. I found a little video of a cat chasing its tail, so I sent that. A peace offering? A bridge of reconciliation? Or just me being stupid?

Kate walked in and told us she'd fallen asleep on the train from Provincetown.

"How'd the talks go?" I asked. Kate had said she never worried about school assemblies, only about after-school and evening talks. She'd said she never knew whether anybody would show up at those—and never wanted to have to say, "Thank you *both* for coming!"

"Good crowd. Thanks."

"Any hot widowers?" Alexa asked.

"I'll ignore that." Kate smiled.

"How are you feeling?" I asked.

"It was harder when I didn't know what was wrong and why I was so achy and run-down. Not that…" She filled her plate. "Girls' night in! So how are *you* guys? And how are *your* guys? Sam? Evan?"

We both mumbled, "Okay." Truth was, things were *not* okay with Sam. And I felt confused and sad.

"Mom, if we tell you anything," Alexa said, "you'll give us a lecture, and a woman in your condition…"

"No free lectures," Kate said. "I get paid to lecture."

. . . .

On Saturday morning, I kept checking my phone but nothing from Sam. I asked Dad if he wanted to play Boggle, and he said sure, so we played a few rounds. He found *gnat*; I found *gnashed*.

"I remember when Mom and I used to let you write down one-letter words," he said. "You'd write *A* and *I* very carefully, with the tip of your little tongue sticking out."

"How often do you think of Mom?" I asked. Now that she didn't live with us or teach at my school, entire mornings or afternoons sometimes slipped by without my thinking of her. Not whole days though. Never a whole day. "Not a day goes by…"

"Every day," Dad replied.

"But you're happy with Kate?" I studied our score sheet.

"Yes. And I have you. And she has Alexa." He looked up at me.

"What about the baby?" I asked.

"Katie says having a baby would be like trying for twenty-one at blackjack when we have two tens. Better to stand pat."

Out the window, a family of skinny deer grazed in the distance. All at once, they picked up their heads as if they'd heard something.

"Lately, though," he conceded, "I've noticed that my patients never ask, 'Do you have a child?' They always ask, 'Do you have *children*?'" He shrugged. "How about you? How often do *you* think of Mom?"

"Every day. It's easier than it used to be." It was hard to admit this aloud, and my nose stung as if I'd had too much wasabi.

Dad nodded. "Having a wonderful mother, then losing her, that's…a lot. But look at you. You're doing well."

"It helps to have a wonderful father," I mumbled, and I could tell he appreciated that. I shook the Boggle cubes and lifted off the plastic cover. "But, Dad," I blurted, "I don't get it. Don't *you* want to keep the baby?"

He didn't answer—just looked for words. And then he looked so sad, I had to turn away and was sorry I'd asked. "It's more Kate's call than mine. Women are the ones whose lives get upended. Men can start a life and walk away. Women can't. And she doesn't really want to start over."

"But you'd never walk away."

"No. Never. Of course not."

. . . .

Alexa gave me a ride to the train station. Kiki and I were meeting at the Museum of Modern Art. "I've been there with my dad," Alexa said. "Say hi to Frida Kahlo for me."

"Frida Kahlo?"

"There's a self-portrait I like. You'll know it when you see it."

"How?"

"Because Frida's holding scissors, and she's surrounded by locks of hair and looks totally badass. Like she's saying, 'Don't even *think* about messing with me!'"

"You want me to say hi to a crazy lady?"

"I studied her in AP Art History. I used to identify with her.

She was full of rage. Her husband, Diego Rivera, cheated on her with her sister."

Huh. I'd known Alexa a long time before I knew her dad was gay or that she knew anything about art. Someday, would someone know me a long time before they knew that my mom died or that I'm half Spanish and used to sing?

At MoMA, Kiki and I met at the coat check, and she showed me a copy of the *Halsey Herald*. "Look at my column," she said, pointing proudly. "'Ask Kiki.'"

"Wow! That's so cool!"

"Yeah but not enough girls write in."

"You can't blame them! It's not exactly anonymous at HSG."

"Good point. I was starting to take it personally." Kiki looked at me. "I guess I needed *your* advice!"

"Sofia *is* Greek for wisdom," I reminded her.

"You should start your own column: 'Sofia Says.'"

I laughed. "No way. I leave that to you experts." I asked Kiki if I could keep her column, and she gave it to me.

The day was mild, and Kiki and I went to the garden and split a sandwich next to a large Henry Moore sculpture called *Family Group*. It was a bronze man, woman, and child with dot eyes. The mother and father were not looking at or touching each other, but both parents were holding the child.

I told Kiki that Alexa had a box of dress-up clothes and also that Alexa's dad, Bryan, lived in Chelsea with his partner, Brian. "Whoa! Whoa! Back up!" Kiki said, eyes wide. I filled her in, leaving out the soggy-cereal part.

"I don't get how Dear Kate married a man who was gay."

"He didn't know. It was a long time ago." Kiki considered this but looked unconvinced. "And maybe even advice columnists don't always make the best decisions?" I added.

We went up the escalator and looked at water lilies by Monet and soup cans by Warhol. But I could tell Kiki was still thinking about Dear Kate. And she didn't even know the top story!

I didn't like holding out on Kiki, but then I hadn't told Kiki right away about Dad and Dear Kate.

I offered another tidbit. "They call themselves the Bryans. Alexa's dad told her he 'didn't know himself for a long time,' but his partner, Brian with an *I*, said he knew he was gay from birth, 'from when the doctor spanked his bottom.'"

Kiki's mouth fell open. After a while, she said, "You used to have a mom and a dad. And now you have a dad who has a girlfriend who has an ex who has a boyfriend!"

"Crazy, right?"

We came across *Self-Portrait with Cropped Hair*, and I told Kiki that Alexa liked this painting.

"Scary," Kiki said.

"You can say that again."

"Scary," Kiki repeated, and we both laughed.

I was hoping I could find a painting that spoke to me. As we walked from room to room, I looked and then I stopped in front of *Christina's World* by Andrew Wyeth. It was of a woman in a field clutching at the grass and gazing at a faraway farm as if she could never get there. I recognized the painting and the yearning, and

I wondered if there would always be times when I'd feel far from home, no matter where I was or who I was with.

"How's Sam?" Kiki asked, as if reading my mind.

"Okay," I said.

"Just okay?"

He and I hadn't talked or texted since the party, and he didn't acknowledge my dumb video. I almost didn't blame him. But how could I tell Kiki that I wasn't spending time with Sam because there was something I wasn't supposed to tell him—or her?

"You making any other friends?" Kiki asked, mercifully changing the subject.

"Starting to." I told her about Gracie, the sophomore in chorus. "She's a soprano, and she knows, like, thirty ways to tie a scarf." Kiki laughed. "Hey, have you talked to Natalie?"

"Yeah. She's doing okay. You should call her."

I nodded.

"And how's my favorite cat?" Kiki asked.

I said that Pepper still doesn't want to go outside, which was just as well, but he looks out the window a lot.

"Fewer cat fights?"

"Fewer cat fights," I confirmed.

"Hey, step-by-step, right?"

Kiki and I left MoMA, and it started to snow, the first snowfall of the winter. We said good-bye and agreed to meet at the Metropolitan Museum next time and to invite Natalie.

When we were little, Mom once took Kiki and me to the Temple of Dendur. Afterward, we had a sleepover, and Kiki said we should wrap all our Barbies in toilet paper and bury them in shoeboxes—turning them into mummies. We did, and we left them buried overnight. But the next morning, I remember how relieved I was when we unwrapped them and they all got to "breathe" again.

. . . .

"I'm home!" I called, then wondered how long I'd been calling Armonk home.

The house was quiet.

"Kate?" Alexa was at volleyball, but unless there was a game, Kate was usually home—and happy to emerge from her office.

"Kate?" I walked into the living room.

She was slumped on the sofa, one arm dangling.

"Kate? Kate! *Kate!*"

I rushed to her side, my blood running cold.

Inside my head, a voice was saying, *No! No! No! This can't be happening!*

Kate opened her eyes. "Sofia." She looked at me and could tell I was about to lose it. "Oh, I'm so sorry. I didn't mean to scare you!"

"You didn't," I lied. "And *I'm* sorry. I should have let you sleep."

"My arm is asleep. Pins and needles." She shook it. "I was having a nightmare—a day-mare. I'm glad you woke me." She was still groggy. And I was still shaken. "I dreamed I had a tiny, knit dress," she said. "It was fluffy and fragile, and I pulled on a string, and the whole thing unraveled."

"Is everything all right?"

"Well, before I nodded off, I bled a little."

"Bled?!"

"Spotted." Kate waved her hand in the air as if to shoo it all away. "I left your dad a message."

"Should I call 911?"

"No, no. He's going to call me back."

"I'm going to call him," I said and ran upstairs and called Dad's office. His receptionist answered, and I said, "It's *practically* an emergency!" then I started to cry. I didn't want to panic Dad, but I wasn't going to hang up until I talked to him. My heart was pounding. "Dad," I said when he got on, "Kate said she bled a little. You should come home, right?" I couldn't disguise the worry in my voice.

"If there was a lot of blood, I'd meet her at a hospital."

"She said 'spotted.' Is that a miscarriage?"

"Spotting is often inconsequential. Was there cramping?"

"I'll ask."

"Wait. Listen, Sofia. Just stay with her and call me right back if there's any cramping or anything. How does she look?"

"Fine. Tired. A little pale."

"I'll be home as soon as I can."

"What should I do till then?"

"Make sure she takes it easy. She can have two Advil or Motrin but *not* aspirin. You got that?"

"Got it. I love you."

I dried my eyes, grabbed two Advil and some water, and ran downstairs. I asked Kate about cramps (she shook her head) and told her what Dad said.

"Want me to call Alexa?"

"No. She's at practice. The Bobcats play Fox Lane tomorrow."

For a second, I felt honored to be the one taking care of Kate, then I felt ashamed for feeling honored.

"Maybe it's just as well," Kate said. "Nature taking its course. A blessing in disguise."

Miscarriage? A blessing? I'd hated when, a year and a half ago, a lunch lady at Halsey handed me soup and said my mother was in a "better place," adding, "God works in mysterious ways." I'd wanted to throw the soup right back at her. God did not need my mom at His (or Her) side! *I* needed her!

"Sofia, I know you like the idea of a baby," Kate continued, "but I'm not a believer in *unplanned* parenthood. And there are so many risks."

"I *do* like babies," I said and told her I used to meet Dad at Mount Sinai outside the big window where all the newborns were lined up.

"I like babies too," Kate said. "Everyone does. This morning, I got an email from a sixteen-year-old who said she was desperate to have a baby. She has no boyfriend, no money, no job, no diploma, and she's 'desperate' to have a baby!" Kate shifted her weight.

My heart was still hammering. "You're right that sixteen-year-olds shouldn't have babies," I said. "Children shouldn't have children." Coconut padded into the room and jumped onto the sofa. "But, Kate, you're a grown-up! And Dad's not going anywhere."

She was petting Coconut, and he was purring.

I couldn't stop myself. "I know you have a lot of answers," I added. "But no one has all the answers. And we could help."

. . . .

Alexa and I were painting our toenails. Mine were pink. Hers were blue.

"Mom said you were 'a comfort' to her this afternoon."

A comfort? Me? All I'd done was get Advil and spoken my mind. I'd even been feeling guilty about it.

"Think we should get her flowers tomorrow?" Alexa asked. "For when she comes home from...you know."

"I guess."

"Mums or dahlias?"

"Whatever."

"Sofia, I know you're big on babies, but I keep telling you: my mom's too old. Besides, how many siblings do you want?"

I studied my pink toes. "Siblings aren't as bad as I thought."

. . . .

My alarm went off, and I pulled on a sweater and jeans and went down to the kitchen. Dad and Alexa were sipping coffee. Kate was looking distracted.

"You okay?" I asked.

"Fine. But I can't break my fast until...afterward," Kate

replied. "I remember when I learned that compound word in school—*breakfast, break fast*. I thought that was so interesting."

"It's the same in Spanish," I said. "*Desayuno. Des ayuno.*"

"What is this, a linguistics class?" Alexa asked, yawning. "When are you guys leaving anyway?"

"In three minutes," Dad answered.

"I'm coming!" I announced.

"Sweetie, that's not necessary," Dad said.

Alexa looked at me and said, "Me too! Like it or not!"

"Well, if you really want to…" Kate said.

Next thing we knew, we were all four putting on coats and piling into Dad's car.

"What time's the appointment?" Alexa asked.

"We're stopping by my office first. I want to do a sonogram. Assuming the fetus is still viable, we'll need to be at the clinic by ten thirty."

"I bet it'll be a first for them!" Alexa said.

"What?" Kate asked.

"You know: middle-aged lady walks in with two teenage daughters, and it's the *mom* with the baby bump." Alexa chuckled. I didn't.

. . . .

At Dad's office, Kate didn't bother undressing or putting on a smock. She just climbed onto the examining table, leaned back, and rolled up her shirt. Dad put on his stethoscope, squirted clear goop onto her belly, and moved a transducer across her skin. He looked at the screen of his ultrasound machine.

"Okay, ladies, we're looking for signs of life." Dad stared at the monitor, and Alexa leaned in as though she were watching an action movie. "If this is too much for anyone"—Dad looked right at me—"just sit down or close your eyes." I sat at his desk and stared at a photo he'd always had of Mom, and now, next to it, is one of Kate and Coco. On Dad's bookshelf, I saw the copy of *Girls' Guide*.

"Found it," Dad said. He pointed to the monitor. "Ten weeks old. About the size of a plum." I glanced at the screen. From where I sat, it looked like a mini ET. "Tenacious little critter."

"I didn't miscarry?" Kate's voice sounded funny, so I got up and walked closer. She'd stood by me in the hospital in July. Standing by her seemed like the least I could do.

"That's the heartbeat," Dad said matter-of-factly.

"Oh my goodness," Kate said, her voice husky. "I'm so relieved!"

"Relieved?" Dad turned toward her. He looked baffled—and maybe a tiny bit hopeful?

"Relieved! Yes!" Kate had tears in her eyes.

"Katie, I don't understand—"

"Gregg, let's cancel that other appointment."

"Cancel? Really?"

She reached for his hand. "Gregg, we can do more tests, of course, but…I want to have this baby!"

"You do?"

Kate nodded.

"You're sure?" Dad sounded afraid to believe it.

I was too. But I could feel myself starting to smile.

"Yes. I'm sure. Gregg, I'm sure!" Dad's eyes got big, and Kate turned to us and said, "Girls, we're having a baby!"

"Whoa, Mom! Whoa!" Alexa looked ashen. "Hang on. Is that a good idea?"

"It's not an idea." Kate laced her fingers on her belly. "It's a baby—it's our baby!"

. . . .

I was late for English. I'd missed class the day before, and I didn't want to have to get a late pass. I ran down the hall—and right into Sam.

"Sam!"

"Sorry, do I know you?"

"Oh, Sam! Can we talk fifth period? I'm late."

"Late?" He made a face. "You're not late, Sofia. You're *absent*."

"Are you mad at me?"

"What's it look like?" He met my eyes. "Do you really think you can press Pause on people and expect them to stay in the picture? That's not how it works, Sofia. At least not for me."

I didn't want Sam to be mad at me, but I hadn't wanted Alexa to be mad at me either, and I guess I was more afraid of her.

Then again, how could I have been so obtuse? And what if Tifini had already asked Sam to the Snow Ball? Or pulled an

Alexa and jumped him? I put my hand on Sam's arm, but he stepped away.

"When I was with Alexa," Sam said, "she called all the shots. Friends with or without benefits—it was always up to her."

"Sam—"

"I don't like getting played. And you and Alexa—"

"Sam, no! I'm sorry." I looked up. "Sometimes, I think I don't know how to have a relationship…"

He rolled his eyes. "Then isn't it time to learn?"

"There's something I haven't told you," I said.

"Great. Here we go. What, you have some guy in the city?"

The bell rang.

"No! It's not even about me. Or you. It's about Kate."

"Kate?" Sam looked impatient.

"She's pregnant."

He looked like that was the last thing he expected me to say. "Kate? Kate Baird? Is that even *possible?*"

"Yes. I guess for a while, it was a maybe baby. But now…it's a baby in May."

"Alexa must be in shock!"

"She almost fainted yesterday in my dad's office. She's not thrilled."

"Why didn't you tell me before?"

"Kate didn't want us to. And Alexa made me promise not to. She didn't want people blabbing."

Sam looked offended. "I'm not *people*, Sofia," he said. "And I don't blab."

"You're right," I said, ashamed. "I've been an idiot." I reached for his hand and hoped he wouldn't pull away. He didn't.

"Listen, Sofia," he said, "you can always talk to me. What are boyfriends for?"

I kissed him right then and there in the hallway. And then I kissed him again. And then I kissed him a third time.

And then I ran to get a late pass.

. . . .

Kate and Dad went to Parents' Night. Dad said it would not be like at Halsey, where some teachers were neighbors, some parents were famous, and some school events felt like a Who's Who—and occasionally Who *Was*.

The electric garage door shuddered, and Dad and Kate clomped up from the basement. I took a homemade pumpkin pie out of the fridge, and Alexa put out plates.

"So what'd you think?" I asked.

Dad went first. "Pretty good, all in all. Mr. Greer praised your 'facility with language.' Dr. Pavlica appreciates your 'lab results.' And your math teacher thinks you should 'work harder.'"

"Like I'm not trying?"

"Oh, and your history teacher, Mr. C, says you came 'very well prepared' from middle school."

"Last year, I had a major crush on him," Alexa said. "It was very motivating actually. This year, I have Mom's old history teacher, Mr. Bagwell. The guy's a bulldog." She puffed out her cheeks.

"Gregg and I also got to meet Señor Muñoz together," Kate said. "Alexa, he's very impressed by how much you've learned."

"Did you guys tell anyone—?" Alexa pointed at her mother's stomach.

Dad shook his head. "No. Too soon."

"Good," Alexa said. Was she still hoping the pregnancy might end on its own?

"Do you realize it was only nine months ago," Kate said, "that I spoke at Halsey School for Girls?"

"Wow," I said.

"A lot can happen in nine months," my doctor dad added.

. . . .

Sam called after practice. And I apologized to him again. "I never meant to freeze you out."

"So come warm me up," he replied.

"How about if you come here? It's been a while. And no one will be home for a while."

"I'll be right over." His words felt like a hug, and as we were hanging up, without thinking, I almost said, "Love you" into the phone.

Minutes later, I opened the door for Sam, and we started kissing in the living room. "Warmed up?"

"Not quite yet," he said.

After a while, I thought I heard Alexa's car turning into the driveway, but I was wrong. And then I couldn't help myself—I asked if everyone knew that he'd gone out with both Alexa and me.

"Who knows? Who cares?" Sam said, and I wished I could feel that way. But it still felt weird that my boyfriend had been my sort-of sister's sort-of boyfriend. "I was stupid to ever tell anybody anything last year," he added, and we agreed that the truth can be tricky—knowing when to share stuff and when to shut up. "Tell you what," he said. "How about if I tell *you* something that *nobody* else knows?"

"Okay..."

He stroked my hair. "Ready? You and Alexa both kissed me first." He smiled.

"Wait. What?"

"It could be that I'm irresistible or that the Baird-Wolfe women are extremely aggressive. Something in the water?"

I decided to confess that I had never made out with anyone before that afternoon in the windmill, that those were my first kisses. He hugged me, but then I ruined the mood by asking when was the *last* time he and Alexa had kissed. "I know about Halloween and the Snow Ball, but..."

"Oh, come on, Sofia. I should never have—you know I hate this subject. Really."

"No secrets?" I said. "I just don't like that, for instance, her volleyball team knows stuff I don't."

He sighed. "Sofia, I *really* don't think as many people know, or care, as you think."

"I care," I said, knowing I was probably being a moron.

"If I tell you, is this going to end in tears?"

"Try me?"

He looked reluctant, then proceeded. "The last time was the end of May. Alexa's mom was going to the city. Actually, I think maybe to see an opera with your dad? Alexa invited me to say good-bye before she went to Canada."

Oh God. I remembered that day! It was when I came to Armonk with Kiki, and Alexa had told us that she'd invited a "hot freshman" to come over and give her a proper good-bye—but "not too proper!"

"Sam," I protested, "you and I had already met!"

"We'd *met,* but we weren't *going out.* And I'm a guy," he added. "And it's not fair if you ask me questions and then get mad at me for answering." He reached for my hand. "We didn't do that much." I knew what he was saying. "And besides," he continued, "I didn't even have your number."

I nodded, swallowed the lump in my throat, and tried to accept this new information. "You have my number now," I finally said, wiping my eyes. "When *did* we start going out?"

"In the windmill. June 18."

"You know the exact day?" I was surprised.

He nodded. "Want to hear a better secret?"

"I don't know. Do I?"

"You were not my first kiss, but you *are* my first real girlfriend."

"Really?"

"Really. Unless you count Rosalind Richelson. We went out for three days in fifth grade."

. . . .

The car phone rang and Kate answered it on Bluetooth. It was Brian, her ex's partner. "Kate, darling, dump that doctor and run away with us." His voice filled the car.

"Hello, Brian. Long time no talk. Where are you two running off to this time?"

"The Galapagos. In three weeks. Want to come?"

"God, yes, but I have my suburban life to lead, remember? Kids. Cats. Carpools. Columns." She looked in the rearview mirror and winked at us. "We're in the car now, going to get kitty litter at DeCicco's. Hey, we might even treat ourselves to yogurt at Peachwave."

"Oh, that silly column of yours," Brian teased. "Can't we do something about it?"

"It's my cross to bear. I write about issues; you write about islands. But send me a postcard, will you?"

"Hi, Brian!" Alexa chimed. "Send me one too."

"Hello, Alley Cat! I don't imagine there's a post office on the Galapagos—just pink flamingos, red crabs, and blue-footed boobies. But we'll be thinking of you—how's that?"

"You coming for Christmas?" Kate asked.

"Wouldn't miss it. We'll bring wine and cheese."

"Sofia's grandfather will be here," Kate said. "So we're going with a Spanish theme."

"¡Olé olé! We'll bring *vino* and cheese-o," Brian said.

"Remind Dad about homecoming," Alexa said.

"Oh, no need. Every night before bed, he mutters, 'We have to beat Pleasantville; we have to beat Pleasantville.'"

Kate laughed. "Well, bon voyage."

They hung up, and Alexa said, "Mom, don't tell me you still haven't told them?"

"I thought *you* might want to after the game on Saturday."

"Mom, we went over this! When you have huge headline news about, say, a boyfriend moving in or a bun in the oven, you don't keep it from your nearest and dearest. That's Life 101."

"Note taken," Kate said, no doubt remembering the scene in the driveway. But I think we all knew that Life 101 was a complicated course.

．．．．．．．．．．

Dad and I spent Thanksgiving in Florida. Grandma Pat didn't travel anymore, so when we wanted to see her, we had to fly south. She'd moved to a senior residence five years earlier and had lots of friends, some in better shape than others.

Dad and I took her to her favorite seaside restaurant for turkey and trimmings.

"Mom, you look terrific," Dad said. "Doing something different with your hair?"

"Eighty is the new fifty!" she said.

"Doesn't she look great?" he asked me, speaking extra loudly.

"You do!" I said, though Grandma Pat didn't exactly look *great*. Her hands were spotted, and her upper arms were fleshy. Still, she looked great for her age. Her light-blue eyes sparkled against her pale skin and snowy hair.

Grandma Pat always used to joke, "Age is a number and mine

is unlisted." But once she hit seventy-five, she started announcing her age to everyone so she could bask in their admiration. I guess she liked being told she looked young as much as she'd once liked being told she looked beautiful.

"Sofia, how's the new school?"

"Good. It's a public school. With boys."

"Well, don't let them take advantage of you." Odd phrase. Was that what Alexa had done to Sam? Taken advantage of him? "Are you still singing?" she asked.

"Yes. My chorus is doing a holiday cabaret." She didn't know what a big deal that was. Even Dad had no idea I had a solo—and I was getting anxious about it. Mr. Rupcich assigned it to me because the song was in Spanish, and though I'd been tempted to say, *I can't*, I'd heard myself say, "Okay."

She asked if I was making new friends, and I told her I'd met a nice girl in chorus who wanted to be a fashion designer. She asked about Kiki, and I told her she was writing an advice column for the *Halsey Herald.*

"Oh, that's neat. She has such spunk."

Neat? Spunk? I didn't add that Kiki had nearly keeled over when I'd finally told her that it was Dear Kate who was, as Alexa sometimes put it, "preggers."

Four years earlier, Kiki and I had visited Grandma Pat by ourselves—partly so my mom and dad could get away for their fifteenth anniversary. Even then, my grandmother had seemed ancient. When she fiddled with the car radio, the car swerved. When she offered to help with luggage, we knew to refuse. And

when she said, "I can still sew, but threading needles is the dick-
ens," Kiki and I had stopped what we were doing and volunteered
to thread a bunch of needles for her.

Still, Grandma Pat had always acted younger than her years.
She even made fun of the Old People ("OP's" she called them mis-
chievously) who, when you said hello, gave a rundown of their latest
ailments. "I don't care for 'organ recitals,'" she said. "Down here,
everyone has aches and pains and senior moments." She joked that
one neighbor's memory was so bad, "he invited people over, and
when they showed up, he thought he was having a surprise party."

Dad laughed. "Listen, Mom, I have news."

"Good news, I hope. It's the only kind I like these days. I
can't bring myself to read the paper anymore. It's all hurricanes
and obituaries."

"Good news, yes." The waiter served us plates of poultry and
sweet potatoes. "You know I'm seeing someone?"

"I know it must be serious because you're living together.
When are you going to make an honest woman of her? You are
setting an example, you know."

Grandma Pat crinkled her nose at me, and I thought, *You don't
know the half of it.*

"My intentions are honorable."

"Then you should have invited her to be with us, Greggie."

"She's in Ohio, visiting her big sister," I said. "She went with
her daughter, Alexa." Since Grandma Pat knew about my bike accident, I chimed in that Alexa had recently made me go for a bike
ride to "get back on the horse."

"Well, have you proposed?" Grandma Pat asked.

Dad looked taken aback. "Uh, with two teens and two jobs, we—"

"Sofia, what do you think?"

I thought about it, then blurted, "Yes. I think they should seal the deal."

Grandma Pat clapped her hands. "Oh goody!"

"It would be a low-key wedding," Dad said.

"I'm so happy for you," she said. "And now I have news: I've met someone too."

What?!

"His name is Dean, and he's a wonderful ballroom dancer. He plays the piano at our chapel and at the health center."

"Mom, that's great."

"Grandma, you little hottie!"

"That's me, a little hottie!" She laughed. "I'm robbing the cradle. He's only seventy-seven."

"A boy toy!" I said.

"Well, he *is* boyish about birthdays. He likes to have a cake full of candles, every year accounted for. How about you, Sofia? Do you have someone special?"

"I might."

"Oh! Come with me, will you? And tell me in the powder room."

Why not? Sam *was* one of my favorite topics. I used to think my grandma and I had nothing to talk about because we didn't like the same music, movies, or magazines. But maybe there were more layers to Grandma Pat than I'd realized. And maybe she was better with teenagers than kids.

. . . .

"She's something, isn't she?" Dad said as we drove our rental car back to the hotel. "I'm glad she has a companion." Grandpa Oscar had died eight years earlier, and Dad didn't seem at all conflicted about his mother's new love life.

"Dad, if he's a candle counter, he'll be able to count backward nine months. When are you going to tell Grandma?"

"After the amnio and a few other hurdles. I'd hate to have to untell her." I nodded. "Sofia, will you help me pick out a ring?"

"Sure. And shouldn't Alexa come too?"

He seemed surprised. "Up to you."

"Dad, I know she blows hot and cold, but if I'm going to be stuck with her…"

He smiled. "Very sensible."

. . . .

Our hotel room had two big beds and one tiny terrace. I gazed out at the black water and starry sky. The hotel lights made the sand look like a field of snow.

Snow? I thought of the Snow Ball and texted Sam "Happy Thanksgiving." But my cell kept saying, "Searching." I hoped Sam could somehow sense that I was thinking of him, searching for him. I also hoped he'd officially invite me to the dance. It was two weeks away!

I took another look at the ocean and thought, *The sea never changes.* Then I realized I had it all wrong. The sea was always changing—the size of the waves, the warmth of the water, the color of the sky, even how much seaweed or sea foam lined the shore.

When we went to sleep, Dad and I left the terrace door open so we could hear and smell the briny surf, and I listened to the whisper of water on sand, water on sand, water on sand. No matter what happened to anyone, anywhere, good or bad, the tides would keep rolling in.

That never changed; the world never stopped.

A year and a half ago, that had seemed so callous and unfair. Now it was also…reassuring.

. . . .

The clock said 6:44. Where was I? What was that line of light on the floor? Oh, right. I was in a hotel room. In Florida! The sun was peeking out from beneath the curtains.

I walked quietly out to the terrace. The sky was pale with wispy, lavender-and-white clouds lit from below. A pink-amber ball of fire peeked out and was beginning to climb the morning sky. A dazzling-yellow stripe zigzagged across the ocean, as if dividing it in two.

I'd seen photos, sure, but had I ever really witnessed a sunrise?

Two couples were on the beach. One was jogging; the other

was looking down, collecting shells, no doubt. I wanted to shout, *Look up! Look up!*

I looked up and watched as the sea became a mirror. The sun kept climbing and its reflection shone in the tidewater. Soon, there were two suns—one high in the sky, one low in the water, both blindingly bright.

"Dad, you have to see this!" I called. It felt like more than the dawn of a new day. It felt, well, Alexa would say, "epic."

. . . .

I pressed KEEKS on my cell phone. "How was Thanksgiving?"

"I ate too much."

"You're supposed to."

"And my dad was disgustingly nice to his new girlfriend and her yappy dog and yappy kid."

"I'm sorry."

"And I just got a C- in algebra. I hate quadratic equations, and I hate Mr. Gruneau, and I hate all the teachers who think that if you're even part Asian, you must be a math genius!"

"That does suck," I said. "If Alexa weren't helping me in math, I'd be drowning." I added, "But I'm helping her in *español*."

"Are you two finally *amigas*?"

"We'll never be besties," I said. "And she's still crabby about Kate's baby bump. But yeah. And when she snarls, I don't let it get to me as much."

"What about Sam?"

"Things are good."

"Has he asked you to that dance?"

"Not yet. What do you think that means?"

"That even perfect boyfriends are imperfect." She laughed.

"I could be aggressive and ask *him*." I thought about explaining the reference, but I didn't. Maybe next time I saw her in person.

"So when are you coming to Halsey?" she asked. "You haven't been back since you left!"

"Maybe for the Holiday Fair?"

"Good idea. Because if you stay away too long, people will think you don't care."

"Okay, Answer Girl." I didn't tell her that Sam had told me sort of the same thing: you can't press Pause on people.

I *did* want to visit Halsey, but I needed to be ready. Sometimes, it felt as if I had a box inside me crammed with memories, and I wanted to be in charge of when to open it.

It was the unexpected memories, the sharp surprises, that stopped me cold. That morning, Dad had dropped off some photos to be developed—he'd found an old disposable camera in a zipper pocket of his luggage. After school, Kate drove me to the store to pick them up. When I got back in the car, I must have looked shaken because she asked, "What's wrong?"

I handed her the bag. It contained twenty-four photos of our spring trip to Florida just over a year and a half earlier. Some were of pelicans and palm trees and Grandma Pat. But one was of Mom, Dad, and me, looking healthy and happy and unmistakably like a family. It was the last one taken of the three of us together—the very last one.

"It's beautiful," Kate said, studying the image.

I stared and stared. Who were these people?

Ah, but I knew. My mom, my brown-eyed, dark-haired mom, smiled so easily. We all did. We smiled like it was nothing, like we didn't realize time was passing—*racing! speeding!*—and that this moment was precious and fleeting.

I couldn't stop staring at the girl in the picture. She looked so innocent, so young, and so like her mother. She had no idea how crushed she was about to feel. She had no idea how tortuous mourning was and how, when you came out of it, when you could finally breathe again, when you woke up from the months of sleep-walking, what you got, at best, was the strength to keep going. That was your reward: strength, resilience, maybe a little wisdom or compassion. But not Mom. You didn't get your mom back.

My eyes had filled with tears. I hadn't prepared myself as I did when I looked at old photos or visited Mom's tree—and as I would when I visited Halsey. "I wasn't expecting these," I said to Kate.

"I'm so sorry," Kate replied.

"How long did it take you to get over it when your parents died?" Alexa had told me that Kate's parents had died long ago.

"Oh, honey." She gave me a hug and held me in her arms. "I'll let you know when I do."

. . . .

"Mom, not to give *you* advice or anything," Alexa said, "but shouldn't you have a ring on your finger now that you have a baby in your belly?" Alexa plopped blobs of oatmeal raisin dough onto a cookie sheet.

I pretended to be fully absorbed in making us gingerbread spice tea.

"Well, as a matter of fact…" Kate extended her left hand and wiggled her fingers.

"Mom, that's a hair band!"

"Yes it is."

"Please don't tell me Gregg gave you a hair band instead of a diamond. That would be, like, seriously disturbing."

"Last night," Kate said, "Gregg pulled this ponytail holder out of my hair and slipped it on my finger. He was joking, but I like it. *We* like it. He called it a 'promise.'"

"Oh God, Mom! If a boyfriend put a scrunchie on my finger, he'd be an ex-boyfriend," Alexa said. "I promise."

"You and I are very different people."

"Yeah. I'm someone who would never let a guy confuse a rubber band with a rock. Would you two even be getting married if it weren't for the little interloper?" She pointed to Kate's belly.

"Yes," Kate said, catching my eye. "Yes, we would."

DECEMBER

W E'RE GOING TO THE DANCE together, right?" Sam texted a week before the dance.

"Right," I texted back. "But that was NOT romantic."

Seconds later, my cell rang. "My very dearest Señorita Sofia," Sam said, "may I have the pleasure of escorting you to the Byram Hills Snow Ball?"

I laughed. "You may."

Now the big night was here.

Alexa and I had gone shopping weeks before. Her dress was black and slinky with spaghetti straps; mine was creamy satin and A-line. We were both wearing heels, but Alexa's were higher than mine, so she towered over me more than usual.

I brushed my hair in front of the oval mirror my mom had looked into when she used to get ready for parties. Alexa stood behind me, trying on a pair of long, sparkly earrings that made her blue eyes look even bluer. I was wearing the pearl studs Abuelo had given Mom when she was a girl.

Kate came in and pronounced us both "stunning," then said, "I just this minute got the cutest email. May I read it to you? It's short."

"Sure," I said.

Alexa rolled her eyes and said, "Knock yourself out, Mom."

Kate read: "Dear Kate, I'm going to a dance, and they always have really slow songs. Help!!! How do you dance with a boy? Please explain it step-by-step. And tell me what to do with my hands!!!"

"I have plenty of suggestions for her," Alexa said and guffawed.

A few minutes later, Sam rang the doorbell, and Dad let him in. As I descended the staircase, Dad said, "Wow! You look beautiful."

Sam did a double take. "You do."

I smiled, too shy to say in front of Dad that Sam looked pretty great himself in his rented tux and bow tie. Dad had us pose for pictures, and I could tell Sam felt self-conscious putting his arm around me in front of him.

"Works even better without the lens cap," I teased. Dad removed the piece of plastic. I was aware he sometimes worried that "Alexa's attitude" was rubbing off on me, so I added, "With all due respect." But even Dad must have known it was good that he and I were no longer treating each other as if we were made of glass.

Evan arrived, and Dad said, "How about a few group shots?" He followed us out into the cold, crisp evening, and we posed some more.

"That's enough!" Alexa said. To me she added, "Your father is a stalker!"

"Have fun, kids," Dad said and went back inside.

Alexa pointed up at Orion. "Welcome back!" she called to the bright constellation. "I love Orion!" she explained. "I miss him during the warm months. Just look at those shoulders!"

Evan rubbed her neck. "You're making me jealous."

"Oh, he's got nothing on you." They kissed.

Sam and I got in the back of Alexa's car, and Alexa and Evan got in the front. "City kids have it so easy," Alexa said, and she turned on the car. "No one even has to be the designated driver because no one drives to parties." She handed Evan a cold bottle of bubbly that she must have hidden in the fridge. "Share nicely, children," she said as she started the car. Evan took a swig and passed it to Sam, who drank some and passed it to me. I liked that he was offering, not pushing. And while I didn't judge anyone for drinking, having spent so many months feeling wobbly, now that I was back on my feet, I liked feeling grounded and present. And like myself—my *new* self?—I shook my head and passed the bottle back.

"Alexa," Sam said, "I can't believe your mom's pregnant."

"I know. If the baby is throw-uppy or tantrum-y, forget it, I'm handing it straight to Sofia."

"You do that," I replied.

"You seem a lot older than when we first met," Alexa said, meeting my eyes in the rearview mirror. "Back then, I was worried I was going to have to babysit *you*." She glanced at Evan. "Crazy, isn't it? That her dad jumped my mom?" She told Evan about how our parents met—or re-met—the night Kate's car had died, but in her version, she made it sound as if Dad had gone and drained Kate's car battery on purpose.

I leaned my head on Sam's shoulder. I was glad Sam and Alexa and I had figured out how to be normal-ish with each other. For a second, I tried to picture Alexa and Sam going to this dance one year earlier. Then I decided it was wiser to stay in the moment.

· · · · · · · · · ·

I liked walking into the Snow Ball with Sam by my side. There were red poinsettias on the tables and white, silver, and blue helium balloon bouquets everywhere. Girls greeted each other: "You look amazing!" "Where'd you get that dress?" Guys ribbed each other: "Check out the penguin suit!" "Dude, you clean up nice."

Girls took group shots of themselves, extending their arms, then hovering over each other to see how they came out. They said, "You have to send me that!" or "You have to delete that!" or "You have to post that!" or "You can't post that!" Larger groups formed, and whoever volunteered to take a photo got handed extra cell phones.

Inside the ballroom, everyone rushed to claim tables. Sam, Alexa, Evan, and I saved seats, and some of Alexa and Amanda's volleyball teammates joined us, looking totally different all dressed up. There were very few freshmen at the dance, but Gracie and another sophomore were at a nearby table. She looked great in a kelly-green dress with a sash of sequins, and we talked about our chorus concert coming up.

Zach was at a table with Zoe and the twins—hard to believe I'd ever had trouble telling them apart. We all waved a quick hi, but I was glad to be sitting next to Sam.

One of Alexa's jock friends teased her, saying, "Only someone as in shape as Alexa could pull off a dress that tight!"

"*I* could pull it off," Evan said, slowly lowering one of Alexa's spaghetti straps.

Amanda examined my shoulder. "That's actually a cool scar, Sofia. It's like a little *X*."

"*X* marks the spot," Sam said and kissed it.

Nevada laughed, and I noticed that her date was a tall girl with beautiful caramel skin. Funny, I hadn't realized Nevada was gay.

Dinner was chicken and rice, and dessert was, of course, a "snowball": vanilla ice cream smothered in coconut and topped with chocolate sauce.

Afterward, everyone rushed to the dance floor, and for a short while, it was as if we were all one happy, unified group rather than splintered clusters of kids with knotty pasts and crossed histories.

I taught Sam a few twirls and jitterbug steps, moves I used to practice with Halsey friends. During a slow dance, he whispered, "I bought your birthday present." We were swaying with the rhythm, and he was being careful not to crush my toes.

"You did?" I pulled back so I could look into his eyes, but then I missed the feel of his chest against my cheek, so I nestled closer.

"I think you'll like it." I loved being so near him, feeling his body next to mine. I loved his face too—sandy hair, pale lashes, sexy smile. I was taking in his every expression. Was this love? Right then, I felt I loved him, but in class or at my desk at home, I was less sure. Besides, I still didn't want to say those three words quite yet. Love was dangerous. When you loved someone, you had so much to lose.

"Give me a hint," I whispered.

"You have to wait a week to find out. But if you want," he said playfully, "every time you kiss me, I'll tell you what it *isn't*."

I kissed him. "It's not a guitar." I kissed him again. "It's not a guinea pig." I kissed him again. "It's not a skipping stone." I kissed him again, a longer kiss. "It's not a red convertible, though I wish it were." I gave him a ten-second kiss. "It's not two tickets to Paris."

I pressed myself into Sam, and I liked how lean and strong he was. I grasped his shoulders, and he looked down and smiled. I wanted to climb right inside him, to hold him as close as I could but still see him and revel in how hot he was, how sweet, how…in love with me?

The last time Kiki had asked for an update on my love life, I'd confessed that I didn't know if I was in love or not. Kiki had nodded and admitted that, for once, she was not with anybody and that it felt "surprisingly okay."

I was glad Sam and I were taking things slowly, neither of us pressuring the other. I hoped we'd have time to get closer on our own terms. Time to take our time.

. . . .

"I told Grandma Pat about the grandbaby-to-be," Dad said. "She's beside herself."

"Should I tell Abuelito before he gets here?"

"I think we'd better."

Abuelo was shocked but glad that I sounded happy. When

I added that Dad and Kate would be getting married, he said, "*Hombre, claro*," which I translated for Dad as a mix of "Of course," and "I should hope so!"

Funny. The verb *casar*, "to marry," comes from *casa*, "house." But in this case, the house had come first.

. . . .

Dad, Alexa, and I met at Tiffany & Co. on the corner of Fifth and Fifty-Seventh to do some stealth shopping. The entire store was decorated on the outside with a giant red ribbon and bow—and it looked like a Christmas present. We took the elevator to the second floor to look at diamond rings. A few couples were sipping champagne—apparently, if you spend enough money, Tiffany's toasts you.

An elegant young woman dressed in black said, "May I help you?"

Dad said he wanted to buy a ring and explained, "I'm marrying this young lady's mother."

"Splendid," she said and encouraged us to look at the rows of rings: some small, some big, some round, some square, some with single stones, some with many. "How much is this one?" Alexa asked, pointing to a large, pale-pink diamond.

"It's extraordinary, isn't it?" the woman began. "Prices vary depending on cut, color, and carats."

"So, like, ten thousand dollars?" Alexa guessed.

"More like one hundred thousand dollars. It's a unique piece. It just came in yesterday."

Alexa's eyes went wide, and the woman steered us to a different counter and showed Dad rows of shining diamonds on simple bands. "These are all classic. And very popular."

Dad pointed to one and asked Alexa and me what we thought.

"Absolutely beautiful," I said.

"Beats the scrunchie," Alexa said.

"This is the one," Dad said with confidence. He and the woman discussed the price, and then she rapped on the desk to summon someone to take Dad's credit card. A third person put the ring in a black suede box and wrapped it with tissue and put it into a robin's-egg-blue cardboard box. She tied the box with a red ribbon, explaining, "We use red during the holidays."

Back in the elevator, Alexa suggested we stop at the fourth floor.

"Why?" I asked.

"To look at baby stuff," she said. "Little rug rat is getting born with a silver spoon in his mouth, right? We should check out the spoons."

. . . .

"May I ask you a question?" I poked my head into Kate's office. She was wearing purple sweatpants and one of Dad's old sweaters. Alexa called it her "bag-lady look."

"Of course. That's just what these girls are doing." Kate tilted her screen toward me so I could see three highlighted emails.

I begged my mom for a cell, and I got one, but I put a bottle of water in my bag, and the cap must not have been on right because the cell got all wet and died, and now I'm afraid my mom's going to kill me.

What do you do when the only person who can make you stop crying is the person who made you cry?

Do you think teenagers are too young to experience love?

"What'd you tell the third girl?" I asked, trying to keep my tone light.

"I said that what teens feel is real and can be incredibly intense but not to rush it. You know me—always trying to get kids to *step* into love instead of *falling* in." She patted her growing belly and gave me an ironic smile. "How's Sam?"

"Good." We both knew Catlover would have said much more. "I wish I could help you with your mail. Kiki keeps asking me to ask if she can be an intern."

"She does? Really? That could work."

"Seriously?" I told her I'd show her Kiki's column. I knew it was in my backpack somewhere.

"She's coming to your concert, right? Maybe she and I can talk about it then."

My concert. I felt a fresh rush of stage fright. Was I really going to sing in public again? What if I panicked? Or forgot the words? I hadn't even told Dad or Kate or Alexa that I had a solo in Spanish.

But I *had* been practicing in the shower whenever I had the house to myself.

"So, did you want to ask me something?" Kate asked.

"It's about Christmas. Do you and Alexa ever put up a tree?"

"Every year! We get the biggest one we can squeeze into the living room. I go a little nuts, and then we keep it up for weeks and weeks. It's a wonder our tree wasn't up when your dad came by last February. Is that…okay?"

"Totally. But what are we waiting for? It's December 15!"

"I thought you'd want to celebrate your birthday first."

"Let's celebrate everything."

. . . .

"I brought dumplings!" Kiki got off the train and handed Dad two yummy-smelling bags. "Mom says Vietnamese food is perfect for the holidays because people get tired of ham, turkey, and roast beef."

"I wish Saigon Sun delivered to Armonk," Dad said.

"It just did!" She laughed. As we drove home, Kiki talked about her new advice column and said she'd printed something funny she'd found called "Why Men Don't Write Advice Columns." She dug a crinkled piece of paper out of her pocket. "Ready? I'll read it. Here goes: 'Dear Larry, Please help. The other day, I went to work and my husband was watching TV. I'd driven less than a mile when my car made terrible noises and conked out. I walked back home and couldn't believe it: my husband was in bed with another woman! He apologized like crazy, but I feel so betrayed! I don't know what to do! Signed, Betsy.' 'Dear Betsy, When a car sputters and stalls after such a short distance, this indicates engine trouble. Have you checked the fuel line?'"

Dad laughed and said she should share that with Kate, so Kiki put the paper back in her pocket.

At the house, Kiki exclaimed over our tree, a Scotch pine, then looked out the window. "Wow! Deer!"

"Rudolph, Bambi, and buddies," Alexa said.

"A lot of birds too!"

"I just dumped sunflower seeds in the feeder. Are you as bad at bird identification as Sofia? Or can you tell a nuthatch from a titmouse?"

"A *tit*mouse?"

"See those two? That's a pair of tufted titmice."

"A *pair* of *tit*mice?!"

"I wouldn't lie about birds," Alexa said.

"She wouldn't," I said. "She and her dad used to go on bird walks." I was beginning to learn Baird family lore.

Kate came out of her office.

"Look at you!" Kiki said. "Omigod, you look great!"

Kate did a pirouette. "I feel great too. The second trimester is easier than the first."

"Mom, if it kicks, do *not* ask Kiki to put her hand on your belly," Alexa said. "That's gross."

"Are you kidding? I want to feel the kicks!" Kiki said.

"Let's get the boxes," Dad said, and we trooped down to the

basement and brought up the Baird and Wolfe ornaments. "It's time to deck the halls."

"I'm so glad you guys are here," Alexa said. "Decorating when it's just Mom and me sucks. No offense, Mom."

"*Un*decorating, just two people, is even worse," I pointed out.

"True that," Alexa said.

Kiki tested a string of lights, then started wrapping the tree. She also helped me hang the red-and-green paper chain I'd made with my mom back in first grade.

In one doorway, I taped our sprig of mistletoe; in another, I taped a golden bell with a pull chain that played "Jingle Bells."

Alexa set up the crèche that Abuelo had carved. She asked where to put the cows, sheep, and donkey. I said, "Near the manger."

"What about the wise guys?" Alexa asked, and Kiki laughed.

The cats went crazy. Pepper jumped in and out of all the boxes, and Coco found her inner kitten and pawed repeatedly at a low ornament until it fell to the ground. Then she picked it up as if it were a dead mouse and dropped it at Alexa's feet.

"A token of her cross-species affection?" Kiki asked.

"I love you too," Alexa said, petting Coco. Coco lifted her butt in the air. "But take it easy, girl, or you're gonna get a reputation."

"Do you have presents to put under the tree?" Kiki asked.

"Lots!" Dad bounded upstairs and Kate went to the laundry room.

Dad came back with gifts but not the small Tiffany blue box. I wondered where he'd put it.

Kate returned with an armload of wrapped boxes, then called, "Kiki! Quick! Feel! Right here!"

Kiki ran over and put her hand on Kate's belly.

"Little hellos from the future," Kate said, beaming.

. . . .

Decorating had taken my mind off the holiday concert, but now I was a bundle of nerves again. I did vocal exercises as I put on my black top, skirt, tights, and heels. Alexa drove me to school and reserved seats in the tenth row before going back to get everyone else.

I had told my family that our chorus would sing songs from around the world, including "O Tannenbaum" and "Il Est Né, le Divin Enfant." What they didn't know was that I'd be belting out the final verse of "Los Peces en el Río" all by myself. I'd been practicing whenever I was alone and planned to silently dedicate the song to my mom. I'd also been "visualizing success," as Dr. G told us to do back at Halsey. But it was one thing to picture myself taking center stage and singing my heart out, another to actually do it.

I unwrapped a honey lozenge, joined the chorus backstage, and did warm-ups with Gracie. Soon, we could hear a crowd begin to arrive and settle into seats.

The butterflies in my stomach were colliding into each other, and a few minutes later, I was following the others onstage. The auditorium lights dimmed, the stage lights went up, and we began singing, first in English, then in German, then in French.

My cue was next. My heart was bonging in my chest, and I took deep breaths as I stepped forward and looked out. I tried to spot Dad, Kate, Alexa, Sam, and Kiki, but it was too dark—which was probably just as well.

Now it was my turn, my moment. I needed to summon my voice from deep inside and give it to everyone in the room. My mom always said that if you have a gift, you have to share it. "¡*Canta!*" I could hear her say. "Sing!"

"This is for you," I answered silently. "*Es para ti.*"

And then I sang, loud and clear, in Spanish and on key, enunciating every word and landing every note. I did it for myself, for the audience, and for my mom.

When I finished, there was complete silence, and I wasn't sure whether to smile or bow, stay in the spotlight or step away. A man in the darkness said, "Wow." And then, thunderous applause.

. . . .

After the concert, I stepped into the bright hallway. Dad gave me a hug and said I sounded amazing. Kate agreed. Sam whispered, "You're incredible."

Kiki said, "I've never heard you sound so good!" Gracie came up, and when Kiki told her she loved her scarf, Gracie said she'd made it out of ties.

Even Alexa was full of compliments. "Jeez, Sofia," she began. "I was kinda spacing out and looking around, you know, and then I heard this killer voice, and holy crap, it was you!"

"Thanks."

"You know warm 'n' fuzzy isn't my style," Alexa added, "but I was impressed by two things. One was your voice. The other was my reaction."

"What do you mean?"

"I mean, while you were singing, I was thinking, *See that kid up there? That's my sister.*" She gave me a shove, so I shoved her back.

. . . .

"Shouldn't we fix the baby's room?" Dad asked.

Dad, Kate, Alexa, and I were peering into what Kate had always referred to as "the little room." It was brimming with textbooks, *Fifteens*, trophies, a sewing machine, a coffeemaker, old skis, boogie boards, clothes, and clutter.

"No need to turn it into a nursery overnight," Kate said.

"You guys don't get it," I said. "My dad *lives* for projects like this. This is his idea of a good time."

Ever since we'd moved, their home—*our* home—was becoming more organized. Dad had been slowly straightening the garage, basement, bookshelves, and cupboards.

"He *is* pretty compulsive," Alexa said.

"In a good way," Kate said.

"I am itching to get in there," Dad admitted. "People who live in apartments dream of finding an extra room…and here one is!"

Dad and Kate pushed up their sleeves, and Alexa and I took a brisk walk around the lake.

"Think we should give Mom a baby shower?" she asked.

"I don't know. I hadn't thought about it."

"I went to one once, and there were these little contests."

"What do you mean 'contests'?"

"Like, each guest brings in his or her own baby photo and tapes it on the wall and everyone has to guess who's who. We even played Baby Scattergories."

"Baby Scattergories?"

"The categories are things like 'children's books' or 'celebrity baby names.' So, for instance, if it's, I don't know, 'things that come out of babies' and the letter is *D*, you can say *drool* or *doo-doo* or *diarrhea*, and you get points if no one else wrote down your answer."

I gave Alexa a long look. "You're kind of getting into this whole baby thing."

She smirked. "I know. Don't tell."

. . . .

"Finally fifteen!" Sam said on December 21. Abuelo had arrived from Spain, and Dad, Kate, Alexa, Sam, Abuelo, and I all went to dinner at the Red Hat on the Hudson River.

Sam's birthday gift to me was a delicate chain with a tiny golden turtle dangling from it. I put it on and loved the way it felt around my neck. It made me happy that he'd noticed that I had a thing for turtles. At dinner, I kept touching the pendant.

Abuelo gave me a jewelry box that he had carved himself. He said I could use it for my pearl earrings and turtle necklace.

"*Gracias*," I said, even though I couldn't yet imagine taking the necklace off.

I got other presents too, and Kate gave me a framed enlargement of the family photo taken in Florida.

When a waiter set down a dazzling chocolate cake glowing with candles, I didn't know what to wish for. So I just wished for it all to keep going—for this happiness to last.

Maybe fifteen would be a good year. Or maybe, I thought, remembering that email Dear Kate had sent Catlover in February, things get easier, then harder, then easier, then harder, then easier and on and on and on. I couldn't blame myself for having been a turtle for a while, for taking it slow and trying to play it safe. Yet somehow I had put one foot in front of the other and I was stronger now.

I looked around the table. Everyone was smiling and laughing and looking happy and healthy. I knew I would never again feel as safe and carefree as I did back when I was a kid, when I thought death had nothing to do with my life. But I was doing okay. More than okay. I *had* gotten out from under the heavy blanket of grief. I was…growing up.

. . . .

"Introducing the Bryans!" Kate exclaimed as she opened the front door. I'd heard so much about them, it was hard to believe I was meeting them for the first time.

"Merry Christmas Eve!" Brian said. "*¡Olé olé!*" He had designer sunglasses balanced on his head. "Kiss me, Kate," he said and gave her air kisses. "Now spin around," he commanded, tut-tutting admiringly.

"Hi, Kate!" Bryan said, stomping his boots. "We're both so excited about your news." He was taller than I'd imagined and very handsome and easygoing. I could see why Kate had fallen for him.

"Come in, come in, it's cold," she said.

"And you, my dear, are *hot!*" Brian was still checking out Kate's full figure. He turned toward Dad. "Gregg, you dog!"

"Wolfe," Dad corrected with a smile. He'd met the Bryans a few times, when he had given Alexa rides into the city.

Bryan handed Kate a basket. "We bought cava, Manchego cheese, and quince paste."

"*Membrillo!* I love membrillo!" I said.

Dad introduced Bryan and Brian to Abuelo, who was wide-eyed.

Alexa bounded downstairs. "Daddy! Brian!"

"Lexi!"

"Alley Cat!"

More kisses, more hugs, more presents—and one tacky ornament. "Don't you love it?" Brian said, showing us how on one side it was a cut-out palm tree and on the other a lady in a bikini with her hands in the air. "Look, it says, 'I took my sweetie to Tahiti'!"

Brian was funny. I could see why Bryan had fallen for him too.

"I thought you were going to the Galapagos," Alexa said.

"We were. We did! But then we kept going. Two separate assignments for two different travel magazines," Bryan said.

"I am *so* in the wrong field!" Kate moaned.

"Not true!" Brian consoled her. "The pay is awful. And we have to inspect every conference room and executive suite— *bor*ing! And the bus rides are interminable!" He clapped his forehead and winked at Bryan. "What we go through to keep our readers satisfied!"

"My heart bleeds," Kate teased. "In fact, here's my teeny tiny violin."

I kept translating for Abuelo, who was trying to take it all in. Then we all moved into the living room, where the fire was crackling.

"Actually," Bryan said, placing the Tahitian ornament on our tree, "we did see an extraordinary sight. There was a full moon, and we saw a moonbow! The captain of the ship said he'd never seen such a thing in thirty years at sea. It was like a rainbow on the horizon but all white and ghosty and beautiful. I took pictures, but they didn't come out. It was just a faint gray arch, shimmering in the moonlight." I translated for Abuelo.

Dinner was *tortilla* (made by me), seafood paella (made by Kate with Dad's help), and Baked Alaska (made by Dad and me, flamed by Alexa). Not the usual fare, but we'd had fun preparing the feast.

Alexa sat next to Abuelo and spoke in slow Spanish. I could tell she was teaching him a few English words, but at the end of dinner, I was surprised when he stood up and thanked us all. "And the next Chreesmees," Abuelo announced with a twinkle, joining his arms and making a rocking motion, "*¡un bebé!*"

· · · · · · · · · ·

On Christmas morning, even Pepper and Coco got presents: catnip mice and plastic balls with jingle bells inside. They sniffed at boxes and played soccer with balled-up wrapping paper. Meanwhile, Abuelo gave us a shepherd made of Lladró porcelain, and I gave him a carved wooden turtle. Dad tried on a new sweater, and Kate modeled much-needed maternity clothes chosen by Alexa and me. The Bryans got a coffee table art book, and Alexa and I opened presents and emptied our stockings, which included Knicks tickets for her and Broadway tickets for me.

Soon, there was nothing left under the tree. Dad said, "Wait, I think there's still one more present." He stood and reached into his pockets and pretended not to be able to locate what he was looking for, but then he patted his jacket, reached inside, and presented Kate with the little blue Tiffany box.

All activity stopped as she pulled on its red satin bow. Everyone's eyes were on Kate, and she looked at Dad and whispered, "I hope this is what I hope it is."

He smiled. So did Alexa. So did I.

The ribbon fell to the floor, and Kate lifted the blue lid to reveal white tissue covering the black suede box. Kate's hands trembled. Coconut rubbed against her, tail high in the air. Pepper settled near me.

Kate was about to open the box when Dad said, "Wait." He knelt in front of her. "Close your eyes." Kate did. Alexa, Abuelo, the Bryans, and I hovered close.

Dad removed the hair band from Kate's fourth finger and said, "Now open your eyes and open the box." Kate opened her eyes, but Dad was gazing into them with such intensity that she didn't look away. When at last she lifted the lid, she gasped.

"Katherine," he began. "I never imagined I would fall in love again. But when I saw you at Halsey, I felt a connection that just keeps growing. I jump-started your car, and you jump-started my life. Now I can't imagine living without you." His voice wavered; her eyes were shining. "You've already let Sofia and me move in with Alexa and you, and we have already, quite literally, started a life together. So it's high time I ask you a very important question." There was no cheering, no translating. Everyone was quiet. Even the cats. "Katherine Baird, will you marry me?"

"Yes," she said. "Yes!"

Dad slid the ring onto her finger. He kissed her hand, and she kissed his lips, and she finally looked at the sparkling diamond, tears in her eyes.

The Bryans said, "Congratulations!"

Alexa said, "I helped pick it out."

Abuelo said, "*Felicidades.*"

I said, "Wow," and realized I really was happy for both of them—for all of us.

Of course, I wish my mom had never died. Of course! But she had. Months and months ago—and there was no turning back time.

Bryan took pictures of Dad and Kate, and in a few, Kate held her hand up so her ring glittered, front and center. He took group shots too. In one, Dad, Kate, Alexa, and I posed together, and Abuelo said, "*La nueva familia.*"

. . . .

"Wanna play Hearts?" Alexa asked as I walked into the living room. The Bryans had gone back to the city, and Abuelo had flown home.

"Sure," I said.

"Mom! Gregg! *Hearts!*"

"No need to holler," Kate said, as she poured us all glasses of eggnog.

"Is it spiked?" Alexa asked.

"I made yours a double," Kate deadpanned.

Dad joined us, and Alexa shuffled the cards and began dealing. "In science," she said, "we learned that mistletoe is a parasite. Too much can strangle a tree."

"Like bittersweet," Kate said.

"You'd think mistletoe wouldn't have a bad side," I said.

Dad sorted his cards and said, "You really do like science, don't you, Alexa?"

"Always have," she answered.

"Maybe you could volunteer with me at the clinic some Saturday. We get a lot of Hispanic teenagers, and it would help if they could talk to someone young and smart in their own language."

"What would I do?"

"Greet them. Take their weight and blood pressure. Make them feel less scared." Dad knew Alexa was as good at scaring girls as at putting them at ease, but he added, "You could make a difference."

"I'd have to think about it."

"What an opportunity," Kate said. "And it would look good to colleges."

Alexa passed three cards to her mother. "Mom, could we *not* talk about colleges during vacation? Amanda just got rejected by Vanderbilt, where she applied early, so her Christmas break is ruined. And Nevada's parents are stressed out because their cleaning lady's son just got offered a free ride at Yale, and Nevada wants to apply there but hasn't even finished her essays."

"Okay, okay. No more college talk," Kate agreed.

"Gregg, different subject," Alexa said. "You always said you liked delivering babies. Couldn't you go back to it now?"

Dad put his cards together, then slowly fanned them out. "I think it was lucky I got to do OB as long as I did."

"I'm just saying, if you got calls in the middle of the night, we'd be here."

Kate put down a two of clubs, but I could tell she was listening. I played my ten.

Dad played his king. "I like my uninterrupted evenings and my lower malpractice rates." He looked at me. "And instead of delivering babies at all hours, I'd just as soon be here with all of you and our new baby." The two cats came racing through the living room and started hissing at each other, wrestling furiously, ears pinned back. "It's nice of you to think about it though."

Alexa played her ace and swept up the first trick. "I guess I could be free this Saturday," she said without looking up. "I don't really have anything better to do."

I peeked at Kate and could tell she was trying not to smile.

·· · · · · · · · ·

"Twelve little grapes," I'd explained. "Every New Year's Eve, when the clocks strike twelve, everyone in Spain stuffs their faces with grapes, one by one, as fast as they can."

"Don't people choke?" Alexa asked.

"No. You use little grapes. Or you cut regular ones in half and take out the seeds."

"Weird," she said. "I prefer the American tradition. You kiss everyone in sight and blow on noisemakers, the kind that curl out like frog tongues."

We were upstairs, getting ready to go to a party with her friends.

The doorbell rang, and I went down. It was Sam. "Happy Almost New Year!" I said. A frosty wind whooshed in, and he kicked snow off his boots and checked to see that we were alone. Then he opened his coat and wrapped me inside.

"Brrr! Your hands are *freezing*!" I giggled and led him under the mistletoe. We kissed—one quick kiss, one slow one.

"Wow, that is a huge tree," Sam said.

"I was just giving it a drink of ginger ale—my mom's trick." I gave him a tour of the tree, pointing out mementos from my childhood, Abuelo's carved figurines, and even the tacky ornament from Tahiti.

"Don't you think it's time you show me the other tree?" Sam asked. "The one in the city?"

I thought about it. I hadn't visited Mom's tree in a long while, but Dad was driving in the next day to go to the New Year's party in our old building. Former neighbors and teachers would be there, and Kiki said she'd go with me if I wanted. But I was an outsider now, and I wasn't sure how it would feel to drop in on my old life or chat about my late mother or soon-to-be stepmother.

Was I ready? Was it time? Kiki and I used to get out my Magic 8 Ball for these sorts of questions. Responses were random, but it always seemed that Kiki got affirmative answers like "You may rely on it," while I got fuzzy ones like "Reply hazy. Try again." I was glad I'd gotten rid of that stupid ball.

I'm fifteen, I thought. I'm ready enough. I didn't need to consult an 8 Ball or Dear Kate or Ask Kiki. I had to use my head and trust my heart.

I told Kiki I'd meet her at the brunch at Halsey Tower, and I decided to tell Sam to meet me afterward at Mom's tree. Why not? I could handle it, couldn't I? And if Sam saw me cry? So what. It wouldn't be the first time.

"How about tomorrow afternoon? We could meet inside Riverside Park."

Sam smiled. "You're on."

JANUARY

D AY ONE OF THE NEW Year. The clouds hung gray and thick. Flurries of snowflakes swirled and sparkled in the cold air.

The annual party in our lobby turned out to be more fun than I'd expected. Mrs. Russell's ribs were delicious, and Mrs. Morris made candy cane cookies, and my former Halsey Tower neighbors all made a fuss over me—and over Dad and Kate and her diamond ring. Kate was wearing one of the loose tops that Alexa and I had picked out, and no one mentioned the baby on the way.

Teachers asked about my new home, and I said, "In a house, you can make all the noise you want without having to worry about downstairs neighbors. But it's hard to get to know your neighbors because, well, no elevators."

Mrs. Russell asked if I had "any boyfriends."

"Just one," I answered with a Mona Lisa smile. Mason came running over and gave me a sassy high five. He repeated "boyfriends" as if it were the funniest word he'd ever heard. I picked him up, and he held on tight.

I liked talking to Mrs. Russell, Mrs. Morris, and Dr. G person

to person rather than student to teacher. Dr. G asked if I was singing again, and Kiki said, "You should've heard Sofia at her holiday concert! She had a solo in Spanish, and she brought down the
house—no, the school!"

When we left, Kiki said, "See? That wasn't so hard. Now you
have to meet Isaiah."

"Isaiah from Dalton? Haven't I met him? You've been friends
forever."

"I think that might be changing."

"Wow."

"Yeah."

We said good-bye, and I walked alone to Riverside Drive. Near
the Joan of Arc statue on Ninety-Third, a sign said "Treecycle," and
I saw a small pile of discarded Christmas trees. I headed down
toward the winding entrance to the park, turning left at the hippo
playground, which stood hushed and empty. The community
garden was stubbly and brown. Even the dog run was desolate.
Two men with strollers walked past me, and two older women were
jogging. But the park was silent—it wasn't vibrant, like in spring
and summer and fall. Yet it had a stark beauty of its own.

I breathed in the cold air and remembered that exactly one year
earlier, on New Year's Day, I'd skipped the building brunch and walked
across Central Park with Kiki. A few days later, I'd helped Dad disman-
tle our dry and droopy tree. My life had seemed to be closing in on me.
Now it was opening up. I'd moved, made friends, started high school,
and was going out with Sam, who was on his way to see me.

People say, "Life is short," and sometimes, that turns out to be true. But for most of us, life is long. And knock on wood, *tocar madera*, my life—I was realizing at last—was mostly ahead of me.

I was glad there was a giant evergreen glimmering in our new home. Glad that Dad and Kate were getting their marriage license, and that in two weeks, the Halsey chaplain was going to officiate a small ceremony. Brian had joked they could make it a double wedding, but Bryan said no, they would take photos of the bride and groom and that would be their wedding gift. Brian added, "Still, you two are inspiring! There could be another wedding down the road."

"Not a shotgun wedding," Bryan added, and everyone laughed.

The most incredible thing was that I was going to be a big sister. Dad kept monitoring everything, and it appeared to be "all systems go": one healthy baby, coming right up. Kate didn't want to know the sex, but I did, so he said he'd tell me if I agreed not to reveal it.

"Can you keep a secret?" Dad asked.

"My father got my pen pal pregnant, and I didn't tell a soul," I replied. "I'm almost too good at secret-keeping," I added.

He beamed. "It's a boy."

I felt pleased that I'd still be Dad's only daughter, favorite daughter. And I pictured myself teaching the baby clapping games and Spanish lullabies. That night, Alexa said she'd show him how to shoot hoops—adding that he'd be "a natural at dribbling."

No doubt the baby would demand a lot of attention, but maybe he'd unite us all more too.

I liked that in our new home, it was always okay to talk about my mom or Alexa's dad. We didn't have to pretend there hadn't been other chapters, other loves, other lives. I was also glad Kate didn't expect me to call her "Mom" and wasn't planning on taking Dad's name. In my mind, I had just one mom, and there was just one Mrs. Wolfe.

I followed the path toward Mom's tree and stood before it. The tree was bare, of course. No leaves, no blossoms. But it was taller than it used to be, strong, sturdy, growing. Alive. Soon, it might be covered with ice, but there would also come a day when it would bloom.

I looked at the tree and whispered, "*Feliz Año Nuevo.*"

The tree was silent.

I did not need or miss my mother as much as I used to. I'd pushed through month after month and had gotten to where I could walk around the hole in my life without falling in, where I could think about her with pleasure, not just heartache. Right now, for instance, I didn't feel like crying. What I felt was that somehow, my mother was with me—*with* me and *within* me. Abuelo had told me he felt her presence when he strolled along the hillside of Castilla too. She was inside both of us. Maybe outside too. Maybe everywhere.

Like a moonbow. I knew this was childish, yet I liked to imagine my mom watching over me. Not in a weird, supernatural way. In a quiet, natural way.

I looked at the spindly branches of the dogwood, and it was as if I heard her answer: *I am watching, Sofia. What could be more natural than a mother watching over her child? Why should love end just because life ends?*

My heart started thumping, and for a moment, the tree blurred. I listened hard, and I heard—or thought I heard—*I'm here. Still here. Right here. I never really left.*

It *was* my mother's voice! Not my mother, no, but her voice, her words, her spirit!

I studied the tree and felt a deep calm. I'd been thinking I might tell her about the Snow Ball and my chorus solo and maybe even the baby. Instead, I put my palms on the small tree trunk, closed my eyes, and whispered, "*Gracias, Mamá.* Thank you."

A hundred yards away, a loud voice boomed across Riverside Park. "Hey, Sofia!" Sam was striding toward me. "There you are!"

I looked up, startled. Then I waved and began to walk toward him.

"Here I am."

ACKNOWLEDGMENTS

Writing *Speed of Life* was not one bit speedy. I spent years writing and rewriting this novel, and I could never have finished without family, friends, and pros. Now it's time to thank all those who offered encouragement along the way. My husband, Rob Ackerman, and our daughters, Lizzi and Emme, read the book not once, not twice, but several times each. My writer mom, the late Marybeth Weston Lobdell, read two drafts. My brothers, Eric and Mark Weston, and sister-in-law, Cynthia, all weighed in, as did Sue Bird, Jean Bird, Sarah Jeffrey, Gene Ackerman, and the Squam Lake Cousins.

Many other students, friends, interns, and experts provided invaluable insights and feedback: Denver Butson, Sam Forman, David Nickoll, Claire Hodgdon, Jennifer Lu, Karolina Ksiazek, Kathy Lathen, Patty Dann, Judy Blum, Michelle Ganon, Nicole Fish, Katherine Dye, Maggie Cooper, Stephanie Richards, Becca Worby, Amanda Boyle, Lucy Logan, Sydney Gabourel, Stephanie Jenkins, Cathy Roos, Rachel Wilder, David Gassett, Nora Sheridan, Suzannah Weiss, Olivia Westbrook Gold, Lily Abrahams, Elise Brau, Juan Antonio Martin, the Farris family, Tom Sullivan, and Eric and Sara Richelson. A special shout-out to Elise Howard, Michelle Frey, Laura Blake Peterson, Tracy Marchini, Jody Hotchkiss, and Peter Ginna. Thanks also to the doctors who came to the rescue with OB/GYN and ER expertise: Stephanie Bird, Adam Romoff, and Jan Johnston.

And where would I be without Susan Ginsberg and Stacy Testa of Writers House? I am also so grateful to the whole Sourcebooks Jabberwocky team, especially my editor, Steve Geck, as well as Dominique Raccah, Heather Moore, Alex Yeadon, Elizabeth Boyer, Margaret Coffee, Katherine Prosswimmer, Gretchen Stelter, Katy Lynch, and Beth Oleniczak.

A toast too to Karen Bokram who, in 1994, asked me to be the advice columnist at *Girls' Life*. And to all the girls who have been sending me letters ever since.

ABOUT THE AUTHOR

Carol Weston's first book, *Girltalk: All the Stuff Your Sister Never Told You*, was published in a dozen languages and has been in print since 1985. Her next fifteen books include *The Diary of Melanie Martin* and *Ava and Pip*, which *The New York Times* called "a love letter to language." After her studies at Byram Hills High School in Armonk, New York, and School Year Abroad in Rennes, France, Carol majored in French and Spanish comparative literature at Yale, graduating summa cum laude. She has an MA in Spanish from Middlebury. Since 1994, she has been the "Dear Carol" advice columnist at *Girls' Life* magazine and has made many YouTube videos for kids and parents. Carol has appeared on television shows, such as *The Today Show*, *Oprah*, and *The View*, and has written for many magazines, including *Seventeen*, *YM*, *Cosmopolitan*, *Bride's*, *Glamour*, *Redbook*, *Cigar*, and *American Way*. She and her husband, playwright Rob Ackerman, met as students in Madrid, Spain, and live on the Upper West Side of New York City, where they raised their two daughters. Find out more at carolweston.com.